Dennis,

You'll see
yourself in
a very good way!
Thank you
for your input.

Karen Lovett

Rise with the Eagle

Karen Lovett

Plicata Press

Rise with the Eagle
©2014 Karen Lovett

ISBN : 978-0-9848400-6-9
LCCN: 2013940413

Cover photograph of soaring eagle by Dick Henderson.

Cover photograph of totem pole by Hugh McMillan.

Cover photograph of Aaron Wayno in canoe by Ed Johnson.

All other cover photos and graphics and design concept by the author, Karen Lovett.

Photo of the author by Richard A. M. Dixon

Printed in the USA on acid-free paper.

Plicata Press
PO Box 32
Gig Harbor, WA 98335
www.plicatapress.com

Introduction

While this story is purely a work of fiction, it was inspired in part by actual local incidents or events. The canoe journey "Paddle to Sqauxin 2012" hosted by the Squaxin Island Tribe took place as described. The Sqauxin crew and Native American tribal members depicted in this story are totally fictitious. Any resemblance to real people is purely coincidental.

Raven Island does not exist other than in the imagination of the author.

Chapter 1

Renee jogged along the path near the shoreline, her legs pumping methodically to the beating rhythm of music from her iPod. Toolie, her long-haired tricolor Australian shepherd, trotted near her side.

A seagull dove beneath the choppy surface. It left the water, a clam clamped firmly in its beak. It flapped away, a second gull in pursuit trying to steal the meal.

Renee observed the birds and her mind flashed back to school. A junior, a boy she knew was trouble, was at it again. She caught him trying to take a cell phone from a freshman that morning. He habitually preyed on younger smaller students, easy targets, and avoided taking responsibility for his actions. She was glad she'd been there to intervene and escort the bully to the principal's office.

The aggressive bird seemed determined to rob another rather than search for its own food, a bully gull relying on another to do its work. Without a guardian to defend it, she hoped the fleeing bird was quick enough to avoid attack and have time to eat.

She loved her job, but counseling students had its ups and downs. Not all the kids fit in well at school. They could be quite a challenge at times, but she believed she could make a difference in some of their lives.

Coming to the beach and the surrounding forest was a peaceful change from the frustrations at work. The briny air filled her senses and cleared her head. She'd sleep well and start fresh in the morning.

She looked ahead to see a teenage girl emerge from the woods. The teen was wearing a rumpled black T-shirt with a toothed, white skull printed on the front, and baggy black denim pants weighed down with loops of heavy silver chains.

The girl called out, "Yo, gotta cigarette?"

Renee stopped and turned off the music. "Were you talking to me?"

"Yeah, got any cigarettes?" Her words were slurred, probably from the silver ball implanted in her tongue.

"No, sorry, I don't smoke." Renee started to walk away, then stopped and turned back. Something about the rough-dressed teen drew her attention.

The girl hadn't budged; her arms hung limply, from slumped shoulders. The narrow, drawn face with the blank expression belied the tough-girl appearance.

Renee asked, "Are you all right?"

Bony fingers tipped with ragged, dirt-embedded nails raked through the unruly tangle of greasy, brown hair, and then tugged nervously at an earlobe lined with a row of small silver rings.

She mumbled, "I'm okay."

Renee suspected that nothing could be further from the truth. She noticed tears welling in the liquid brown eyes and trailing down grimy cheeks. She pulled a tissue out of the pocket of her khaki shorts. "Here, use this."

The girl wiped her eyes and blew her nose, then stuffed the wadded tissue into a large, sagging pants pocket.

"Thanks."

"My name's Renee. What's yours?"

After a long pause, she said, "Addie."

"Addie, it's a pleasure to meet you." Renee extended her hand.

Addie took her hand; a narrow smile formed on her pale lips.

"This is Toolie." Renee reached over to pat the head of her canine companion. "We like to come here."

The dog wagged her plumed tail and licked Renee's hand at the mention of her name. She sat down next to Addie and raised her foreleg.

"She likes to shake hands," Renee said.

Addie reached down and took hold of the paw. After she let go, Toolie pawed at her pant leg and continued to hold up her foot.

"I wish I'd never taught her that trick." Renee laughed, leaned down to scratch the dog's back. "It's hard to get her to stop. She can be very persistent." The shepherd pawed Addie's leg again.

Addie held the dog's foot. "She has awesome eyes. I love the pale blue one, and the brown one's almost the same color as mine."

"She was so cute when she was a puppy. I fell in love with her the minute I saw her. Those big mismatched eyes seem so mysterious. I knew she was meant to be mine."

Addie let out a deep sigh. "I wish I had a dog. We used to have one . . . Toby . . . we had to give him away."

"Oh, I'm sorry."

"I gotta go," Addie blurted.

"Do you live nearby?"

Addie broke into sobs and turned away.

"Addie! What's wrong?"

The girl ran into the woods, shoving branches aside as she fled. Her hair caught on vegetation as she fought her way through the underbrush. Renee started to follow, but turned back to the path when Addie disappeared into the brambles. Toolie whined as they turned to leave.

Renee knew the girl needed help. She turned up the volume on her iPod and hoped her nagging worry would diminish with the silken voices of Celtic Women.

The vision of the black-clothed figure fleeing into the woods plagued her and dampened her mood as she picked up the pace.

Irritated shrieking overwhelmed the music, suspending her thoughts. She looked out over Puget Sound. A pair of kingfishers flew a few feet above the surface. Toolie halted, barking at the noise

Renee turned down the music. "Toolie! No! Be quiet."

The dog stopped barking, but her eyes followed the two large-beaked birds, blue-gray wings beating rapidly just above the waves. Raucous calls diminished as they circled away and disappeared behind the bare cliffs of a rocky point.

Renee turned up the music and regained her pace, Toolie panting beside her.

Chapter 2

Addie tromped on sword ferns and fought her way through the thick barrier of dark green salal. Salmon berry thorns tore at her clothes and pricked her hands and arms. She regretted avoiding the trail, but the nagging fear that clenched the pit of her stomach prevented her from taking the easier route. It was necessary to guarantee she wouldn't be followed. She paused beneath a tall western red cedar and peered silently from behind the two-foot thick trunk, searching the woods listening for rustling or cracking branches. But the woods were still, her own heavy breathing was the only sound.

She heard the high-pitched drone of a mosquito and turned her head attempting to pinpoint the bug. Too late. She felt the prick, slapped her neck, looked at her palm. Tiny crushed wings and a gray and white striped, bloodied body—her blood—smeared the inside of her hand.

"Gotcha."

A large, itchy red bump would form and itch for days. "Dammit, I hate this place."

She tore at the bark of the cedar, shredding a few reddish-brown strips from the tree. She twisted the bark and rubbed it against her hand, erasing traces of the flattened bug, then tossing the remains aside.

A woodpecker tapped in the distance. She looked in the direction of the drumming but couldn't see the bird.

At least the woman's not following me. It's safe to move. She fought her way deeper into the forest until she found a narrow path where the going got easier. She came to a wider trail and turned right, shuffling her worn tennis shoes through the brown, needle-covered ground toward the familiar smell of wood smoke emanating from the wispy, gray plume rising ahead.

Emerging from the woods, she crossed the clearing and walked up to the circle of rocks surrounding an open fire pit. She picked up a couple of pieces of split alder from a nearby woodpile and placed them atop the glowing coals. The fire surged higher, licking the blackening bark, sending crackling sparks skyward. She stared at the dancing bright yellow-orange flames and moved closer to warm up.

Her mother peeked out from behind the mosquito netting on the front of the tent. "Addie, you're back. Where have you been?" She unzipped the netting and pushed it aside.

"Around."

"Around where? You know, I need some help." She stepped out of the tent and zipped it closed before she walked over to stand beside her daughter.

"Where's Dad? Why can't *he* help?"

"Honey, he heard about a job and went to see if he could find work."

"Yeah, like that'll happen." Addie flopped down into a white plastic chair and burst into tears. Loud wracking sobs tore from her throat. She buried her face in her hands.

Myra stood by helplessly and thought, God knows, Addie's cried enough for all of us. Will we ever get our lives back on track? She placed her hand on her daughter's shoulder. Warm tears flowed silently from her own eyes, running down her cheeks and dampening the collar of her blue denim shirt.

"Mom!—Mom!—Guess what!" Ethan was running down the dirt road, a broad grin spread across his freckled face.

Addie said sourly, "What are you so happy about?"

"I found a new friend. Look what he gave me."

He reached into his pocket and took out a small wooden eagle with widespread wings.

"See, isn't it cool?"

Myra picked up the carving, marveling at exquisite tiny feathers that appeared to catch the wind. Every detail of a salmon clutched in the talons was remarkably lifelike. "It's beautiful. Who is this new friend? He's a wonderful craftsman."

"Walt. He's a Native American. He lives on the other side of the woods. His dad showed him how. He's gonna teach me."

"How did you meet Walt?" Myra asked.

"On the beach. I was skipping stones. He was sitting on a rock, bird-watching and carving. He said you can learn a lot by watching animals. I watched him carve the eagle and then he gave it to me."

Myra handed the eagle back to Ethan. "That was very generous of him."

"He said I can go to his house to learn. He lives close by."

"Ethan, you don't really know this man. I don't want you going to see him until your dad and I meet him and find out where he lives."

"I told him you'd want to see him first. He said you and Dad are welcome to come. Can we go when Dad gets back?"

"We'll see. It depends on how tired he is. We have to eat dinner when he gets home."

"What's for dinner?" Addie asked.

"Macaroni and cheese."

"Again. That's the third time this week." She screwed up her face.

Myra forced a smile. "I know. I'm sorry. I don't like this any better than you do. Under the circumstances we're fortunate to have anything to eat . . ."

"Fortunate? Get real, Mom. I hate it here. Living in a tent. No heat. I can't see my friends. I want my own room. We don't even have a bathroom!" Addie leaped out of the chair and ran sobbing down a trail.

"Addie! Where are you going? Addie!" Myra started after her, but halted when she realized there was no way she could keep up.

She walked sadly back to camp. "I'm sorry, Ethan." She wrapped her arms around her son and clutched him close to her chest. I know you kids deserve better than this." Her eyes brimmed with tears.

Ethan returned her hug. "I don't blame you or Dad. I know things will get better. Besides, I have my new friend, Walt."

The sound of the familiar car engine rumbling down the narrow, dirt road grew louder.

"Dad's back! I wanna show him my eagle." Ethan launched himself down the road and ran alongside the black Ford Explorer.

The SUV pulled up near the tent and Nick got out.

"Dad, look at my eagle."

Nick accepted it from his son and looked at the bird. "Well, that's quite a carving. Where'd you get it?"

"My new friend. Walt. He gave it to me. He's gonna teach me to carve. Mom said we can go there after dinner so you can meet him."

Nick handed the eagle back to Ethan. He walked over to Myra, enfolded her in his arms and kissed her.

"That's not exactly what I told him. I said if you weren't too tired, we could go after dinner."

"It was a workout. I split and stacked two cords of firewood. Made a hundred bucks."

"That'll help." Myra tried to sound positive.

She ran her fingers through his hair and buried her face against his chest. "You smell so good."

"I stopped by Mike's. He washed my clothes. I took a shower and got cleaned up. "Wish I could find a full-time job. I hate what this is doing to you and the kids." The lines on his forehead deepened. "We can't keep going on like this. Things have to improve."

"They will, you have to believe that." God knew she prayed every night for their lives to get back on track. She still had faith that it would happen soon."

Nick looked around the campsite. "Where's Addie?"

"She was in another one of her moods. Ran off a short while ago when I told her we were having macaroni. This isn't much of a life for a girl her age."

"I know. I'd give anything to change our situation."

"Honey, I know. You're doing the best you can. We'll get by until things turn around. I have faith. This is just a temporary situation."

He put his arm around her waist. "You're my rock. I couldn't get through this without you."

She brushed her fingers along his dark beard and then slipped out of his grasp. "Let me get dinner ready." She set a rebar tripod above the fire, hung a pot above the coals and poured water from a gallon jug. They sat down and waited for the water to boil.

Nick ruffled his son's flaming red hair. "Ethan, I think going to meet your friend is the perfect way to spend our evening. We need a change of pace."

Myra looked away from the pot as Addie shuffled slowly back to camp and flopped down into a chair. Her face contorted in a grim frown.

Nick leaned over and touched Addie's arm. "Hi, sweetie, how's my girl?"

She glared at him, but said nothing.

"We're going to visit Ethan's friend, Walt, after dinner. Would you like to come?"

"Nope."

Nick said, "Honey, I think getting away from here would do you good."

"Yeah, right, and go see some old man who lives out here, in the woods. Like that's supposed to cheer me up."

"Addie, I'm sorry you're so upset. This isn't easy for any of us. Please don't shut us out. We need to stick together. We're a team." He pleaded, "Please, come with us."

"Okaaaay."

Myra drained the macaroni and mixed in the cheese sauce and margarine and some powdered milk and water. She set out paper plates and plastic forks and spoons.

"Dinner's ready."

They sat at the round white plastic picnic table to eat. After dinner, they discarded the dishes in a garbage bag.

Nick clasped Myra's hand and they followed Ethan down the road, and then turned off onto a path through the woods. Addie lagged behind.

They came to a clearing where an unfinished dugout canoe sat parallel to the driveway. A totem pole towered above them in the front yard. A wood bear stood on its hind legs, a salmon clutched in its paws near the front steps of a log house. Carved poles supported the cedar-shingled roof above the porch. A cougar crouched, his head turned toward the center of the yard.

Myra marveled at the realistic wood work, "It looks like a museum."

"Yeah, it sure is impressive," Nick agreed. "The guy's definitely got talent."

Myra watched as Addie stood fixated in front of the two-foot wide totem pole. Her hand ran along the fine lines of the large bear at the base. An eagle looked out from its perch at the top. She was still there when the door of the cabin opened.

A stocky man with a long silver braid walked out. "Ethan, it's good to see you." A smile filled his line-etched face.

Ethan said, "Brought my family."

The older man came down the steps and extended his hand. "Walt Tilton."

"Nick Matheson." He returned the firm grasp then motioned, "My wife, Myra."

"Pleased to meet you," she said.

"The pleasure's mine." Walt looked her in the eye.

"That's our daughter, Addie," Myra gestured across the yard.

Addie remained silent, but moved away from the pole and stood near them. Her eyes shifted to the standing bear. She stared into the large, wide-open, tooth-filled jaws. The great beast looked so real, it was almost scary.

Walt noticed her studying the life-size figure. "The bear, our revered mother, is a teacher. She taught the people of the water how to fish and find berries. That is what the spirit of the bear signifies. Those legends have been passed down from generation to generation by the storytellers.

"Woodcarvers preserve our history. My grandfather and father taught me. Now, I must pass on that knowledge to the next generation. My son did not like to spend time learning the ways of our ancestors. I've been teaching my grandson. He's a very willing student."

Myra looked puzzled. "You speak of your son in the past. Did something happen to him?"

The lines in his face deepened. "He was killed by a drunk driver two years ago."

"Oh, Myra's voice softened, I'm sorry."

"It's been especially hard on Sophie, my daughter-in-law." He looked away, but his expression brightened when he nodded toward the boy. "When I ran into Ethan, I told him about the animals and our relationship with them. He seemed eager to learn. I showed him the eagle I was working on. I would like to teach him how to carve if he wants to learn. Boys should have a purpose in life. Perhaps Ethan will find a calling working with wood."

Ethan looked up at his father, "Can I Dad?"

Nick stroked his beard, "Well, I don't see why not. As long as you help out with chores and get your school work done."

"Don't worry, I will." Ethan grinned and looked at Walt. "When can I start?"

"How 'bout Saturday morning?" Walt looked at Nick. "Say, ten o'clock?"

Nick nodded. "I think that'll be fine." He turned to look at his wife. "You have any problem with that, Myra?"

"No, how long will he be?"

"Oh, let's say until two. He's young and will need a break." Walt winked at the boy. "I'll fix lunch so we won't be working the whole time."

"All right, but if he gets to be too much trouble, send him home." Myra glanced at Ethan.

"Oh, I don't expect him to be a problem." Walt smiled at the freckled face.

Nick took Myra's hand. "We've taken up enough of your time. Ethan will be here on Saturday. Come on, let's head back to camp."

Ethan strode ahead. Addie shuffled slowly behind, then stopped at the totem pole and looked up at the eagle. The piercing eyes looked out into the trees across the road.

Myra turned and looked back. "Come on, Addie."

Addie moved on and followed them at a distance.

Walt watched them go. A strange, uneasy feeling overcame him. A premonition?

He spoke to himself, "That girl has a troubled spirit."

Chapter 3

The bearded senior picked up his backpack and slung the strap across his shoulder. "Thanks, Miss Stuart."

"You're welcome, Ross. Keep up the good work. Check back in if you need to. June's only two months away. We want to make sure you graduate with your class."

"I know." He walked out of the counselor's office and closed the door behind him.

Renee picked up the phone and pushed the extension for the receptionist. "Marcia, you can send in my next appointment."

She set the phone down, leaned back in her chair and massaged her aching neck, wondering what happened to Addie and wishing she could do something to help her. Addie wasn't one of Renee's students so she didn't know how to find her. What's that girl going through and what's going to happen to her?

A knock on the door interrupted her thoughts. "Come in."

"Miss Stuart, you want to see me?"

"Yes, Derek," she gestured to a chair facing her desk. "Please have a seat."

The stocky youth sat down and stretched his legs in front of him. He brushed a few loose strands of long black hair away from his face. A band held the rest behind his head.

Renee said, "I just want to touch bases with you. Are you having any problems keeping up with your community service hours?"

His eyes shifted down to the floor. "Nope."

"Are you getting in enough time?"

"Yeah." His fingernails scratched at the fabric of his blue jeans on his thigh.

"What are they having you do?"

"I've been painting, and unloading boxes of food at the food bank."

"How do you like working with Mr. Grayson?"

Derek looked up and scratched his elbow. His tone changed and the hint of a smile lit his face. "I like him. He's a nice guy."

"I've heard good things about him. I'm glad things are working out."

His brow furrowed and he looked away again. She paused, noticing the change in his demeanor. "Are you having trouble getting your homework done?"

"Sometimes. I have a lot to do." He twisted a few strands of hair. "I'm managing."

"Let me know if you run into any problems. Be glad you got off easy. Things could have been much worse. I know it's not easy to fit everything in, but in the long run you'll come out of this a stronger person."

He rubbed the back of his neck. "I guess."

"Go back to class now and don't forget to keep me posted on how you're doing. I need to know if you're having a difficult time keeping up." She stood and followed him to the door.

"See ya." He strode down the hall.

Renee returned to her desk and clicked her mouse. The screensaver blinked off and documents filled the screen. She scrolled through Derek's records and read the long file. He seemed to be doing better. His attendance was regular and his grades were improving. That was a good sign. Whatever was going on with him, Simon Grayson seemed to be making a difference.

She'd never met the YMCA Friends and Services Coordinator, but she was aware of the positive influence he had on a number of students she counseled. They held him in high regard. He managed to help them get their lives turned around. She wished the results with all the students she counseled were as positive.

Again she thought of Addie, the troubled wild child, who seemed to be living on the edge. Their brief, fleeting encounter left Renee unable to get the image of the girl out of her mind. Of all the students she came in contact with, something about the sad-eyed girl cried out for help.

Renee shut down the computer as the bell rang, and walked out into the hall to watch the students leave. She looked for Addie among the flowing mass of chattering teenagers making their way out to the buses and parking lot. Addie wasn't there. Of course, she could have gone a different direction. With the large number of students attending the high school, unless Addie was assigned to Renee, it was doubtful they would have met. Perhaps she was home-schooled.

The roar of car engines diminished and noise in the hall died down. Renee picked up her purse and walked to her car. A fine drizzle dampened her skin and coated the window. The windshield wipers pulsed intermittently, scraping minute droplets off the glass.

She drove across the Purdy spit and looked out over the gray water. The tide was out and a crew was working on the beach harvesting farmed oysters. Traffic snaking slowly up the winding hill was halted by the red flashing lights of the yellow school bus. Forty minutes later, after a stop at her Post Office box half way down the Key Peninsula in the almost-town of Home to collect her mail, she pulled into her driveway. She could hear Toolie barking in the house as the key turned in the lock.

The dog ran circles around her, out the open door, along the chain-link fence and back inside.

Renee changed into her running clothes and fixed herself a snack. She clicked the leash onto the dog's collar and they jogged toward the beach.

The tide was rising as waves lapped gently against the rocky shore. A fish jumped sending a circle of ripples. The sun burned through the clouds, drying the damp air. A great blue heron waded on stilted legs, prodding its sharp bill beneath the surface in search of food. Renee paused to watch the long-necked bird wade stealthily through the shallow water.

She moved on a few minutes later and wondered if she'd run into Addie. That hope dwindled as they continued along the beach with no sign of the teen.

She looked down a path running into the woods and considered trying to find her, but decided that wasn't a good idea and continued on.

A bank of gunmetal-gray clouds loomed in the sky and blotted out the sun, again. Light dimmed in the ominous shadow of the imminent storm. A sudden gust of wind tore at her jacket. She started to run, and tugged the hood up to cover her head and secured the ties. Heavy drops of rain pelted the purple, waterproof fabric, glistening droplets beaded up as she ran. A flash of lightning lit up the sky before the thunder boomed. The rain no longer fell in haphazard drips, but blasted in bone-chilling silver sheets driving in at an angle to the ground.

Renee held her hand in front of her eyes, in a futile attempt to keep the blinding downpour from blocking her vision. She ran as fast as she could, Toolie splashing through puddles beside her. Renee took the steps two at a time and turned her key in the lock. The dog rushed past her, then stopped in the hall and shook her long soaked coat, sending a spray of water onto the walls and across the floor.

"Oh no, Toolie."

Once wasn't enough. The shepherd shook herself again, sat down in the growing pool, mouth open in a toothy grin.

Renee groaned, hurried into the bathroom and grabbed a towel. She wrapped it around the dog, rubbed her coat, and dried Toolie's feet. "Now, you can go," she said, patting the moist head.

She stripped off her coat and hung it up, left her shoes by the door and carried her soaked clothes into the bathroom, dropping them into the hamper. She ran the water in the tub and climbed in, settling comfortably into soothing warmth.

* * *

Myra stuffed a towel in the doorway of the tent in an effort to stem the flood of water flowing in. Tears started to roll down her cheeks as she looked sadly at Addie and Ethan sitting glumly on their cots at the other end of the tent. The billowing fabric snapped loudly in the blustery wind. Not far in the distance, the sharp crack of a breaking tree followed by a loud "thwump" as it hit the ground, startled them with the very real threat of a new terror.

Addie shrieked, "A tree's gonna fall on us!"

Myra moved across the damp floor and faced her daughter. She put her hands on the terrified girl's shoulders. "No, don't worry, honey. We'll be fine." She hoped she sounded more confident than she felt. She said a silent prayer the storm would pass quickly and leave them unscathed.

Thunder reverberated.

Addie huddled beneath a blanket. Her rigid fingers twisted the plush fabric and pulled it over the top of her head. Myra knew her daughter took little comfort as she clutched the soft pink remnant of her former life and snugged it around her, shuddering sobs wracking her trembling body.

Ethan looked at Myra. "Mom, when's Dad gonna get back?"

"Ohhhh, I wish he was here. He's at the library searching for jobs on-line." A slight edge crept into her voice. "I'm expecting him any time." She moved back to the entrance and stared at rustling trees swaying in the howling wind. Rain ricocheted up from the widening pool forming around their tent. She looked up. "God please stop the rain."

She placed another towel on the floor. "Why don't we play cards? Maybe that will take our minds off the storm."

"Okay." Ethan said.

Addie continued to sob.

"Addie, would you like to play?" Myra asked.

"No."

"It might make you feel better."

"I don't want to!"

Myra turned to Ethan. "Well, I guess just the two of us will play." She removed a deck of cards from a small black case.

Ethan set up the small white plastic table. She sat down opposite him, shuffled the cards and dealt the first hand.

* * *

Nick drove down the peninsula highway on his way back from the library. The windshield wipers fought against waves of water that severely reduced his vision. Leaves and branches tumbled from trees landing on the road and SUV. Suddenly, a strong gust ripped through a large maple. One section of the tree succumbed to the force of the wind. The huge limb cracked and split, crashing onto the road.

"Damn!" Nick slammed on the brakes. The Explorer fishtailed. Tires skidded across the asphalt leaving a trail of rubber across the wet pavement before screeching to a halt just as the bumper gouged a ragged tear in the bark of the downed tree. Smaller branches scraped across the grill and hood. He reversed, pulled to the side of the road, and got out to survey the damage. For once, he was lucky. The tree blocked both lanes and lay across a splintered fence on the far side.

Another car pulled up to the tree and stopped. A stooped silver-haired man joined him. The gravelly voice could barely be heard above the sound of the rain. "Looks like we'll have to get this cleared out of the way."

"I've got a chainsaw in the back of my SUV." Nick walked back and opened the trunk. "Good thing this is in here."

Water ran down the back hatch and soaked into the carpet while he checked the fuel tank and added a bit more before taking off the blade guard.

Nick carried the saw to the tree and pulled the cord. The engine revved up, and then settled down. He laid the chain against the trunk. Chips flew as the teeth bit into the wood. First, he sliced off the branches. As they fell, the other man hauled them to the side of the road stacking them into a large pile. Before long, a thirty-something woman and her teenage son joined their impromptu work crew. Once all the branches were out of the way, Nick went to work making vertical cuts across the trunk. He kept working his way across the road.

A few more drivers showed up and pitched in to help. No one complained as the squall tore at their rain-soaked clothing, chilling exposed skin. Wind whipped up tiny chunks of wood, swirling them through the air like confetti, coating hair and clothes of the motley crew. They persevered in spite of discomfort. Rounds were rolled to the side. Before long the road was clear except for mounds of wet, chunky sawdust and small twigs. The group of strangers climbed into their vehicles and drove their separate ways.

Nick's wet clothes clung to his clammy skin and his tennis shoes squished when he walked. He crammed in as much wood as he could and set the saw on the floor up front. Water dripped from his hair into his eyes and ran from his beard. He brushed off his clothes as best as he could and got into the car. Shivering, he turned up the heat. He wiped the foggy window with his sleeve. Visibility through the smeared glass was only marginally better.

Defrost improved the problem slightly. He waited a couple of minutes before pulling onto the highway. He squinted through the streaked, rain-blotted windshield, barely able to see the side streets. He almost missed the intersection, but made the turn in time and followed the muddy single-lane road that wound between stands of alder, maple and evergreens to their camp.

He sloshed through the shallow pool that formed in front of the tent, unzipped the mosquito netting and stepped over the pile of saturated towels.

"Thank goodness you're finally back. What took you so long?" Myra hugged him. "You're soaking wet!" She ran her hand across his sleeve. "Why are you covered with woodchips?"

"I almost got hit by a tree that fell in front of me on the road. Had to cut it out of the way. Several people helped. We all got soaked. For once, I was lucky. A few more seconds, and it would have all been over."

Ethan blurted, "How big was the tree?"

"A large maple, about this big." He held his hands about a foot and a half apart. "It landed across the road plus another thirty feet and that wasn't even the whole tree."

"Wow!" Ethan said.

"Oh, my gosh. Thank goodness you're all right! You better get out of those wet clothes before you get sick." Myra helped him pull off his sweatshirt. She rubbed his back with a towel then handed it to him.

He dried his hair and face then blotted his torso. Myra handed him a dry sweatshirt and hung a blanket across a corner of the tent while he took off his shoes. He stripped off his pants and pulled on a dry pair behind the screen. Cold and shivering, he climbed into his cool sleeping bag.

Addie hadn't spoken. Nick noticed his daughter shrouded in the blanket. Her face was turned away. He wasn't sure if she was awake or asleep.

"Addie," he spoke softly.

She didn't reply.

"Addie," he raised his voice slightly.

She remained silent and didn't move.

Myra looked at him sadly. "She's been upset all afternoon."

Nick was still cold, but climbed out of his sleeping bag to take his daughter into his arms. "Addie, I'm sorry things are so bad right now. I really wish they weren't. We've all got to pull together. We aren't the only ones struggling. That's the problem. There are so many people out of work; it's really hard to find a job. If there was any

way I could get us out of this mess right now," his voice
choked up, "believe me, I would."

He loosened his arms and she turned to face him. He
ran a fingertip down her cheek.

With a sobbing wail, Addie let go of the blanket and
wrapped her arms around her dad's firm body. She
snuggled against him just as she had as a young child. "I
love you Daddy," she said with a muffled sob.

"I love you too, baby girl." He kissed her forehead.

Chapter 4

Simon Grayson arrived at the food bank just before a faded blue Dodge Ram drove up.

Derek got out. "Thanks, Mom. See you at three-thirty." He waved as the pickup circled away.

Simon saw the boy dressed in a gray paint-spattered T-shirt and blue jeans with the knees torn out. His neatly braided hair was fastened with a beaded, rawhide strip. "I see you're ready to paint?"

"Yeah." Derek shoved his hands in his pockets and followed Simon downstairs to the back room.

Simon got out cans of paint, brushes, trays and sheets of plastic. He mixed the paint and laid the plastic across the floors and shelves. Derek got a brush and poured some paint into a tray.

"Start painting the beams at the far end." Derek went to work, dipping his brush in the paint, trying not to drip any on the floor or shelves.

Volunteers and other community service workers tried to avoid wet paint as they boxed or shelved food and loaded shopping carts.

People signed up for food baskets and picked through bread racks out front while volunteers loaded bags and boxes with canned goods, cereal, meat, dairy products, and produce into shopping carts.

Elderly men and women, young mothers or fathers with children, single adults or large families with a house full of kids, people from all walks of life, who, for whatever reason, found themselves down and out. Circumstances led them to the doors of the food bank. Some loaded as much as they could carry into backpacks and trudged away down the road.

The food bank was going through increasing amounts of food and other necessities as the number of unemployed grew. Donations were dwindling and with the increasing demand, times were getting tougher.

The Explorer pulled into the parking lot. Nick and Myra got out and walked to the front door. A silver-haired woman limped out pushing a shopping cart.

"Let me help you with that." Nick reached for the cart.

The woman held onto the handle. "I can manage, but thank you for offering."

Nick watched her move slowly across the driveway as he held the door for Myra.

A young mother looked over the pastries. A toddler clung to her jacket.

An older boy looked at the shelves. "I want cupcakes."

She selected a plastic container of chocolate cakes frosted with blue icing and placed it in her cart.

"Yum." The boy's face lit up.

"Cookies," the little girl chimed.

A box of chocolate chip cookies went into the basket.

"Goody." She clapped her hands.

"What do we need to do?" Myra asked the man sitting behind the counter.

"You can help yourselves to bread and pastry. Signs on the shelves explain the limits of different items. If you qualify for a food basket, you need to sign up here. I'll need to see a photo ID and a light bill or other envelope with your physical address on it."

"Oh." Myra's face took on a pained expression. "We don't have a physical address . . . not anymore. We're camping in a tent in the woods." She struggled quietly over the words. "We have a P. O. box."

"That's okay. I can put you into the system with a photo ID. Are you the head of household?"

"No, I am." Nick pulled out his wallet.

"How many are in your family?"

"Four." Nick replied.

The manager, Stan, requested more information and entered everything into the computer. He slid a notepad across the counter. "Here's a list of extras you can choose. Check off what you want."

Nick marked items: flour, rice, beans, oatmeal, sugar, coffee, creamer, toothpaste, hand soap, shampoo, and laundry detergent.

When Nick was finished, Stan took the list. "I need your signature."

"Family of four!" Stan called out. A young woman came to the window and Stan handed her the list. "You can also take whatever you want from the shelves outside in front of the building. Use the bags from the bread room. Someone will be right out with your basket."

"Thanks." Nick left the counter.

Myra picked up a plastic bag and filled it with bagels, hot dog buns, rolls, two loaves of sliced bread and a couple of loaves of long, crisp French baguettes.

Nick looked over the sweets. "How about an apple pie? It looks really good." He shifted some of the containers. "Double chocolate muffins." He picked up the package and set it on top of the pie. "I've got dessert."

Myra looked at his choices. "That'll go right to my hips."

He looked at her thin frame. "A bit more curve wouldn't hurt," he teased.

"Are you saying I'm too thin?" She frowned.

"No, but a little bit of padding would make you a little softer to snuggle up to," he said with a smile.

An alarm beeped followed by a door opening to the back.

A cheerful woman greeted them. "Nick. Have a nice day."

They set the bread and pastry on top of the cart and went out. Cases of granola bars lined the bottom shelf. Nick grabbed a package while Myra picked through bins of onions, potatoes, lettuce, apples, and bags of salad.

She added the produce to the rest of their supplies and said, "They're a little old. The quality isn't as good as shopping at the grocery store, but we can cut off the bad parts."

"We'll make do." He rolled the cart across the parking lot and loaded everything into the back of the Explorer.

"I know." Myra sighed. "At this point I'm happy for anything. Wonder why they call it a basket when it's a box and bags?"

"Nick shrugged. "Don't know and don't care. I'm just glad we can get it."

Myra said, "Me, too." She opened the door and got in.

He shut the back and returned the cart. After getting in and fastening his seatbelt, he leaned over and laid his arm on Myra's shoulder. "I still can't believe we've ended up in this mess. I never imagined it." A heavy sigh escaped.

She reached up and touched his hand. "Nick, it's not your fault. We're in the same boat as thousands of other families. I know that doesn't make our situation any easier, but we didn't do anything wrong. Things won't always be this bad. Remember how broke we were when we first got married?"

"I remember. All the meals of tuna noodle casserole, but we were young. We had our whole lives ahead of us. I thought we'd seen the last of those days. Now we have the kids to think about, and we don't have as many years to recover from this." He closed his eyes and tilted his head back.

Myra sat silently. A couple of minutes later, Nick pulled his arm back and put both hands on the steering wheel. The engine started and they drove back to camp.

* * *

Simon examined a beam. "Derek, it's almost three. Time to clean up. Don't forget, you need to sweep and mop the floor where we were working."

"Okay." He washed his hands and started on the floor. After sweeping he got out the bucket and mop. He hurriedly ran the mop across the mottled floor. He finished and rinsed the mop before dumping the bucket.

Simon looked at drops of paint and ran his finger across them. "Derek, did you mop the whole floor where we worked?"

"I think so."

"What about over here?" He held up paint-smudged finger. "You missed this spot."

Derek frowned and picked up the mop again. He went over the area Simon pointed out then rinsed out the mop for the second time.

"That's good." Simon smiled with approval. "You can go on home. I'll finish putting things away. See you next week. Have a good weekend."

"You too, see you on Wednesday at noon." Derek went out the door and waited for his mom in the front parking lot.

He climbed into the truck and fastened his seatbelt.

"Well, how was your day?" Sophie asked.

"It was okay." He rolled down the window.

She looked at the spots of brown paint in his black hair. "I see you've been painting."

"Yeah, we still have a lot left to do, but we're making progress."

"Good, is Mr. Grayson pleased with your work?" She backed up and drove onto the highway.

Derek thought about the spots on the floor. "I think so." He didn't sound very convincing.

He turned away from her look to stare out the window. They drove the rest of the way in silence.

The truck pulled into the driveway and came to a stop in front of a wooden wolf sitting with his muzzle in the air. Derek looked at the howling figure. "I want to spend time with Grandpa this weekend."

"I'm sure he'll be pleased to have you come by." He darted off while she walked up the steps.

* * *

Derek went behind the house and followed the well-worn path through the woods. The trail wove between the trees and opened into a grassy field. An eight-foot long gray, black and white-flecked, flat-topped granite boulder protruded three feet above the ground on the other side of the meadow. Derek strode through tall, damp grass and bolted onto the rock. This was his thinking rock. He felt at peace here. He listened to rustling leaves and serenading songbirds in the nearby trees. All his problems seemed to vaporize and blow away, carried away on the wind.

The high pitched call of a bald eagle caught his attention. His eyes panned the sky searching for the great bird. Wide-spread wings soared from behind the trees and circled gracefully, as the eagle scoped the ground. Derek watched the bird intently, his eyes roaming the sky in the bird's path. After a few minutes, the bright white head and tail vanished, borne by black outspread wings and disappeared behind the screen of towering trees.

Derek closed his eyes and visualized himself as an eagle. What would it be like to take to the sky, fly above Mother Earth and view the world below? He could feel himself grow weightless, the vision consuming him. Trees appeared small, the forest running together in various shades of green. An undefinable human presence entered the vision. His body started to tremble.

Rain started to fall. He opened his eyes and climbed down from his rock. He scanned the tall rough-barked evergreens rising around him as he passed through the forest wondering what the strange vision meant.

Chapter 5

Ethan crawled out of his sleeping bag and went outside. Nick and Myra were sitting by the fire sipping steaming mugs of coffee.

"Good morning," Ethan said.

Myra noticed his beaming smile. "Good morning. You certainly sound chipper today. Would you like a cup of hot chocolate?"

"Yes, please."

She tore open a packet of cocoa and emptied the brown powder and dehydrated marshmallows into a mug, then ladled some hot water from the pot over the fire.

"Thanks, Mom."

"You're welcome."

His easygoing, cheerful acceptance of their plight was a pleasant respite from the stress of dealing with everyday problems. His optimistic outlook lifted her spirits.

He picked up a spoon and stirred, blowing on the steamy chocolate as marshmallows swirled and swelled.

"Today's Saturday, I'm going to Walt's. This is my first day learning to carve."

"Have some oatmeal before you go." She spooned some into a bowl and poured some powdered milk, sugar and hot water over the top.

Ethan took the bowl, stirred the contents, and began slurping the thick mush. He polished it off and licked the bowl.

"Ethan, have some manners," Myra chided.

"Aw, Mom, we're camping."

Nick set down his cup. "That doesn't matter, listen to your mother."

"Okay." He washed his bowl in the basin and rinsed it.

"I'm going to Walt's." He waved and sprinted down the road.

Ethan ran all the way, his tennis shoes making little sound on the soft loam. He burst into the clearing and slowed down when he saw Walt sitting on the front steps. He stopped in front of Walt and bent over, hands on his knees, gasping to catch his breath.

"Well my young friend, you need to learn patience and pace yourself." His fingers worked a knife across the surface of a piece of cedar as he spoke. "Boys are always in a hurry. They have no time to waste. You'll find that time moves faster and faster as you grow old. Slow down and listen to the voices of the creatures and forces of nature around you. They have much to say. How can you hear them, if you are in such a hurry?"

Ethan straightened up and sat beside Walt on the steps. He watched as callused fingers skillfully controlled the knife, shaving thin curls of wood, releasing the as-yet unidentifiable form from the rough block.

"The most important thing you have to know is how to take care of your tools. The blades must be kept razor sharp." Walt held up the blade of his knife and ran his thumb along the side. "Don't run your finger across the edge. You'll get cut. It should leave a shiny cut through the wood. A nick in the blade will leave a streak."

"Oh."

Walt shifted the wood. "You want to cut down with the grain or diagonally across. If you cut upwards against the grain, or across the grain, it will tear or splinter the wood." Walt rotated it and held it out so Ethan could get a closer look. "See how the wood is not slicing off smoothly?"

Ethan studied the cut. "Uh-huh."

"That means the knife is going against the grain. I have to turn the wood to go with the grain." He repositioned the block and sheared a smooth piece off. "Now, you try it."

Ethan took the cedar in his hands and turned it around. "How should I hold it?"

"Are you left or right-handed?"

"Right-handed."

"Look closely at the grain. Make sure you hold it in your left hand. Keep the left hand behind the knife and use the left thumb on the blunt side of the blade to act like a lever to control the cut." Walt positioned Ethan's left hand and fingers and then placed the knife in his right hand. "Now, make your cut."

Ethan pushed with his right hand. A strip of wood peeled off. He grinned and looked over at Walt. "Like that?"

"Yep, that's the idea. Now, think about the form you're carving. I drew a shape on the wood. See the lines?"

Ethan looked at the block again. "Yeah."

"Visualize the frog in the wood. He is there. You are going to free him. He is a symbol of rebirth and cleansing of the spirit.

"When you choose a piece of wood, imagine the figure. Make sure it fits well and works with the grain. I chose the frog for your first project. As your technique improves, I'll give you harder subjects."

The two sat on the steps for a while, a small pile of shavings collecting at their feet. Walt offered suggestions and gave pointers when necessary. Ethan concentrated on the form taking shape in his hands. He repositioned the block to work on the other side.

"Grandpa."

Walt's face lit up, "Well, you came at a good time. I'm teaching my young friend to carve. Ethan, this is my grandson, Derek."

Derek walked across the grass and leaned against the head of the bear near the porch. "You have an excellent teacher. Grandpa is the best."

Ethan stopped carving and looked at the teenager's face, noticing the resemblance to the older man minus the etched creases of age. "It's nice to meet you."

"You too. Whatcha making?"

"A frog." Ethan held out the block.

Derek took the wood, turned it over in his hand and examined the cuts. "It's coming along. Takes time." He passed it back.

"Grandpa's been carving his whole life. He makes it look easy."

"Yeah, I know." Ethan's eyes narrowed and his brow furrowed as he scrutinized his progress.

Walt tapped the porch. "Come here. Tell me about school."

"All right." Derek sat next to Ethan.

"First, how about your obligation at the food bank?"

"We're getting the painting done. It's tedious, taking a lot of time. I'll be glad when it's done, but I'll miss Mr. Grayson." He stood up, strode across the yard, and leaned over the canoe. He ran his hands along a rough side. "Thought I'd work on this today. Been thinking about it all week."

"Good idea." Walt turned to Ethan. "The canoe's a big project. Derek and I've been working on it together for about a year. We still have a long way to go, but it's getting there."

"That's really cool." Ethan looked down at his small, unfinished frog. "Guess I've got a lot of practice to do."

"Very few know how to make a canoe anymore. Grandpa's very knowledgeable about the old ways and culture of our people. I'm glad he's teaching me." Derek started to walk around the side of the house. "I'll get the tools."

The knife moved in Ethan's hands shaving more thin strips. "This sure goes slow."

"Patience, my friend. That is part of the lesson. The young are always so impatient. Everything has to be in a hurry. Good things take time." He laid a scarred, callused hand on Ethan's shoulder. "You will learn that someday. I will teach you the value of time." He nodded toward his grandson as the youth reappeared from behind the house and started to jog over to the canoe. "That one still has much to learn," he said with a smile.

Ethan squinted at the wooden handled tools in the teen's hands. "What are those?"

Derek changed course and walked back to the porch. "They're adzes." He raised his right hand, turning the hatchet-like handle so Ethan could see the steel was longer and slimmer than an axe. The straight blade on the end was turned ninety degrees like a narrow, sharp hoe.

Ethan set down his knife and wood and reached for the adze handle. He grasped the smooth wood and moved the tool in a pounding motion.

"Whoa, careful son, that blade has a very sharp edge." Walt leaned back, throwing up his hands in mock fear, but his face was serious.

"Sorry." Ethan stopped his hand and ran the fingers of his left hand across the metal avoiding the sharp edge. "What's the other one?"

"This is a curved adze. It's similar, but the sharp edge is rounded." Derek lifted the tool and swapped it for the one in Ethan's hand so Ethan could examine the second blade. These are used to strip larger pieces of wood. You'd never get a log done if you could only use a knife." He took the adze from Ethan. "I'm gonna get to work on the canoe."

Ethan picked up the knife and his unfinished frog. Narrow strips peeled away from the block. He stopped and shook his fingers. "My hand's sore."

Walt reached for the boy's hand and nodded at the blistered skin. "It takes time to build up calluses. You'd better stop now. Give your hands a break."

"Okay, where shall I put these?" He held out the knife and block.

"I'll keep them here at the house for you." Walt turned and went inside.

Ethan leapt off the porch. He reached up and batted the bear's nose as he passed by then stopped beside Derek next to the canoe. Derek was bent over the top, his arm moving methodically along the inside. The adze bit into the log, tearing off a curved chunk of wood with each stroke of the sharp blade.

Ethan studied the action, impressed by Derek's skill and strength as he wielded the simple tool. His own very brief experience with the knife gave him an increased appreciation for the patience, and artistic talent necessary to be a good wood carver. He wondered if he would ever become skilled. He was already beginning to have self-doubts.

Walt came out and handed Ethan a glass of lemonade and a sandwich. "Someday, you'll be able to help us on another big project."

"Cool. What is it?

"If you keep coming over and practicing, you'll find out. After your hands and arms get accustomed to the work, it'll get a lot easier. Then you can handle a big job. If you get to that point, I'll use your help."

Walt nodded toward Derek. "That one started out like you. He was much younger of course, but he had the desire. My son never wanted to learn. I see a will and strength in you like just like my grandson. He has the spirit of the eagle, our family totem, and communicates with the Great Spirit. His skill and patience guarantee the history and culture of our tribe are safe. The knowledge of the past will pass to future generations through his voice and hands. I can go in peace when it is my time, knowing Derek will continue our traditions."

Ethan chewed a bite of his sandwich then looked up at the craggy face. "What's a totem?"

"Aahhh . . . a totem is a guide . . . a spirit. It takes the form of an animal and stays with you throughout this physical life and then goes with you into the spirit world."

"How do you know what it is?" Ethan looked at the eagle perched at the top of the totem pole.

Walt looked up to the sky. "You need to be observant. Pay attention to the animals around you. It can come through dreams, or be an animal that you are attracted to. You can learn lessons from your totem, but only if you pay attention to what it is telling you. Be open to learning from the guide and trust what it is saying—"

At that moment the high-pitched cry of an eagle interrupted the conversation. Their eyes scanned the sky searching for the unseen bird.

Derek pointed as the great black wings soared out from above the trees. "There it is."

The bird circled above them several times before it disappeared from sight behind the trees.

"He has come to check on us," Derek smiled. "He does that often."

"That's awesome." Ethan said.

"Yeah, it is." Derek nodded and returned to work on the canoe.

Ethan finished eating and handed the glass to Walt. "Thank you for lunch and for helping me. I guess I'd better get back to camp. I want to tell Mom and Dad what I learned today. See you, Derek."

Derek nodded. "Catch you later."

Walt waved. "Come back soon."

"I will." Ethan moved slowly down the path looking up between the branches as he passed between the trees. He walked into the campsite.

"Hi, Dad."

Nick had the hood up on the Explorer and was bent over the engine wiping off the dip-stick. He looked up, and smiled at Ethan. "How'd it go?"

"Good. Takes longer than I thought." He flexed his fingers. "Had to quit 'cause my hand got sore. Walt told me it takes time to build up calluses, then it won't hurt anymore."

Nick reinserted the dip-stick into the tube, and slammed the hood. "Walt's been carving his whole life. I'm sure he knows what he's talking about." He tucked the rag into a plastic bag and set it in the back of the vehicle.

"Yeah, I know. I met his grandson, Derek. He was working on the canoe. He's a carver too." He walked over by the fire and flopped into a chair. "Where's Mom?"

"She went for a walk. I imagine she'll be back soon." Nick sat down next to Ethan.

Ethan picked up a stick and prodded the glowing coals. "Do you know what a totem is?"

"I think it's an animal form that is significant according to ancient cultural traditions. Different animals mean different things. Some people believe that an animal may have an influence over their lives."

"An eagle flew over us while I was there. Walt said the eagle is their family totem. He said it connects them to the future and the spirit world."

"I don't know much about those things." Nick clasped his hands behind his head and looked up at the sky. "I suppose it's important to native beliefs, but I'm not sure if it has any actual impact on their lives."

"Walt said if I pay attention to animals I might find my totem."

Nick placed his hand on his son's knee. "Well, I don't know about that. I guess it doesn't hurt to look."

Soft thudding footsteps and rustling branches were barely perceptible. They both turned to look.

"You're back," Nick reached a hand out to Myra as she leaned over him and brushed her lips across his cheek.

"Did Addie come back yet?" she asked.

"No. I thought you might have run into her."

"I hoped to, but I don't know where she went." Myra sat down and scratched a welt on her ankle. "A mosquito bit me. Wish we had money for repellent."

Ethan said, "I bet Walt knows what to do. I'll ask."

Chapter 6

Addie stopped rowing and looked down into the choppy water, squinting to see beneath the blue-green surface. She rubbed her aching arms and looked at the blisters on her hands.

The familiar beach she left behind formed a pencil line in the distance and the island, her destination, was still a long way off. The sun, high in the sky when she started out, glowed behind clouds as it moved lower toward the mountains. A stiff breeze picked up, chilling her clammy skin.

She groaned as the muscles in her arms strained with her renewed efforts. The blisters on her hands throbbed. What had once seemed like a good idea was becoming misery.

When she'd discovered the row-boat just above the beach, it had seemed like a miracle—her escape. In her eagerness to put distance between her and her family, she hadn't taken the time to formulate a plan. It was too late now. She pulled against the oars, willing her body to comply. Spending the night in the small craft was not a pleasant prospect. The sky darkened as clouds blotted out the sun and drops of rain splattered against the dull aluminum.

She turned to look at the nearing shoreline and pulled harder. The wind whipped her hair against her face as she fought the waves. At last, the hull scraped across the bottom. She dropped the oars and leaped over the bow, sliding on green seaweed as she stumbled on the slimy barnacle-encrusted stones. She pulled the boat up near a large rock and lifted out her damp backpack. After slipping on a windbreaker over her hoodie, she trudged up the beach and stared into the dark, unwelcoming forest. The dense tangle of brambles lining the shoreline offered little hope of shelter.

In the dimming light, she scanned the shore. "I'd better stay here," she grumbled. She walked over to a large uprooted tree that lay on the upper beach and hung her backpack from a protruding root, then dragged a few pieces of sun-bleached driftwood over in an attempt to create a makeshift shelter.

After eating a granola bar for dinner and washing it down with a bottle of water, she moved her backpack under the log hoping it would stay dry. She settled back against the tree shivering in the bone-chilling rain. The moonless, starless sky loomed dark above, enveloping her in seamless inky blackness. She spent a sleepless night hunched miserably in the pummeling rain listening to the wind whistling through trees as waves slapped against the shore.

At last, the rain let up and a silver sliver of light gleamed from the edge of darkness and spread slowly across the sky. Addie stared out across the gray water bathed in a blanket of dense fog. She stood up and looked up and down the beach, eyes searching for the boat. It had to be there. But it was not. The tide came in farther than she'd expected, and she hadn't taken the time to secure the boat. At last, the fog lifted and she saw the boat floating far out on the choppy water. Icy fear clutched her heart as terrifying reality struck her. She sank to her knees sobbing.

* * *

Myra sat on the edge of the cot, fists clutching a black T-shirt, tears rolling from red, puffy eyes.

"Honey, did you get any sleep?" Nick rolled over and put his arms around her.

Myra remained motionless then collapsed into the warm arms of her husband. He ran his finger down her face, tracing a tear.

"I'm sure she'll be all right." He tried to sound more comforting than he felt. In truth, Nick was very concerned about Addie. He hadn't slept either. Wondering where his daughter was during the stormy night had weighed heavy on his mind.

"What if she's been kidnapped? What if a sexual predator has taken her?" Myra's strained voice verbalized Nick's worries.

"She probably hiked out to visit a friend." Nick prayed silently for the best case scenario. "You know how much she hates being here."

Myra said, "We need to file a missing person report."

"It's too soon. Her backpack, blanket, several bottles of water and all the granola bars are missing. The police aren't going to do anything. We're just going to have to be patient."

Myra pushed him away and stood up. "She's only fifteen . . ."

"I'm sure she'll be back. Let's get up and have some coffee. Maybe she'll show up in a couple of hours." He hoped that would be the case, but he had a sinking feeling in his heart.

They got dressed and went out. Nick struggled with the fire in the damp mist. The thick fog unsettled his nerves as he stared at his cup of coffee. The hot mug warmed his hands in the cool morning air.

They were sitting by the fire sipping their drinks when Ethan unzipped the tent flap and came out. "Did Addie come back?"

Nick handed him a cup of cocoa. "Not yet."

"We gonna look for her?"

"That's a good idea, son. Shall we all go together?"

Myra said, "You go. I'll stay here in case she shows up. Have some breakfast first."

Monday morning, Nick and Myra dropped Ethan off at the grade school and drove to the state patrol office miles away. Without a phone or physical address, the only contact information they could give was a P.O. box and an email address. The local library was their main link to the outside world. Myra had a photo of Addie in her wallet, and the deputy taking down the information made a copy.

"I'll send out a bulletin, but I can't activate an Amber Alert. That can only be used if there is a known suspect and we know for certain the child has been kidnapped. More than likely your daughter's a runaway." He finished taking down their report. "Check with all her friends."

"Please keep us informed," Myra pleaded. She leaned against Nick's shoulder as they walked out expecting little help from the Sheriff's Department.

Nick started the engine. "Let's go to a copy store and get Addie's picture enlarged. "We need to make fliers."

After parting with some of their very meager funds they drove to the library and typed up a poster. The librarian helped them add Addie's picture to the page and allowed them to make free copies. Nick tacked a copy of the notice on the bulletin board before they left. They used more precious gasoline driving around the area posting signs and talking to strangers, praying someone would be able to help them find Addie.

* * *

Addie was cold and hungry. She ate a granola bar and drank half a bottle of water. After breakfast, she decided to explore the island. A thicket of salal and salmonberries made walking into the woods a difficult task. She decided to walk along the edge of the forest to look for a path. Discovering a narrow break in the line of undergrowth, she changed direction and ventured inland. Light was dim in the shadows of the dominating Douglas firs and hemlocks. Progress was slow. Thorny vines tore at her clothes as the woods enclosed her. She pushed branches aside, penetrating deeper into the gloom.

Her feet sloshed through a deep puddle soaking her already damp shoes and socks. "Dammit!" Cold and miserable, she shivered in the diffused light and hoped the sun would shine. As if to deny her wish, a fine drizzle fell and increased her suffering. She looked at her watch - 11:20 - and tried to suppress the niggling worry. What was she going to do? She brushed her running nose with her sleeve as tears ran down her cheeks and slogged on.

A fallen log blocked the trail and she decided to sit and rest a while. She unzipped her pack. A frown filled her face as she looked at her dwindling supplies: two bottles of water and a half a box of granola bars. The realization hit her. How could she be so stupid? Hungry and thirsty, she opened a bottle of water, but took only a sip before returning it to the pack.

Her chest heaved as a deep sigh escaped. The perilous consequences of her reckless decision to come here were beginning to invade her thoughts. No one knows where she is. She could die here. Loneliness and fear were grim companions.

She continued on, but found nothing in the woods that would alleviate her situation. She gathered some fern fronds to make a bed.

A woodpecker drummed somewhere ahead of her. Her eyes scanned the trunks in the direction of the sound, but failed to see the bird. By late afternoon she discovered a semi-dry clearing beneath the sheltering branches of a large cedar. She spread the fronds on the ground and lay down on her new bed. Exhausted from her sleepless night and day of working her way through the woods, her heavy eyelids closed and she drifted into a restless sleep.

By Monday morning, the Mathesons still had no sign of what happened to Addie. They searched everywhere they could think of and spoke to many people, but no one had seen her. They dropped Ethan off at the grade school and left a poster of Addie at the office then drove on to Addie's school.

Nick and Myra took some posters to the high school and asked to speak to the principal. Mrs. Ringwold welcomed them into her office. Myra slumped in a chair and struggled to speak, but was too choked up, words were garbled and she was unable to continue.

Nick explained the mystifying circumstances of their daughter's disappearance. The principal listened silently as he asked for any assistance the school could provide in the search. When he was finished she said, "I'll have a copy of your flier posted in every room and we'll hold a special assembly this afternoon to notify everyone. Her friends and fellow students will be upset." She held up one of the fliers and examined the girl's face. "Maybe someone here knows something."

Nick hung his head and admitted, "I'm out of work and we lost our home. Addie's been very distraught over our situation. She may have run away. We want her back and hope nothing has happened to her." As the Matheson's stood to leave, Mrs. Ringwold promised, "We'll do everything we can." She squeezed Myra's hand. "You take care. Addie will be back soon."

Mrs. Ringwold watched them walk away and hoped her words would hold true, then went out to the secretary's desk. "I need to call a special assembly at one o'clock. Please run plenty of copies of this." She handed her a copy of the sign with Addie's picture.

Chapter 7

Renee stared at the flier that was just delivered to her office. She recognized the photograph. The same girl she met near the beach. The memory of their brief encounter flashed through her mind again. What happened to you?

She listened as Mrs. Ringwold addressed the staff and members of the student body in the assembly room. It was a somber message, and students were instructed to come forward with any information if they had any knowledge of the whereabouts of Addie Matheson. The principal also suggested that anyone suffering with emotional distress should see the school psychologist. The normally noisy halls were strangely quiet as everyone shuffled back to class.

Renee attempted to give each student her undivided attention, but her mind kept drifting back to the memory of the wild-haired girl dressed in black running away from her into the woods. Addie Matheson. Now she had a name. No wonder she hadn't known her before. She counseled students with last names beginning with N-Z. Matheson wasn't in her section.

She looked at the clock frequently, and walked quickly to her car as soon as the final bell rang. Renee couldn't wait to get home. With luck she'd make it out before the long backup of traffic.

Toolie bounded out, tail wagging briskly as soon as the door was opened. Renee changed out of her work clothes and slipped into a comfortable pair of jeans and a sweatshirt. She tied her shoes, put on her waterproof jacket, attached a bottle of water to the holder in her belt and grabbed the dog leash. No iPod. She didn't want to be distracted or have her hearing impaired by music.

Toolie sat obediently while Renee fastened the leash to her collar then the pair took off at a quick jog. They ran along the beach until they got to the location where Addie had appeared. Renee stopped and looked into the woods. She decided to walk down a path near to where the girl had run into the forest. She moved slowly, studying the woods as she progressed. She didn't expect to find her there and certainly didn't want to find a body, but she continued.

She smelled smoke and headed in that direction. The path emerged into a clearing and Renee was surprised to find a large green tent set up near a campfire. "Hello!"

A thin woman was sitting in a chair beneath the tent awning. Unwashed, chin-length auburn hair framed her face. Dark bags sagged beneath liquid brown eyes that were sunken below puffy red eyelids. Her facial structure bore a strong resemblance to Addie. Her light green jacket had food stains on it and was smudged with ashes.

Renee cautiously approached the woman. "I didn't know anyone was camping here."

Myra was leery of disclosing their circumstances and unauthorized camping to a stranger. She hesitated before responding, but decided the situation with Addie warranted an explanation. She sensed she could trust this woman.

"We've been here for a few weeks. My husband and I are both out of work and we came here when we lost our home."

"Oh, I'm sorry." Renee extended her hand. "I'm Renee Stuart, a guidance counselor at Puget Sound High School. This is Toolie," she nodded toward the dog.

"Myra Matheson." She shook Renee's hand. "Would you like to sit down?"

Renee sat next to Myra. Toolie lay down in front of her feet. "Are you Addie's Mother?"

"Yes. How did you know that? Do you know her?"

"I often jog along the water. We met briefly about a week ago not far from here. You look like her. I read her name on the flier."

Myra's voice was strained, "She's missing. Sheriff's Department won't help. They think she's a runaway."

Renee paused then spoke softly, "I know. I learned about it at school today. What can I do to help?"

"We need more people to search for her. We've looked everywhere we can think of and asked her friends if they know where she is. No one has any idea what happened to her. She just vanished. We need everyone to look. She went missing on Saturday. It's been wet and cold, I'm so worried. I just don't know where she can be." Myra wiped her eyes on her sleeve.

"She's been so angry and depressed since we lost our home. It's been tough on all of us, but especially hard on Addie.

"My husband, Nick, and I also have a ten-year old son, Ethan. He's been a real trooper through our ordeal, but I know he's suffering too."

"Are you getting any kind of help?"

"The local church and food bank are helping and we get food assistance, but my husband was not eligible for unemployment. He's a self-employed contractor, and there's been almost no work. I get very little in benefits." Her voice broke as tears ran down her cheeks.

Renee reached over and clasped Myra's hand. "I don't have any paper or pens on me. I'd like to leave my contact information with you. I'll do everything I can to help."

Myra stood up and went to the tent. She came out with a notepad and pen. She handed them to Renee.

Renee started writing. "I'm giving you my phone number and email address so you can contact me. I live nearby. Here's my address." She handed the pen and paper back to Myra. "I'll stop by every day to check on you."

She gave Myra a hug. "I've got to go. I'll be searching for Addie. We'll get a whole team together. We *will* find her." She waved, then she and the dog reentered the woods.

Renee followed the path back to the beach. The light drizzle turned to a heavy rain. She looked out over the water, but the curtain of rain limited visibility over the steel-gray waves. "Addie, where are you? I hope you're not out in this weather."

She looked down at the wet dog. Drips rolled off the ends of the shepherd's long hair. "Guess we might as well go home, Toolie."

The dog looked at her and whined.

Renee turned back to the path and the two of them ran home.

Chapter 8

Addie's misery was due only to her lack of judgment. She'd blamed her parents and the rest of the world for her family's troubles and had turned that anger and frustration into something far more serious. Now, in a very real life-threatening situation of her own making, the folly of her irrational, impulsive action hit home. All the 'what ifs' and 'if onlys' couldn't change her situation no matter how much she wished she could undo the events she'd set into motion.

She forced herself to concentrate. Feeling sorry for herself wasn't going to solve anything. If she was going to survive, she needed to come up with a plan. Water was the first priority. She decided to do something about that while it was still raining.

She slung the backpack over her shoulders and started to walk farther down the trail to see if there was a source of water anywhere. After stumbling along for about half an hour she spied a shallow pool just off to the right.

She slipped off the pack, dropped down on her knees and removed the three empty bottles from the bag. The submerged bottle just cleared the rain-splashed surface when laid on its side; bubbles of air glugged out. She lifted the full bottle and replaced the cap and repeated the process with the other two empty containers. Uuuhhhg. She scrunched up her nose as she inspected the brown-tinged liquid in the bottles. At least I won't die of thirst. Not for a while anyway.

Her stomach growled noisily and her thoughts turned to food. She stared at the vegetation on both sides of the path as she progressed. April was too early in the year for berries.

The brief uplifting of her spirits at the success of acquiring water subsided, replaced by the serious problem posed by damp clothing and the cool temperature. The windbreaker wasn't near enough protection from the downpour. The dark, cloud-filled sky gave no indication that the relentless rain would let up any time soon.

The trail came to the edge of the woods and Addie walked out onto the beach. Damn, this place is sure small. She stared across the rocky beach. Her stomach growled again. She was down to her last two granola bars.

A large, flat-topped rock was lodged on the upper beach. Addie sat down on the granite and ran her hand along a smooth curved edge. She scanned the shoreline. Waves curled and broke against the rocky shore sending white-lace foam across the sea-polished stones. It was so isolated. Close to people, but so far. She'd purposely distanced herself from everyone in her life lately: family—friends—teachers. She'd turned away from the people who could help the most. Unable to accept the changes in her life, it was easier to avoid contact with people rather than admit the humiliation she felt.

Loneliness overwhelmed her as she sat on that isolated beach far from anyone. She buried her face in her hands. Gut-wrenching sobs tore from her throat as she rocked back and forth, her body washed by the rain as she sat on her ancient perch. She cried until she could cry no more. Her chest muscles burned from the effort. Spent, she stared across the water in silence.

A great blue heron flew through the rain and spread its wings to land nearby just offshore, a welcome intruder to her private space. The bird waded through the shallows balanced on tall green stilt-legs. He stood very still for a time, the narrow black head plume danced in the rain. The long neck extended down and the sharp spear-bill extracted an unfortunate crab from its sanctuary. Addie observed the bird as it focused intently from one area to another, methodically hunting and capturing selected crabs, mollusks or fish. It swallowed the creatures whole, making capturing food look easy, seemingly unbothered by the weather.

The rain slowed to a fine drizzle. She wrapped her arms around her abdomen as she watched the heron hunt and swallow his meal. She closed her eyes and envisioned a hamburger oozing with melted cheese. The smoky rich smell of meat taunted her nostrils; her mouth watered hungrily. When she opened her eyes, the smell of salty, sea air and seaweed filled her senses, replacing the imaginary burger.

She stared at slimy seaweed clinging across the rocks. It almost resembled wet bright green lettuce. She slid off the rock and walked over to a patch and pulled up a handful of the plants and stuffed some into her mouth.

"Yuck."

She forced the bite down and took another. The unappetizing meal was not very appealing, but at least it was food. She wouldn't starve. She gathered her dinner of the unfulfilling stuff. Her lips tasted strongly of salt. She slaked her thirst with a bottle of tinted water.

The memory of Walt entered her consciousness. His ancestors survived here long before the white man intruded into their world. They didn't just survive, but thrived in this area. That thought was small comfort as she shivered in the cold.

Hunger and thirst temporarily alleviated, now she had to contend with hypothermia, a much more difficult problem to solve. She had a lighter, but in the saturated environment there was no hope of building a fire.

Finding shelter became the next immediate priority. She left the beach and returned to the forest. At least the sheltering trees offered some protection from the wind and rain. She discovered a large fallen log supported at one end by a rotting stump, where a space of about two and a half feet in depth beneath the moss-covered log looked inviting. With a little work, it could serve her purpose.

Leaving her backpack underneath the tree, she went back to the beach and gathered suitable pieces of drift wood and piled them near the trailhead. It took several trips to haul them back to her new "home." She leaned them up at an angle on one side forming a slanted wall. Fallen branches and limbs placed across the top made up the next layer. Next, she chose salal, breaking off branches of the dark green, thick-leaved evergreen and wove them into the wooden framework. Sword fern fronds topped the almost-satisfactory roof and made a reasonably soft bed to finish the project. She laid her blanket on the ferns.

She stepped back to survey the results of her efforts. Her raw, green-stained hands hurt and every part of her body ached, but she felt a sense of pride at her accomplishment.

She shivered in the cold. Her damp clothing wasn't going to dry out in this weather and the windbreaker wasn't enough protection. She gathered some twigs and sticks and took her book and lighter out of the pack. She tore some pages out of the book, crumpled them up, and managed to ignite a small fire. It wasn't much, but her hands warmed a little. She took off her wet socks and draped them on sticks near the fire. She had one spare pair and put those on.

With little light left, she added more sticks to the fire and crouched beside the meager flames. Exhausted, she crawled into her makeshift shelter. Unable to sit up, she lay on her side, and tugged her hoodie around her damp hair. Wrapped in the blanket with a thick layer of ferns on top, she watched the rain until darkness swallowed her.

In her exhausted state, she managed to sleep in spite of the dampness. She awoke shivering, listening to the cheerful serenade of unseen songbirds, a sign that the rain had subsided. She peered into the dim light of daybreak. The fire was out and her socks were still wet.

Hunger pangs reminded her of the necessity of finding food. She was going to have to find something more substantial than seaweed. She ate half of the last granola bar.

Addie crawled out and stretched her aching limbs. If only she had a tent. She thought back to how much she hated and complained about living in the tent at the family's campsite. The irony of her longing seemed almost funny except for the seriousness of her current plight. She never imagined a tent would seem like an unattainable luxury. What a downturn her life had taken.

A new appreciation of how hard her parents were trying to make their lives bearable under adverse circumstances added another component to her mental anguish. Guilt. She put those thoughts aside and trudged to the beach to search for food.

"Arraaackk!"

Addie looked up and saw the heron, long neck and legs extended, flying above the water in her direction. He landed just offshore and took his stance not far from where she stood. The tide was out and she moved to the water's edge where small waves lapped against the shore.

Blue mussels clustered, firmly attached to the surface of a rock by the thread-like, brown-fibrous byssus. Addie pried one off and placed it on another rock. She hit the shell with another stone. After a few bashes, she managed to break the shell. She looked at the soft body exposed inside and scooped it out of its protective home. She held the slimy mass in her fingers and pushed it into her mouth.

"Bleeaahh." It didn't taste bad, but the texture was disgusting.

She broke another one, easier this time, but instead of picking it out of the shell, broke off the top shell and used it to detach the body, then held the lower shell up to her mouth and scooped the mollusk into her mouth with a finger. She swallowed it as quickly as possible. It was a time-consuming process and the tide was starting to come in. Addie pried a number of them off and carried them farther up the beach. A couple of cone-shaped limpets clung to a rock by strong feet. She used a shell to pry one off.

Oysters covered many of the rocks on the beach. She tried to pry off a rough, ridged shell.

"Ouch! I hate oysters!"

The bird eyed her, but did not move away.

Blood ran from cuts on her hand. She picked up a rock with three oysters on it and added it to her growing food supply.

Occasionally, she looked up to watch her feathered companion, admiring the fringes and plumes of the graceful bird as he expertly accomplished the task of finding food. She wished she could get food as easily as he did.

Satisfied with the number of shells, Addie sat down on the rock to eat. She picked up a stone and hammered an oyster. Bits of shell broke off. Finally, the ruffled mantle was exposed. Scraping the slimy mass out of the pearly hollow, she slid it into her mouth and swallowed.

"Yuck!" Slime ran down her chin and she brushed it off with the back of her hand. She picked up her hammer-stone and attacked another one.

She finished her meal. Her stomach was full, for now. Goosebumps rose on her cool skin. She shivered in the cold and returned to the shelter. Hypothermia was another very real threat. She had to rebuild the fire and find a way to get warm.

Chapter 9

Renee stared at the computer screen where Addie's image superimposed itself over the document she needed to complete. Someone needed to take action. She called the Sheriff's office. They considered Addie to be a runaway and weren't willing to instigate a search.

She would coordinate the effort to get a search underway. She called the YMCA, and local radio and television stations to request more volunteers. After a few more calls to get a phone chain going on the Key Peninsula, she brought up a blank page and began typing a bulletin requesting volunteers to meet at Joemma State Park on Wednesday, tomorrow in the afternoon right after school to search for the missing student. Notices were posted around the school and announcements made to the classrooms.

After lunch there was a knock on her door.

"Come in."

The door opened and Derek Tilton walked in. "Miss Stuart."

"Derek, what's up?" It was unusual for him to instigate an office visit on his own.

"I want to help look for Addie Matheson."

"I'm sure her family will appreciate your help."

"I met her brother. My grandpa knows her family. I'm sure he'll want to be there too. I'll pass the word on."

"Good. You're my first volunteer."

He slipped out as fast as he slipped in, leaving her to stare at the door and worry.

After school, Renee stopped at the Cost-N-Save and picked up things she knew the Mathesons would need: paper towels, toilet paper, Wet Ones, insect repellant, soap, propane, a powerful flashlight, and batteries. Things food stamps wouldn't cover and the food bank provided in minimal amounts if at all. She loaded the items into her car and hurried home to change.

"Toolie, let's go for a ride." The dog ran to the car and jumped onto the passenger seat as soon as Renee opened the door. Five minutes later they were at the Matheson's camp.

"Hi, Myra. Any word?"

She shook her head. "No . . . nothing. Renee, this is my husband Nick."

"Nice to meet you, Nick." She offered her hand. "Renee Stuart, I'm a counselor at Puget Sound High School. I brought some things I thought you might need." Renee walked to the back of the car and opened the hatch.

"You didn't have to do that." Myra objected. Tears pooled in the corners of her eyes.

"I know. I did it because I wanted to." Renee started to lift out a package.

Nick said, "I'll get those. Thank you so much. We're very grateful."

Renee handed him a box. "Our principal, Carolyn Ringwold, has made finding Addie a school-wide cause. A lot of students have volunteered to help. Everyone's keeping an eye out for her. The kids have been busy posting fliers. The whole community is working on it. A search party is coming out tomorrow after school. Derek Tilton has been a big help. "

Myra asked, "Walt's grandson?"

Renee said, "I've never met his grandfather. Derek said he knows your family."

"Walt's been spending a lot of time with our son, Ethan. Teaching him woodcarving." Nick closed the back of the car. "Ethan thinks the world of him. The man's quite the carver. He's great with kids. Real patient. Ethan's even picking up some knowledge of Native American culture in the process."

Myra looked at Toolie sticking her head out of the open car window. "Why don't you let your dog out? She won't hurt anything."

Renee went to the other side of the car and opened the door. Toolie jumped out and followed Renee to her chair and lay at her feet.

Nick reached out a hand in front of the dog. She moved to sit in front of him and placed a paw against his hand. "Okay." He took the foot then let go and scratched her back. He stopped and she pressed against him. "You're not going to let me stop are you girl?" He rubbed behind her ears.

He smiled briefly, then his expression saddened. "We had to give our dog, Toby, away. And now Addie—" his voice choked up.

Myra put her head in her hands, unable to control her muffled sobs.

Renee touched her shoulder. "We'll find her. You have to believe that. Addie seems like a tough girl. I'm sure she'll be back soon."

Myra looked up, tears streaked across her cheeks. "She looks tough. All her body and ear piercings, and those heavy chains. Dressed in black. But that's just a phase she's going through. She's not really like that. Emotionally, she's very fragile right now. She's had a terrible time dealing with what's happened to us. We all have. I just want her back."

Renee looked at this woman, her stained jeans and coat and unwashed hair. She couldn't help but think: What would she do if she were in that situation? Could she cope? She guessed we all did what we had to. But could Addie?

Another thought popped into her head. "Why don't you come to my house and take a warm bath. You can wash your hair and do your laundry. You can both come."

Myra's eyes opened wide and she raked a hand through her straggly hair. "Oh my, that does sounds wonderful . . . too tempting, really." She paused then said, "But, we can't leave. What if Addie comes back and we aren't here . . . and Ethan, he'll be coming home from school soon."

"Honey, don't worry, you go and pamper yourself. You deserve it. I'll stay here." Nick looked at his watch. "Ethan will be home in just a few minutes. If you don't mind waiting, Renee, could you take him with you? He could really use a bath. We can get the laundry together while you wait."

"Sure, that's no problem at all."

Myra got to her feet.

"I'll take care of it." Nick stood up. You relax and visit with our guest. I'll get the clothes." Toolie looked up and brushed against his leg. "Sorry girl, you'll have to get someone else to give you a rub."

Myra looked at her dirty fingernails, "You're doing so much for us. Someday we'll pay you back."

"Don't worry about it. I don't want you to. Have you heard the saying 'Pay if forward?'"

Myra shook her head, "No."

"It's a great concept. You help someone, then that person helps another person on down the line. People helping people, it makes our world a better place. I'll help you, and then whenever you're able, you help someone else."

"Oh, I like that." Myra's lips curled in a narrow smile.

Nick brought out a full large black garbage bag and loaded it into the back of the Focus. He closed the back.

"Dad! Who's here?" The boy came at a run.

"Ethan, meet Renee Stuart. She's a counselor at the high school."

"Hello, Ethan. It's nice to meet you."

He slung off his pack. "Hello. Did they find Addie?"

"No," Nick shook his head.

"Then why is Miss Stuart here?"

"I came to help your family. The high school will be spearheading a search party tomorrow."

"Can I go?"

Nick touched his shoulder. "You'll be in school, but right now Miss Stuart's going to take you to her house to have a bath, wash your hair, and do laundry."

"Oh Dad, do I have to?" He screwed up his face.

"Yes, you definitely do."

Renee nodded her head when she looked at his dirty jeans, stained shirt and greasy red hair. His freckles were almost hidden beneath a layer of dirt.

Ethan looked down and noticed Toolie. "You have a dog!"

He put his hands out for her to sniff. She sat down and lifted a paw.

"She likes to shake hands." He laughed and shook her foot.

Renee grinned, "Yes, she does."

"Her eyes are different colors! The blue one is cool!" He chuckled, his expression turned serious. We had a Pug. His name was Toby. We gave him away."

"I know. That must have made you sad."

"Yeah, Dad says we'll get another dog someday." He threw his arms around Toolie and hugged her to his chest.

She licked his face. When he let go, she crouched down and barked. Then jumped up and ran in circles around him.

Renee laughed. "You're her friend now."

"She's my friend, too."

Renee looked at her watch. "We'd better get going if you're going to get done at a reasonable time. I'll fix dinner at my house. We'll bring you some back, Nick."

Myra turned to Ethan. "Bring your school books. You can do your homework while I do the laundry."

"Aw, Mom."

She put her hands on her thin hips, "Don't *aw Mom* me. Come on."

He picked up the backpack.

Renee said, "You can put that in the back with the laundry."

"Can I ride with Toolie?"

"Sure." Renee opened the back door.

He tossed the bag over the seatback. "Toolie, get in."

She jumped on the seat and moved over. He slid in next to her and fastened his seatbelt.

Renee drove a short distance before turning down a dirt road, then made a left into her driveway. Bright colored hyacinths filled flower beds in front of the small white-trimmed, pale green clapboard house. A chainlink fence surrounded the yard.

They all got out and Ethan chased Toolie as she bounded around the yard.

"I'll bring in your laundry," Renee said. She held out the key "Here, Myra, you open the door."

Myra walked up the steps and unlocked the deadbolt. She crossed the threshold and looked around. Framed watercolors lined the walls: seascapes, landscapes, flowers, birds, and animals.

"What beautiful paintings," Myra stood in front of a family of raccoons feeding beneath a madrona tree.

"That's my backyard."

Myra read the signature on the bottom then studied the name on the painting next to it: a blue heron standing on the beach with a fish in his bill. "You painted all these? They're beautiful. You're a very talented artist."

Renee set down the bag. "Thank you. I've loved art my whole life. Took up painting when I was a kid. I've been doing it ever since. That's one reason why I love living in the country. Lots of time to observe nature and native animals in their natural habitats. Watercolor's my favorite medium, but I also do oil and acrylic."

"I wish I could paint," Myra sighed. "I've never even been able to draw a straight line."

"I could teach you. It's a great stress reliever." She picked up the clothes and carried them to the laundry room. "Why don't you put a load in first, then you can take a bath."

"What about the hot water? You'll run out."

"No, I have a demand system. It runs on propane and only heats the water as I use it. Never runs out. It's much cheaper that way."

"What a good idea. Wish I had hot water." Myra's chest heaved as a heavy sigh escaped. "Don't think I'll ever want to go camping again as long as I live." She looked down at the stained clothes she was wearing. "I need to wash the things I have on. Hope they'll come clean."

"I have a robe you can borrow. It'll take more than one load to get your laundry done. The bathroom's just down the hall to the right. Go ahead and have your bath. Take as much time as you want. Give yourself a good soak, relax, enjoy yourself. The shampoo and soap are next to the tub. There's a robe hanging on a hook on the bathroom door. It's clean, go ahead and use that one. I'll put in the first load and get Ethan started on his homework."

"You're treating me like a queen. I can't thank you enough."

"I get something out of this, too. Makes me feel good to help other people. I've been divorced for fifteen years. I don't have any children, and my parents were killed in a car wreck. My sister lives back in New Jersey and I never see her. It feels good to have someone to look after, gives my nurturing instinct something to focus on for a change."

She smiled and tapped Myra's shoulder. "Go take your bath."

Renee listened to the water running in the other room as she separated the clothes. She stared at the smelly, dingy socks. I'd better use some bleach with these whites. She added a dry scoop of septic tank-safe additive.

Ethan came in breathing heavy gasps. Toolie circled around him wagging her tail, then she ran to the laundry room and sat down next to Renee with her tongue lolling out.

Renee looked down at the panting dog. "Did you wear out Ethan?"

She walked out of the laundry room and called. "Ethan."

"I'm in the kitchen. Can I please have a glass of water, I'm dying of thirst."

"Sure." She filled a glass and handed it to him. "Help yourself if you need more. You better get started on your homework. You can sit here at the kitchen table."

He took his books out and started to work.

Myra put her hand in the water and adjusted the temperature down just a bit. When it was comfortable and the level was up, she undressed and stepped in. She lay back and submerged herself in the warmth. It felt so good. She lathered soap on her arms and legs and scrubbed. The water turned a dingy brown. Next she washed her hair, massaging the shampoo into her scalp. After a second wash she closed her eyes and just lay back relaxing in the soothing heat.

Myra came into the kitchen wearing Renee's plush pink robe and a white towel wrapped around her head. "How's the homework coming?"

"Okay."

Renee was stirring something on the stove.

Myra walked over and looked into the pan. "That sure smells good. What are you cooking?"

"Stroganoff, it'll be done soon. Ethan's bath will have to wait until after we've had dinner and his homework is finished. By then he should have some clean clothes to wear. I have a sweatsuit you can borrow until your clothes are dry. I set it on the coffee table in the living room."

Toolie was in the living room gnawing on a piece of rawhide.

Myra was smiling when she came back into the kitchen. "I can't tell you how good it feels to be clean. I always took having a bathroom for granted. I can't tell you how luxurious it felt just to soak in the tub for a while and wash my hair. I was so dirty. I had to scrub the tub out good. After Ethan uses it, I'll have to use cleanser."

"Don't worry; I'll take care of it."

Myra said, "Ethan, clear your things off the table. Take them out to the living room until after dinner." She turned to Renee. "I'll set the table. Where are the plates?"

Renee pointed to a cupboard. "I'm afraid we'll have to eat in the kitchen. I've got a bunch of art projects cluttering the dining room table."

"That's quite all right. It's a treat to be inside at any table." Myra laid out the place settings. "Ethan, go wash up, then come and eat!"

"Renee, I'm going to pull the clothes out of the dryer and put in the next load. I'll be back in a couple of minutes." When she came back, Ethan was already sitting at the table. "Let me see your hands."

He held them out in front of her. "See."

"They aren't too bad. They'll look better after your bath."

Renee asked, "Ethan, what would you like to drink?"

"Milk."

"Milk it is." She set a steaming bowl of stroganoff on the table next to another one of stir-fried vegetables.

Myra took a bite of stroganoff and closed her eyes. She chewed slowly and swallowed, "This is wonderful."

"It's great." Ethan said. He cleaned his first plate in a hurry, and helped himself to another.

Myra lifted a forkful of vegetables. "Save some for Dad."

"How about some ice cream?" Renee got up and took the serving bowls to the counter.

"Ooo! What flavor?" Ethan smacked his lips.

"Chocolate Chip"

"Yummm."

"How 'bout you, Myra?"

"Not right now, maybe later."

Renee scooped some ice cream into a bowl and placed it in front of Ethan. She started clearing the table.

Myra pushed back her chair. "Let me help."

"No, you just sit back and relax. I've got a dishwasher. I'll just rinse them off and load them in."

Ethan finished his ice cream. "That was awesome, Miss Stuart. All of it. Even the vegetables. Thank you."

"You're welcome, Ethan. Now you go in and take your bath."

"Guess I'd better fold clothes." Myra went back to work in the laundry room while Renee took care of the dishes.

Myra finished the whites and rejoined Renee in the kitchen. "Would you mind showing me more of your paintings?"

"Not at all."

Myra followed Renee into the dining and family rooms. She paused to look at each painting along the walls. Orca whales, their sleek black and white bodies, rising out of swirling blue water; in another, a pair of bald eagles circled the sky. A doe with a pair of spotted fawns emerged from a woodland.

They reminded her of the beautiful grounds around their campsite. These same creatures roamed the area. She'd seen some of them, but the paintings made her realize the special co-existence between the animals and her family as they shared the forest and water.

"Why do you work at school if you paint like this?"

Renee chuckled. "I do make some money selling cards and paintings, but I still need my day job to pay most of the bills. Besides, I enjoy working with the kids. Eventually, I'll get a pension when I retire from the school system."

Myra looked down at the floor, reminded of her family's situation.

Renee put her hand over her mouth. "I'm sorry. That was insensitive of me. I didn't think—"

"Don't apologize. I'm the one who brought it up. Let's have our ice cream."

They sat on the sofa eating dessert and chatting.

Ethan came out with a towel wrapped around him. "Mom, I'm done."

Myra went back to the laundry room and came back with his clean clothes. "Here, put these on. I'd better finish folding the rest."

A few minutes later, Ethan was dressed in a clean sweatshirt and jeans, hair combed.

Myra said, "You look like a different kid. You even smell clean. Go ahead and finish your homework.

"As soon as the laundry's done we'd better be going. I know you have to get up early, Renee. Ethan needs to be in bed at a reasonable time."

"I promised Nick I'd send some dinner home with you. I'll heat it up."

Myra packed the clean clothes into a new bag and carried them out to the car. About thirty minutes later they pulled into the campsite. Nick opened the car door for his wife and helped her out. "Mmmm, you smell good."

"I *feel* good." She smiled.

He gave her a hug and kissed her on the mouth. "You certainly do."

She changed the subject. "Laundry's in back."

He took out the bag and carried it to the tent, then walked back to the car.

"I brought you some dinner." Renee handed him a covered pie tin.

"It's still warm." He raised it to his nose and lifted the foil. It smells wonderful. Thank you."

"You're welcome. I need to get going."

"Thank you for everything." Myra hugged Renee.

"Remember, the search party will meet at the Joemma parking lot at three tomorrow."

Nick said, "I'll arrange to have Ethan go to a friend's."

"We'll be ready." Myra held Nick's hand and waved goodbye.

Chapter 10

It was three p.m. and the grassy area beside the parking lot was crowded with people, members of the Sheriff's Department and YMCA, students and faculty of the high school and middle school, friends and locals. The community had pulled together. Everyone came out to look for Addie Matheson.

Renee stood with the Mathesons at the edge of the group. Derek Tilton joined them, accompanied by an older man. "Miss Stuart, this is my Grandpa, Walt Tilton."

"Walt, I'm glad you could come."

Walt scanned the sea of bodies. "It's nice to know so many people are willing to help. A person can survive only so long in the woods in this weather. If she's out here somewhere, we'd better find her soon."

Derek pointed towards a tall, thin blond man. "Mr. Grayson!"

Simon Grayson looked around. The youth waved his arms. Simon threaded his way through the throng of people to where Derek was standing. The younger Tilton introduced him to his grandfather, the Mathesons and Renee.

"I'm sorry about your daughter," Simon said. "We'll do everything in our power to bring her back."

Renee waved to catch the attention of the deputy. "I think everyone must be here by now. We'd better get started. We only have a few hours of daylight."

The Sheriff's Department had divided the area into grids and assigned teams of searchers to cover the sections. They would start on the west side and work their way east.

The deputy announced, "Everyone, call her name now and then. This is a rescue mission, not recovery, but keep your eyes open. If you find clothing, anything suspicious, her body, don't touch anything. Shout out. The Sheriff's Department will take it from there."

No one wanted to find her corpse. If the search turned up nothing, she could still be alive somewhere.

The dense undergrowth made for slow progress. The teams struggled through the brambles and pushed aside branches to look beneath the bushes for any signs of the missing girl or disturbed soil. Sounds of voices calling for Addie and thrashing brush replaced the normal tranquility of the forest. Search and rescue dogs scoured the area.

The Sheriff called the search off at 7. "I don't want anyone out here after dark. They marked the area with surveyor's tape to keep track of which sections were done. They all returned to the starting point.

The sheriff said, "Thank you for volunteering your time. We'll continue tomorrow. Anyone who's available, show up here at nine a.m."

Everyone drifted off to their vehicles. Renee drove Nick and Myra back to their camp. Simon followed and they were joined by Walt and Derek. The mood was somber, but the fact that Addie hadn't been found left them feeling hopeful.

"She's alive, and out on the street somewhere." Myra said. "I'd feel it in my heart if she were dead."

Renee rubbed her hand where a bush had ripped her skin. "I'm sure you're right, but we have to eliminate the possibility that she's here."

Nick shook his head. "It's just so strange no one's seen her. How could she disappear without a trace? It doesn't make sense. Someone has to know where she is."

Walt said, "There are a lot of places she can hide on the Key Peninsula."

Myra's voice cracked, "Without shelter, or food—"

Derek interrupted, "Maybe she found a shed or a cabin somewhere. There are old trailers hidden around in the woods."

"Honey, that's a possibility," Nick agreed. "You know how much she hates living in the tent. What if she found a better shelter?"

"She'd tell us. You can't think she'd just take off like that." Myra rubbed her forehead. Her temple was throbbing.

"I don't know what to think. Nothing is normal. Addie certainly hasn't been herself. I want everything back the way it was. I wish I still had work and we were still in our house. I never planned to end up like this—"

"I know you didn't." Myra gave in to her pent-up emotions and tears flowed freely. She wiped her eyes and struggled to regain her composure, embarrassed that she lost control in front of other people.

The men and boys looked away. Renee touched Myra's hand. "There's no one to blame. Some things are beyond our control. I know your situation is bleak right now, but it will get better. Addie will be back."

Simon said, "I'm glad I met you. Just wish it were under different circumstances. I need to get going."

Renee moved a few steps back. "Me, too, I'll see you tomorrow."

Simon walked Renee to her car. His dark blond hair and ruggedly handsome face reminded her of Robert Redford. She'd heard so much about him, now that they finally met, she was intrigued by the man whose clear blue eyes lit up his face and met her gaze with a curious intensity.

She felt an emotional spark that left her feeling exposed in spite of the serious nature of their meeting. "I'd better be getting home."

She drove down the dirt road, his face visible in the rearview mirror until she rounded the bend.

Chapter 11

Addie opened her eyes and turned over, pushing the blanket back under the log to keep it covered in case it rained. She crawled out of the shelter and stretched her arms out to the side. It felt good to be able to sit up. The tiny shelter managed to keep her fairly dry, but gave her little room to move around.

Her forehead was hot and muscles ached. She coughed, trying to clear the ragged pain searing her throat. Her eyes closed and her head rolled back. "What am I gonna do? Thank God it's not raining." She repeated, "Oh, God." Coughed again, trying to clear the raspy sounding croak from her voice. Her chest hurt as she took deep gasping breaths feeling like she couldn't get enough air. Her chest burned with the effort. She doubled over with deep wracking coughs that left her eyes watering and chest muscles aching.

She wished for a warm bed, cup of hot chocolate, and a steaming bowl of chicken noodle soup, the warm liquid coating her ragged throat. Tears pooled in her eyes and she started to cry. She thought of all the things she'd hated about her life before she came here. Now, those things didn't seem so bad. She was so cold. The nagging fear returned. Would she ever see her family again? The thought that she might die in this place, alone, unnerved her.

She stuck a bottle of water into a pants pocket and forced herself up, then made her way to the beach. Billowing white clouds hung in the pale blue sky above the deep blue-green water. Clams had been added to her diet of mussels, oysters, limpets and seaweed. She picked up her latest tool, a thin piece of driftwood with a slight curve that served as a somewhat satisfactory hoe. If she held it with both hands, she could scoop away rocks and sand to uncover the buried bivalves. They were more difficult to harvest than mussels and the shells were harder to crack, but they tasted better.

She uncovered about a dozen and rinsed them off. Addie piled them onto a piece of blue plastic tarp she found washed up on the beach. It wasn't big enough to be of any use as a shelter, but the two-foot square served as an adequate bag to haul food. The effort of digging the clams sapped her waning energy. After adding some mussels to the pile, she picked up the corners of the tarp and carried it and her tool to her rock to break the shells open and eat.

After her morning meal she carried her empty water bottle back to the watering hole and refilled it, then returned to camp. Her skin was damp and cool; large inflamed patches burned beneath her wet clothes. Addie rolled up her pant legs and sleeves to expose her extremities to fresh air. She hoped that would help. She felt like she was freezing. Her teeth chattered as she lay shivering, arms and legs tucked in fetal position.

Her sixth day on the island passed uneventfully as she curled up, covered with the blanket and ferns, inadequate protection against the moderately cool weather. She skipped a midday meal unwilling to get up to search for food, and fell into a restless sleep.

"Addie, I brought you some soup and hot chocolate."

She reached out her hand. I'm so cold. So cold. She tried to pull her blanket around her. She opened her eyes. Her mother wasn't there. She had no blanket. The dream ended.

A memory of being tucked in her warm bed when she was sick flashed through her mind. She looked around. Moss-covered trees and ferns surrounded her. Reality kicked in. I'm on the island. I'm starving.

It was late in the day. Giving in to hunger pangs, she got up to gather dinner. A rough cough wracked her chest and she stopped, doubled over, lungs sucking air. She pulled her pant legs and sleeves back down and stumbled along the path.

Too weak to spend much energy procuring food, she watched the heron. I wish you'd get my dinner. Her wish went unanswered. She consumed her meager meal consisting mostly of seaweed. At least it's slippery so it doesn't hurt my throat. In fact, the salt slightly helped soothe the rough, scratchy irritation.

She tramped heavily back to camp and curled up to sleep. She tossed and turned throughout the night, suffering through a burning fever and icy chills. Fits of coughing rumbled from deep in her chest and pulled at sore muscles.

When the sun finally rose in the morning, she lay moaning on a torn-up bed of ferns, battered by her wild thrashing. She stayed there for the rest of the day, too weak to get up and search for food. She drank the rest of her water, but didn't get up to refill the bottles.

By morning her lips were dry and chapped, and her throat was swollen and parched. She drifted in and out of consciousness, chilled to the bone. I'm gonna die here and no one's gonna know. The thought ran through her mind at every rare waking moment.

Chapter 12

Saturday morning, Derek woke up early and ate a quick breakfast. He'd gone out with the search party every day as they looked for Addie. He thought back to the strange premonition he'd had on his thinking rock and decided to hunt for her on his own. He jogged to the beach and looked out across the water. A few feathery wisps of clouds broke up the otherwise pale blue sky. His eyes scanned beyond the shoreline.

An eagle flew overhead and circled high above the gentle waves in front of him, then soared further out toward Raven Island. Its shrill call reverberated across the water as it grew smaller. Derek squinted as he struggled to focus his eyes on the great bird until it nearly disappeared from view. It circled back. He sensed it calling to him as he watched the eagle make another pass before it flew toward the island again.

He stared at the island trying to focus on the shoreline, but the distance was too great. Concentrating his field of vision on the fluid surface, his attention was drawn to something drifting on the waves about a mile offshore, halfway to Raven Island. He used a pair of binoculars he'd borrowed from his Grandpa. It was a small boat. His heart raced as he realized it was empty.

A lump formed in his throat. Addie. Could she have taken a boat out and drowned? It was possible. He turned and ran to Walt's house. His grandfather was sitting on the front porch etching the figure of a deer onto the side of an antler prong.

"Grandpa, I need to take the canoe out."

"Oh?" Walt looked up. "Are you going fishing?"

Derek let the question hang before he finally answered. "No, I just want to go out for a while." He didn't want to say anything about the boat he'd seen until he had a chance to check it out.

"You want to take some food? You might get hungry. There's smoked salmon and geoduck, and deer jerky."

Derek was in a hurry, but he didn't know how long he'd be gone. "That's a good idea."

"Let's get you fixed up. It's always important to be prepared." Walt groaned as he stood and rubbed his aching knee. He left his tool and antler on the chair then went inside and put packages of meat into a canvas bag. He tossed in an apple and a couple of oranges. "Don't forget water. Pulling a paddle's hard work."

"I'm in good shape."

"I know, but that's not an excuse to go without provisions." Walt grinned. "You're a growing boy."

Derek tried to suppress his desire to hurry and took the bag. "Thank you."

"I'll help you carry the canoe down to the water." Derek set the bag down and went to get a paddle from a rack on the wall in the shed. He carried it to the twelve foot canoe sitting upside down on blocks in the back yard above the beach. They turned the canoe and Walt picked up the front end while Derek heaved up the back. They walked across stones smoothed by eons of tumbling with the sea's waves. They set the canoe down at the water's edge. Derek went back for the paddle and food and set them inside. The boy shoved off, jumped in, took his seat then grabbed the paddle. He raised it vertically in the air and pointed it towards shore.

"Thank you! See you later!"

Walt waved and walked back to the house.

Derek headed in the direction where he'd seen the boat. His paddle dipped too deep into the water and he pulled back hard. One side then the other, he corrected his pacing, smooth deliberate strokes. He settled into a smooth familiar rhythm. His pace was constant as he glided across the murky blue-green inlet. It took him an hour to reach the boat.

The oars were still fastened in the oarlocks and turned inside. Nothing was out of place. There was no indication that anyone had fallen overboard. He leaned over to grab the boat's rope. The canoe rocked, nearly capsizing and he paused to regain his balance. Then he tied the boat to the back of the canoe.

He wondered if Addie was on Raven Island. It wasn't far away.

The rowboat slowed his progress slightly. It tugged and lurched against the rope, making it difficult to keep up a smooth pace. He neared the shoreline an hour and a half later, and gazed along the coast visualizing where she might have gone ashore. He coasted in, jumped out onto the beach, and dragged both boats above the tideline.

Guess I'd better have a look around.

Derek saw the driftwood tree and noticed a pile of opened shells next to the clump of roots. He picked one up and examined it. Fresh. She could be here. He continued along the shoreline around the other side of the island inspecting the beach and woods for signs of a human. He noticed the large rock with the fresh pile of opened shells, more proof someone was gathering food.

He searched the brambles for a path and discovered the break in the underbrush. Leaving the beach he made his way carefully along the path, following the trail through the woods. Broken branches and trodden moss and ferns led the way. Then he spotted the fern-covered makeshift shelter leaning against a fallen log, propped up at one end by a rotting stump.

"Addie." He spoke softly not wanting to frighten her.

No response. Could be a squatter's shelter. He bent down to look underneath.

He called louder. "Addie." He caught his breath, extended his hand and shook her gently on the shoulder. "Addie . . . Addie." He panicked when she did not respond.

A moan escaped, but she didn't move.

He rolled her out and touched her hand. It felt very cold. A tangle of matted brown hair hung across her dirty, pasty-white face. She bore little resemblance to her picture on the posters. "I've got to get you back soon or you're gonna die out here."

Derek groaned as he lifted her up, bent beneath her weight. He staggered along the path and almost fell as he tripped over a branch. Her foot got hung up in clump of salal. He stumbled, almost dropping her, and set her down.

"I gotta rest," he gasped.

Addie's breathing was weak, her chest rattled and she started coughing. Her eyes fluttered open and she stared at his face. Her voice was barely audible.

"Who are you?"

"Derek. Derek Tilton. I'm gonna get you outta here."

He picked her up again and struggled back to the beach. He laid her down at the waterfront. "I gotta go get the boat. I'll be back."

He stopped for a couple of minutes to catch his breath and wondered what to do. Rowboat or canoe? He decided it would be better to put her in the canoe and leave the row boat. He'd come back for it later. The canoe would be more cramped, but he could move faster, and he figured Addie didn't have much time. It was better to get her back in a hurry. She needed to get to a hospital.

He ran to the canoe and tugged it into the water, then paddled back to where he'd left her.

A blue heron wading in the shallows stepped away as he neared the beach. Derek carried Addie to the canoe and placed her up front where he could keep an eye on her. He pushed off, taking up the paddle. He sensed the heron watching as they pulled away from shore. Then it spread its wings and took to the sky.

Addie's chest continued to rise and fall. Derek listened to her raspy breaths and watched her as he paddled, his arms forging ahead with strong brisk strokes in spite of the fatigue his muscles were feeling from the day's workout. He was gasping now too as they approached the shore. He jumped into the water, pulling the canoe onto the beach, running for the house calling,

"Grandpa! Grandpa!" He burst around the side of the house and stopped hunched over to catch his breath.

Walt came out of the house. "What's wrong?"

"I found Addie! She's in the canoe. We gotta get her to the hospital!"

"What?" Walt ran across the yard as fast as his arthritic knee would allow.

"Hurry, help me get her into your truck!" Derek was already running back to the canoe.

The older man got to the canoe as Derek was pulling it higher up on the beach. Walt reached in and gathered Addie in his arms. He carried her to the pickup. Derek rushed to open the door.

Walt slid her across the seat. "Run in and get blankets. Call 9-1-1. Tell them we found her. We're bringing her to the hospital for a hypothermia emergency." He tucked the blankets around her.

"We need to let the Matheson's know." A couple of minutes later they were bouncing down the dirt road to the campsite.

Derek jumped out. "I found Addie! You gotta get her to the hospital!"

Nick and Myra ran to the truck and peered inside. "Jeeze!" Nick's face contorted at the shock of seeing the grime-covered unconscious girl. His daughter. His fingers tightened on Myra's arm as she sank silent, to her knees.

Walt said, "Why don't I drive her to the hospital in Gig Harbor? Myra, ride with me. Keep an eye on her." He turned up the heat.

She climbed in and pulled off Addie's wet coat before tucking the blanket around her and fastening their seatbelts.

"Derek, why don't you come with me?" Nick was already climbing into the Explorer.

Derek flung open the passenger door and jumped in. Nick took off following the maroon Chevy Silverado. Forty minutes later they pulled up to the emergency room entrance at St. Anthony.

Walt lifted Addie out of the truck, her head sagging against his shoulder. He laid her on a waiting gurney.

A nurse came through a door and motioned for him to follow. "Bring her back here."

Nick rushed in followed by Derek. "My daughter was just brought in—"

The receptionist handed him a stack of papers attached to a clipboard. "You need to fill these out."

Walt walked back into the waiting room. He saw Derek seated next to Nick. "I'm going out to move my truck." He came back a few minutes later.

Nick sighed, scowling at the papers. He plowed a hand through his hair and wrote down their P.O. box, but left a number of lines blank including the spaces marked Employer and Phone. After filling out as much as he could he handed it back to the receptionist.

She looked at the forms. "You need to put your contact information."

"We only have email. We're homeless."

Her voice softened. "Just write homeless on the form."

He filled in the blank and handed her the clipboard.

"I'll take you back to see your daughter."

He walked in and looked at Addie. Her mouth and nose were covered by a mask pumping oxygen from a BiPAP. Plastic tubes ran fluid through IVs into both arms and a heart monitor patch was attached to her chest. A nurse sat beside the unconscious girl collecting a blood sample while a doctor listened to her chest.

The doctor finished with the stethoscope and laid it around the back of his neck. He turned to look at the anxious couple and motioned them out of the room. "She's suffering from hypothermia and fluid in the lungs . . . pneumonia. She certainly wouldn't have lasted another day. I doubt she would have made it through the night. You got her here in the nick of time. I'm sending her right up to the Critical Care Unit on the third floor. They'll take good care of her."

He spoke to the nurse, "We'll need to get help to transfer her onto a gurney and send her up to CCU."

Myra closed her eyes and leaned against her husband's shoulder. "Thank God." She thought of Derek and Walt waiting in the reception area. "Nick, I've got to thank the Tiltons, especially Derek. They must be wondering what's happening. I'm sure they'll want to go home.

"Ben's mom will be dropping Ethan off. I forgot all about him. Maybe they can check on him. Let's go out and thank them."

She said, "Doctor, we'll be right back."

"Don't worry. It'll take a few minutes to get her ready. She'll be right here."

The couple walked out to where the Tilton's were seated. Myra noticed loose strands of hair sticking out from Derek's black braid. Her voice was soft. "I don't know how you found her, but we can't thank you enough. You saved her life. We owe you a great debt."

Derek looked into her red-rimmed eyes. "You don't owe me a thing. I'm just glad I could help. I probably would have found her sooner if it hadn't been raining all week. After the weather cleared up, I was able to see the boat she'd used floating out there. I was curious and went out to check on it. Glad I did."

Nick smiled. "Son, what you did was remarkable. You're a hero."

Derek looked down at the floor, his face reddened, but his eyes lit up.

"We'd better get going," Walt said. "Is there anything more we can do for you?"

Nick asked, "Would you mind checking on Ethan? He's been at his friend's house. He wasn't there when we left. He's gonna wonder where we are."

Walt held his palm up, "No problem. We'll stop on the way home. I'll pick up Ethan and keep him with me."

Nick shook the older man's hand. "Thank you so much . . . for everything."

Walt led Derek to the parking lot. "It really was a miracle you found her. What made you think to look out there?"

"Yechhola. An eagle led me to her. Well, he pointed me in the right direction. Yechhola came to me and circled around, then flew to Raven Island. He called for me to follow, so I did. That is the truth. If he hadn't shown me the way, I would not have found her."

Walt looked at his grandson and grinned. "Your spirit was guiding you. Your connection to the eagle is strong. That is good."

Chapter 13

Nick and Myra sat at Addie's bedside in the Critical Care Unit. Her filthy clothes had been stripped off. Beneath a stack of heated blankets, she wore a thin cotton hospital gown.

Myra put Addie's reeking clothes in a plastic bag and tied the bag to seal them. Even wearing clean clothes, Addie stank.

"Can I give her a sponge bath?" Myra asked an attending nurse.

"Why don't we wait until tomorrow? It's extremely important to get her stabilized first. We'll worry about hygiene after her breathing and temperature are under control. She's still hypothermic. We've got to get her warmed up and hydrated. That's far more critical than cleaning her up. I'll be back in a little while to check on her. Call me if she needs anything." The nurse got up and left them alone.

Myra finger-combed her daughter's hair and pulled it away from her face. "She looks so fragile. What possessed her to go out to that island by herself?" Her voice cracked as she readjusted the blankets around Addie's shoulders.

"Where did she get the boat? I should have known she would try to run away. Didn't pay enough attention to her."

Nick reached for Myra's hand and pressed her fingers to his lips. "Honey, she wasn't herself lately. Don't blame yourself. Neither one of us could have prevented this. I've tried every way I know to reach out to Addie. She refused to open up to us. Ever since we lost our home she's been angry and hurt. If anyone's to blame, it's me. I should have tried harder to find work."

Myra brushed away a tear rolling down his cheek. "Nick, I don't blame you. I know how hard you've been trying to find a job. I haven't had any more success than you. It's just the times." Her stomach growled as the sun started to sink below the treetops visible from the window. "I didn't think to bring anything to eat." She wrapped her arms around her stomach. "I want to stay here tonight. Why don't you go on back and have dinner and take care of Ethan."

"Are you sure you don't want to come with me? We can come back later." Nick stood up and leaned his chin on her shoulder.

"No. I'll be fine. I'd like you to bring me some clean clothes and food in the morning."

Nick dug his hand in his pocket and pulled out his wallet. "Here's ten dollars. At least buy yourself something to eat."

"I don't want to spend any money for food. I can wait until tomorrow," she protested.

"You'll get sick too if you don't eat. Addie's going to need you to be strong. She wouldn't want you to starve yourself."

Clutching the bill in her hand, Myra got out of her chair and snuggled against his chest. Nick wrapped his arms around her and kissed her tenderly on the lips then pushed back the curtain. She followed him into the hall and watched him walk away.

She stopped across the hall at the nurse's station. "I'm going to stay here tonight," she told the receptionist.

"Would you like to stay in the family area? It's more comfortable in there. Or, if you prefer, I can have blankets and a pillow brought to your daughter's room. You can sleep on the bench by the window."

"I don't imagine I'll sleep much tonight. I'd prefer to stay in her room. I do need to get something to eat first. Can you tell me where to find the cafeteria?"

"The café's on the ground floor, but don't worry. I'll have the kitchen send you something."

Myra settled back on the cushioned chair beside the bed to eat her meal.

Moaning beneath the mask, Addie twisted and raised her arm. The monitor started to beep.

The nurse hurried in. She held Addie's hand and laid it back down. "You need to keep your arm straight. The IV gets cut off if you bend your elbow. We didn't want to run the IV into your hand. You have so many cuts and abrasions."

Addie opened her eyes and blinked. She moved her hand and tugged the facemask off. "Where am I?"

Myra leaned over. "You're in the hospital."

The nurse replaced the mask over Addie's nose and mouth. "You're awake. You need to leave the facemask on and keep your arm straight. The Bi-level Positive Airway Pressure helps you breathe while you're unconscious and your lungs are so inflamed. When your lungs clear up we'll be able to take you off the BiPAP and change you over to a C-PAP, continuous flow oxygen line. You'll be a lot more comfortable without that mask on your face.

"Just relax, Addie, and try to get some sleep. If you need anything, you push this button with the red cross. I'll come right in. My name is Lindsey." She smiled and squeezed Addie's hand. "You're my only patient. I'll be taking good care of you."

Myra tried to sound cheerful, "I'll be here with you, honey. I'm staying in your room all night." Addie lifted the mask off again. "How long have I been here?" Her raspy voice was barely above a whisper.

Myra touched Addie's forehead. "Just a few hours, you gave us quite a scare. Your dad left a little while ago. He'll be back in the morning. Do you need anything?"

"I'm cold."

The nurse touched the blanket. She said, "It's starting to cool off. I'll go heat some more for you and be right back."

"Can I have water? Ice?"

"Yes. I'll be right back."

A few minutes later, Lindsey was tucking warm blankets over Addie's body and around her feet. She studied the pulsing lines on the monitor, checking heart rate and respiration. "Now young lady, it's time for you to get some sleep. I'll be right across the hall."

Myra sat beside the bed and held her daughter's hand. Long after Addie drifted off to sleep, Myra started to slump in the chair and her head tilted down to her chest.

Lindsey came in and tapped her on the shoulder. "I put a blanket and pillow on the bench," she whispered.

"Thank you." Myra yawned and walked to the bench. She stretched out and the nurse covered her with the blanket as though she were the patient. Giving in to exhaustion, she closed her eyes.

Early the next morning, Jenna, another nurse, came in. She changed the IV bags and checked the lines running into Addie's arms. Jenna stretched the bands holding the mask and lifted it off Addie's face. "How are you doing today?"

Addie's voice was a raspy whisper. "Okay, I guess," Can I have some ice?"

"You sure can." Jenna went out and returned with a glass of ice chips and two warm blankets. Addie sucked on the chips while Jenna tucked the heated blankets around her.

Myra pulled off her blanket and walked across the room. She smiled at her daughter. "You're not so pale today. How do you feel?"

"A little better."

The nurse asked. "How's your chest? Are you having difficulty breathing?"

"Not as bad as yesterday." She started to cough.

"Try not to talk too much. I need to listen to your lungs." She placed the stethoscope on Addie's chest and moved it around to a number of places. "The doctor will be here in a couple of hours. We'll see what he has to say."

* * *

Dr. Sanford came in and stood next to Addie's bed. "Well, how are you this morning, young lady?"

"A little better," she rasped and rubbed her throat.

He studied her charts and listened to her chest. "I think we can take off the BiPAP and switch you to a C-PAP."

Addie nodded.

"I've got you on antibiotics. We need to leave the IV in and keep you on oxygen. You were in pretty bad shape. You're young and strong. You should make a pretty rapid recovery once we get the infection under control." He listened to her lungs and heart. "Make sure you eat all your meals and get lots of rest. You'll be back on your feet in a few days, at school with your friends. I'll be here to check on you later." He smiled and then added notes to the medical chart.

"Doctor, how long do you think it will be before we can take her out of here?" Myra asked.

"I'd say about three days, but we won't know for sure until we see how quickly she recovers. I'll have a better idea when I get the results back from the lab."

"Thank you." Myra managed a smile and followed him out. "Do you think it would be all right if I gave her a sponge bath? She's awfully dirty."

"I don't think that'll cause any problem. Just make sure she doesn't get cold. I'll be back late this afternoon."

Myra walked to the nurse's desk and spoke to the attendant.

A nurse came in carrying a plastic basin and bathing items. She set them on the table then removed the face mask and looped an oxygen line around Addie's head and ears, bringing it up to her patient's nostrils. "You should be more comfortable now." She rolled the BiPAP out of the way and turned to Myra. "Would you like some help with her bath?"

"No thanks, I can handle it."

Myra started with Addie's face. The water turned a muddy brown. "Guess I better change the water. You certainly managed to get dirty."

Addie lay silently as Myra worked over her body.

"Ouch, that hurts."

"I'm sorry. I'll be careful." Myra inspected Addie's hand. With the dirt removed, she could see numerous cuts and scrapes crisscrossing the long fingers and hand. After she finished washing Addie's body, Myra worked in dry hair shampoo.

A nurse's aide came in and helped dress Addie in a clean gown. She left with the used supplies and returned with some freshly heated blankets and covered her. "We don't want you to get cold." She tucked them around the shivering girl. "I'll see you in about an hour unless you need anything before then." She carried the used blankets in her arms.

Myra sat down and looked at her daughter. "It smells much better in here, now. I'm sure you'll feel better without all that dirt. Your skin must have been covered with germs."

"Uh-huh." Her lips turned up slightly, then Addie closed her eyes.

Nick walked in carrying two large bags. He set them on the counter then put his arm around Myra and kissed her. "How's she doing?"

"Better. The doctor left a little while ago. He'll be back this afternoon."

"I brought your clothes and food. I threw in some soap and shampoo so you can take a shower."

A smile lit her face. "Thank you." She slipped his arm off, walked over to look into a bag and pulled out a banana. "I am hungry."

He sat down beside the bed and touched Addie's fingers. "She looks so helpless," he whispered softly.

"I know." She looked down at him, then took a bite of her banana.

They were sitting beside the bed when a young woman walked into the room. "I'm Paula Hyatt, a social worker. The hospital called to let me know you are homeless."

Myra looked warily at Nick, but didn't say anything.

Nick looked down at the floor. "That's true, but it's just temporary." He looked into her eyes. "I'm sure things will pick up soon."

"I hope that's the case." She turned to Myra. "I'm here to let you know we have services to help."

"We already get food stamps," Myra admitted.

Paula handed her a business card. "I can sign you up for housing. We don't have anything available right now, but I can put you on a waiting list. I just need to have you fill out some paperwork."

Myra took the forms and glanced down the page. "Can I fill these out later? Now really isn't a good time." She set them on the counter behind her.

"Sure, you fax them from the hospital or Children's Home Society for free. If you prefer, you can mail them or come in and drop them off at our office. Do it as soon as you can."

"I will," Myra stood up and set the stack of papers on the counter by the bags.

Paula pulled the curtain back and walked into the hall. "Good luck."

'Thanks." Myra sat back down and looked at her daughter's pale face. "When she's well enough to leave, how can we take her back to a tent in the woods?"

Nick shook his head and sighed. "What choice do we have?"

Myra touched his beard and exhaled loudly, "I don't know. I wish I did. This is so hard on Addie. We almost lost her. We've got to do better."

Addie opened her eyes and looked around the room. She started to lift her arm, but the IV needle tugged uncomfortably. She laid her arm back against the bed. "I'm hungry."

"That's a good sign." Nick smiled.

"I'm sure they'll bring you something to eat soon." Myra stood up and put her hand on Addie's head. "How are you feeling?"

"Chest hurts. Sore throat. Lips . . . hands . . ."

A short time later, a nurse's aide brought in a tray with lunch and some juice. Addie ate everything on her plate. "That was really good." She smiled for the first time in weeks.

The nurse came in and walked over to the monitor. "You're looking much better."

Chapter 14

Renee stopped at the drive thru and placed her order. She paid the clerk, then took the bag and drove to the hospital following the signs to Critical Care. Nick and Myra were seated beside the bed when she walked in. "I thought you'd be here." She held up a paper bag. "How's Addie?"

"Improving," Myra answered with a smile. "She ate all her lunch. Fell asleep about a half hour ago."

"Good." Renee handed her the sack. "I thought you could use something to eat."

"That's so thoughtful of you." Myra opened the bag and looked inside. She inhaled deeply; the warm enticing aroma of burgers and French fries wafted into the room. She offered a hamburger to Renee.

"No thanks, these are for you. I had lunch a little while ago."

Myra passed the bag to Nick. He pulled out a box of fries and squeezed a packet of ketchup onto a napkin. "How'd you know we were here?"

"The Sheriff's Department notified me. Addie's rescue's been all over the news. The media have been interviewing Derek Tilton. All the kids at school are touting him as the hero of Puget Sound High. He came to see me. He's always been a quiet loner. He's embarrassed by the publicity. "

Nick stood. "I'll get you a chair." He removed a wooden chair from a closet and unfolded it.

Renee sat near the foot of the bed. She looked out the window at the evergreen covered hills. "Addie sure was lucky to end up here in this hospital. St. Anthony is exceptional."

"I've sure been pleased with the wonderful care she's been getting here. Everyone is so nice and they're always so cheerful." Myra wiped her chin with a napkin. "It's not like any hospital I've ever been in."

Nick dipped a fry into the ketchup. "Did you see the canoe hanging on the wall downstairs? This is certainly the appropriate place for Addie, isn't it?"

Renee settled back in her chair. "Yes. I saw the canoe. It's beautiful. The paintings on the walls, the building, the pools and fountains, it's so unlike any hospital I've ever seen. The Native American artwork is a nice touch. Even the walls are painted in pleasing colors. The architect and interior designers for this facility did a fabulous job. I can certainly appreciate the effort that went into this place."

Myra swallowed a bite of her hamburger. A blob of sauce dribbled down the front of her shirt. "Oh great, the burger's so juicy. I'm such a slob."

Nick crumpled the hamburger wrapper and tossed it into the trash. "Remember, I brought you a clean shirt."

"I know, but it's so hard to get laundry done."

"Don't worry about that," Renee said. "I'll help you. Just take care of your daughter."

A beep was followed a minute later by the entrance of a nurse. "Well, more visitors. How's our girl." She walked over to check the IV.

"She fell asleep after lunch." Nick yawned. "I could use a nap myself."

"Would you like to lay down in the family room? It's right down the hall."

"I'm all right for now, but I'll keep that in mind." He nodded his head.

"Let us know if you need blankets and a pillow."

Addie opened her eyes and looked around the room. "Who's in here?"

"Jenna, your nurse." She grinned broadly. "How're you feeling?"

"A little better. My throat's not quite so scratchy."

"Good. We're making progress. I need to add some fluid to your IV." She removed the empty bag and replaced it with a full one. "I need to listen to your lungs." She inserted the earpieces of the stethoscope and placed the bell against Addie's chest. "You sound better already." She looped the stethoscope around her neck. "You'll start feeling stronger in no time." She winked. "Bet you can't wait to get back to school."

Addie frowned. "I don't think so. What is everyone going to think of me now? It was bad enough before this happened."

Jenna looked at Myra. "I'll be just across the hall." The soft soles of her shoes padded out quietly.

Addie stared at Renee. "Who are you?"

"You don't remember me?"

"Should I?"

"My name's Renee Stuart. We met near the beach. I was running with my dog. You came out and talked to me and then you ran off into the woods."

"Oh, yeah. I sorta remember. Why're you here?"

"I'm a counselor at your school. I met your parents. We're friends. I heard you'd been found. I came to see how you're doing."

"Ohhh." Addie leaned her head back into the pillow and closed her eyes.

"Guess, I'd better get home and let Toolie out." Renee stood up and put the chair back into the closet. "I'll come back tomorrow." She gave Myra a hug.

Myra followed her into the hall. "I'll walk you out."

They stopped to look at the fountain.

"I'm sorry she was so rude to you," Myra apologized. She hasn't been herself since we lost our house."

"Don't worry about it. Remember, I work with teenagers. I'm used to dealing with their behaviors on a regular basis. I've seen it all." She pulled her keys out of her purse. "We'll get her through this. Things will get better."

Myra shoved her hands into her pockets. "I certainly hope so."

"It's going to take some effort to get her back on track. But cheer up, you found your daughter and she's recovering."

"True. I need to look at the bright side. It could have been much worse."

Renee walked toward the parking lot and turned and waved. Myra watched the crystal clear water cascading down in a continuous sheet into the shallow, rectangular pool below. She closed her eyes and listened to the soothing drone of the splashing drops. She thanked God for her daughter's life and included Derek in her prayers. She hardly knew the boy, but he had an extraordinary connection to Addie or the spirits—something. A few minutes later, she went back inside.

Chapter 15

Derek got off the bus and went straight to his room. He slung the backpack off his shoulder and dropped it on the desk. After eating a peanut butter and jelly sandwich and drinking a glass of milk, he went back outside.

Sword fern fronds and salal branches brushed against his legs along the familiar path between the trees. In the field beyond the woods, the high grassy carpet flattened in a line behind his footsteps ending at the flat-topped boulder. The hard granite felt cool beneath his outstretched body as he studied the billowing clouds gliding across the gray sky from the northwest. Since he'd found Addie, his life had become more complicated. He tended to be a loner, preferring to avoid attention. Now, he was thrust from relative obscurity into the eye of the public and he was feeling uncomfortable and overwhelmed with his new-found notoriety. He needed to be alone—time to think.

A woodpecker tapped nearby, the rhythmic drumming a pleasant diversion. His eyes caught sudden motion at the edge of the forest. A doe emerged into the clearing followed closely by a pair of yearlings. She paused and tested the air, eyeing him cautiously for a couple of minutes. His unmoving form did not appear threatening and the trio ventured further into the meadow. Reassured, she lowered her head to nibble tender shoots.

His eyes drifted away from the deer and returned to the cloud formations in the sky. He looked for a sign in the clouds, but they drifted in undefined shapes. Bird calls filled in the woods, and a flock of crows flew overhead cawing loudly. He thought about Addie. What happened to her? What was she like? He knew very little about her.

The familiar call of an eagle broke the silence. He looked to the sky. Two great birds soared together. He watched as they dipped and rose, danced in the sky. One broke away and landed in a tree nearby. The second bird settled on the same limb and touched the other, beak to beak.

Derek could hardly breathe. This was a sign. He watched the pair unnoticed as they continued their interaction.

At last, one bird raised its wings and rose into the air flapping to gain altitude. Its mate followed and the aerial display continued. They circled father away then disappeared behind the trees.

When they did not reappear, Derek finally dared to move. He visualized the eagles and wondered what the vision meant. What were they trying to tell him?

He felt a connection to the girl he didn't even know. He thought he should visit Addie in the hospital.

He slid off the rock. The doe raised her head and watched him, ears twitching. He moved in the opposite direction, but she bounded across the grassland and disappeared into the woods, the twins close behind.

He made up his mind to visit her the next day. He didn't know what he'd say to her—wasn't even sure why he felt such a strong urge to see her. His mind was made up. He'd ask Grandpa to take him.

* * *

Addie was sitting up in bed, an IV still hooked into her arm and an oxygen line pumping a continuous flow to her nostrils.

Myra sat at the bedside thumbing through the pages of the local newspaper. She turned the page and saw a picture of Derek Tilton standing in front of a beach beside a canoe. "Here's an article about Derek and your rescue." She handed the paper to Addie.

Addie studied the photograph before reading the story. "Ohhh . . . this is sooo embarrassing. The whole world's gonna know how stupid I am." She crumpled the paper.

Myra reached for it and tried to smooth it. "I want to save that."

"Mommmm. I just wanna forget it."

Myra shook her head. "You'll put it behind you and move on with your life. But, you'll never forget. We learn from our experiences and they help shape our lives."

Walt Tilton pushed the curtain aside. "Hello. Can we come in?"

Myra smiled, "Of course."

He entered the room. "How are you?"

"Getting better. It's nice of you to come."

Derek followed his grandfather and looked at Addie. "Hello."

"Hi." Her brow furrowed as she studied his face.

He moved closer. "Do you remember me?"

"Sort of, I don't remember much of that day. I was kind of out of it."

"Walt, have you seen the Native American art and the canoe downstairs?" Myra winked and nodded towards the door. "I'd be happy to show you." She got up and he followed her out.

"Let's give them some time alone," she whispered as they walked down the hall.

Derek looked out the window, then glanced around the room before he met Addie's gaze. "Nice room."

"Yeah, not bad for a hospital." She smiled thinly. "Thank you for saving my life. I wouldn't have lasted another day."

"Glad I found you." He was thinking that cleaned up and hair combed, she looked a lot prettier now than the first time he'd seen her.

"How did you find me? It sure was lucky."

"I don't think luck had anything to do with it. My totem led me to you."

"Your totem?" She frowned.

"Yechhola."

"Yuck whata?

"Yechhola. That's Lushootseed for eagle."

"What's loo shoot seed?"

"Lushootseed, the language of our ancestors, the Coast Salish Indians. I am of the Squaxin Island tribe. Noo Seh Chatl. People of the Water.

"Yechhola came to me with a message. Called me to follow him. That's when I saw the empty boat. I thought maybe you drowned. But when I got out there, I figured you were probably on the island. I followed the trail." He shrugged his shoulders. "That's how I found you."

Addie frowned crookedly. "Hmmm. yeah . . . right . . . What's a totem?"

"My animal spirit guide. The eagle is my family's totem. Eagles have sharp vision and are great hunters. They communicate with the Great Spirit." He paused, looked out the window. His eyes closed and he tilted his head back. Finally, he opened his eyes and met her gaze. He licked his lips and swallowed, then continued. "The Great Spirit knew where you were. He sent the eagle to show me so I could find you and bring you home."

Her eyes narrowed. "That sounds hard to believe."

"Believe it or not, it's the truth."

Her expression changed. Her thick lashes fluttered. Doe brown eyes opened wide and locked on his. Then her facial muscles relaxed and her eyes narrowed slightly. "How do you find your totem?"

He pulled a chair closer to the bed and sat down. "A totem finds you. It may come in a dream or a vision. An animal may come to you in life. Often, it will spend time with you. Totems are teachers. We learn from their wisdom."

"Can anyone have a totem?"

He crossed his arms and leaned back. "I don't know why not."

"When I was on the island, a heron came every day. He stayed nearby while I searched for food." She scratched her head and looked out the window. When she turned back she met his gaze unblinking. "I watched him hunt. He was my only companion for the week. I didn't think about why he was there. He was just part of the surroundings." She pulled the blanket closer around her. "Could he have been my totem?"

Derek brushed his hand across the top of his head. "I saw him. He wasn't there at first, but when I carried you out of the woods to the beach he was wading in the water close by. Perhaps the bird was watching over you."

"Maybe he was. I wished he would get me something to eat. He didn't. Watching him motivated me to find food. I ate mussels, clams, oysters and seaweed. It was hard work, but I had food." She lifted her hands, opening and closing them slowly.

He noticed her scratching at a long scab on her palm. "You should leave that alone. It could get infected."

She rubbed her palm against her chest. "It itches. My hands got cut up breaking the shells. I was doin' okay 'till I got sick and too weak to gather food. It probably would have been all right if I had a dry shelter. I was always so wet and cold." She snuggled the blanket under her chin.

"It feels so good to be warm and dry. So glad I don't have to search for food anymore. Even being in the hospital, wearing this funky gown feels wonderful."

Addie relaxed against the bed and ran her hands through her hair. "Dry shampoo didn't do a perfect job, but it sure feels good to be clean." She looked at Derek's long dark hair. "Is your hair tied with leather?"

"Yeah. Deer hide. Grandpa tanned it himself." He smiled shyly. "I think you look pretty good. A lot better than the last time I saw you." He noted the look of surprise in her eyes. His face felt hot. He stepped away and stared out the window.

"No one's told me I look good lately. I don't know you. Why did you want to find me?"

Derek faced her again and looked in her eyes. "Grandpa knows your family, especially your brother. I wanted to help."

"I can't thank you enough. I don't remember seeing you at school. I transferred from Orchard High last year. I don't know many kids at Puget."

"We haven't had any of the same classes." He looked down at the floor. His fingers pinched the inside of his thigh. "I had to do community service. Been busy. Done with that now."

Addie's raised her eyebrows. "Community Service? What for?"

"I was stupid." He shrugged and gave her a strange look. "Smoked dope. Got busted."

"Oh." She paused. Finally, she said, "I've been feeling so sorry for myself. I guess I haven't noticed; I'm not the only one with problems."

"Well, it's over now. Learned my lesson. Besides, working at the food bank was a good thing."

Derek turned his head when he heard Myra and Walt walk in. He saw her smile.

"You're certainly cheerful." Myra pulled a chair out of the closet, unfolded it and sat down near the window. She motioned towards the other chair, "Have a seat Walt."

"You're looking much better than the last time I saw you. It's good to see some color in those cheeks and sparkle in your eyes," Derek's Grandpa said with a grin.

"I'm feeling better."

"That's good to hear. You gave everyone quite a scare."

Addie's cheeks flushed. "I didn't mean to freak everyone out. Just needed to get away for a while. Didn't plan on getting stuck out there."

"We know." Myra laid her hand on her daughter's arm. "We're so glad to have you back. We came so close to losing you. Without Derek's help . . . " her voice choked off.

His Grandpa looked at Derek. "Everything will be fine."

Addie's gaze shifted from the older man to Derek. "You look so much alike. Same dark eyes, same nose and lips. You even wear your hair the same way. Derek your Grandpa must have looked just like you when he was young."

The nurse entered. "You're certainly popular today."

Addie nodded with a smile. "Yeah, seems like it."

Jenna stood beside the bed, took a package out of her pocket and removed a syringe and test tube. "I need to take some blood."

"Again." Addie frowned.

"Sorry, I just need a small sample. It won't hurt much. I promise." She wiped Addie's arm with an alcohol pad.

Addie closed her eyes and bit her lip as the needle went in and the tube filled with blood.

"That didn't hurt much did it?" Jenna removed the needle and taped a gauze pad over the puncture.

"No." Addie opened her eyes.

Jenna tipped the sample back and forth and labeled it. "I'll be back in a while and the doctor will be here in a couple of hours." She smiled and disappeared behind the curtain.

Derek said, "Grandpa, I need to get home and work on my schoolwork."

"I guess, we better let Addie get some rest," his Grandpa said.

"I'm so glad you came by." Myra said.

"Yeah, I'm glad you came. Come and see me again sometime." Addie smiled at Derek.

Derek stood up. "Sure, guess we can do that if Grandpa doesn't mind."

The creased face chuckled. "Oh, I think we can manage that."

"Good." Myra followed them out.

"We'll stop by tomorrow," Walt said.

Myra looked into Derek's eyes. "Addie really perked up when you showed up. Thank you."

Derek's cheeks burned. His fingers pinched into his thigh. "I'll see you tomorrow." He walked next to the older man as they got on the elevator.

Neither spoke as they left the hospital and walked across the parking lot. After they got into the truck and fastened their seatbelts, Walt looked at Derek before he started the engine. Grandpa said, "Addie is a very troubled girl. Maybe you can do some good. Give her direction. She needs a friend."

"Yeah, I know. She wanted to know how I found her. I told her about the eagle and our totems. I think she found her totem, the heron. She said there was one near her every day."

"That's not a common spirit, but it is possible. She's not of the tribe. Not familiar with our ways. Maybe she could have a totem. The bird must have sensed her need."

"I guess. I saw the heron. He watched as I took her away."

"He must have been looking out for her." Walt turned the key, the engine started and they pulled out of the parking lot.

Derek noticed Grandpa's face sag. He thought about Grandpa's family. "How's Uncle Ray doing?" Derek asked.

"Not good. I should call Arleen when I get home. Ray is very frail. He doesn't have much time left. The cancer . . ."

Derek looked silently out the window. A crow picked at the body of a rabbit lying dead on the shoulder of the road.

Chapter 16

Renee answered the phone. She tried to keep the surprise out of her voice. "How are you Simon?"

"Keeping busy."

"Me, too. Things have eased up some since Derek found Addie. He's quite the hero around here."

"I can imagine. He's quite humble. Bet he hates all the attention."

She chuckled. "That's an understatement."

"After all the stress of the past week I can use a break. I know it's short notice, but I was wondering if you'd like to go out to dinner tonight?" After a brief pause, he continued. "I have some ideas on how to help the Mathesons. I'd like to get your input."

"So, it's a working dinner?"

"Well—not exactly," he hesitated. "I have an ulterior motive. I thought it would be a good chance to get to know you better."

"So, you're asking me out on a date?"

"Yes. Yes I am."

"Sure, I'll go out to dinner with you. Do you have a place in mind?"

"Do you like Italian?"

"I do."

"How about the place in Purdy? I hear the food's good there."

"Mario's? I've been wanting to try it sometime. I don't go out to eat often."

"Does six o'clock work for you?"

"Yes." In truth she wasn't busy any night.

Renee turned and looked outside. She could almost see the restaurant from her window. "Why don't I meet you there? I can stay at school late and catch up on some paperwork, then I can go over to the hospital and see how Addie's doing before I meet you."

"Why don't we make it an hour earlier? You won't have so much time to kill."

She looked at the clock. "Sound's good. I'll be at Mario's at five."

"Great. See you then."

She pushed the off button on the phone and stared at the handset before replacing it on the base. That was out of the blue. She hoped he hadn't detected the real reason she preferred to meet him at the restaurant rather than have him pick her up at home. She hardly knew him and didn't want to have to worry about having him in her house.

It had been a long time since she'd been on a date. She'd been calm on the phone, but now her heart was racing. He did seem nice. She hoped he wouldn't turn out to be a jerk.

* * *

Renee locked her office. She called, "Goodnight," to the janitor as she left the building.

Fifteen minutes later she walked into Addie's room at the hospital. The bed was empty. She crossed the hall to the nurse's desk. "Was Addie Matheson released?"

"No," the nurse answered. "She's been moved to room 212 on the second floor. "She doesn't need to be in CCU anymore."

"Oh, that's good news." Renee walked away.

"Do you need help to find her?"

"No thanks."

On the second floor, a man in scrubs pointed her in the right direction.

"Hello." She announced cheerfully as she entered the room and walked over to Myra and gave her a hug.

Renee let go of Myra and turned to look at Addie lying on the bed. "You're looking a lot better." She noticed the color had returned to Addie's cheeks and the girl was breathing without the aid of the BiPAP machine.

"Thanks," Addie said. The trace of a smile lit her face. "I remember you, Renee."

"That's right." Renee reached out and wrapped her fingers around the bedrail. "You're going to be out of here in no time."

"They're talking about releasing her soon." The tone of voice and drawn facial expression on Myra's face indicated to Renee that her friend was worried about Addie's return to the campsite.

"That's good news." Renee looked at Myra then smiled at Addie.

Addie's brow furrowed, her eyes narrowed and the frown returned. Her voice had a grim tone, "I suppose."

"Aren't you looking forward to getting out of here?"

Addie looked across the room and stared out the window. "They're really nice here. It's warm and dry. The food's pretty good."

Myra stood up, leaned over and grasped Addie's hand between hers. "Honey, you know you can't stay here."

"I hate going back to the tent." Addie sighed. "I know it'll be better than living out on that island, but I want to live in a house. I hate camping." She started to cry.

Myra sat back down, closed her eyes and exhaled a long loud breath.

Renee pulled a chair from against the wall and sat down next to Myra. "We'll come up with a solution. Simon Grayson's working on something. In fact, I'm meeting him in a little while to discuss it." Her face felt warm as she glanced at her watch. It was almost four.

"Really? That's interesting. Maybe he wants to get to know you better. "

"No." The reply sounded sharper than she intended.

Myra reached over and touched Renee's arm. "He seems so nice. He's good with kids. Maybe he noticed what a wonderful woman you are. You live out in the country alone. It would be nice if you found a nice man to share your life."

"I'm not alone. Toolie keeps me company. I stay busy." Renee looked at the floor. She wondered how the conversation turned to this. "I'm not doing so bad. Everything's going on an even keel."

"No, professionally, you are doing very well. But don't you get lonely?"

"Sometimes, I guess. But I don't let it get to me."

"Things may be going badly for us right now, but I can't imagine what life would be like without my family. Nick is my rock. We'll get through this as long as we have each other." Myra nodded. "I know we'll turn our lives around." She walked over and combed her fingers through Addie's hair. "There's no doubt in my mind."

Addie looked at her mother and said, "I never knew you were so strong."

The curtain in the doorway opened. Nick and Ethan walked in. "How're my girls." He leaned over, wrapped his arms around Myra and hugged her to his chest.

"Look who's here." Myra motioned toward Renee.

"It's good to see you, Renee. How have you been?" A grin spread across his face, lighting his eyes.

"I've been doing well. How about you?"

"Still looking for work. I've managed to pick up the odd job here and there."

"Guess you must have been looking for work when I stopped by a couple of times."

"Could be."

Renee stood up. "Take my chair, I need to leave anyway."

"You don't have to run off on my account," Nick said with a wink.

"I'm not. I have an appointment." Renee walked past him. "Let me know if you need anything."

"Thanks for stopping by." Myra waved.

"I'll see you soon."

Renee arrived at Mario's ten minutes early, decided to go in and wait, and found Simon already there.

"You're early." A smile lit up his eyes. "Thought I'd better get here early just in case. Didn't want to keep a pretty lady waiting."

"Are you ready to be seated?" the hostess asked and picked up menus.

"Yes please." Simon swept his arm down and to the side indicating Renee to lead. He followed as they were led to a table overlooking the water.

"How's this?" the hostess asked.

"Perfect." Renee said.

"Yes." Simon seated her and sat across.

The hostess placed menus on the table. "What would you like to drink?"

Renee opened her menu. "Just water for me, please."

"Make it two," Simon looked at Renee. "Care for hors d'oeuvres?"

The hostess filled their glasses. "Your waiter will be right with you."

The waiter came with a basket of fresh bread and a dish of seasoned olive oil and took their order. A starter of Calamari Fritti and the seafood linguine to split between them.

The calamari came right away and the waiter refilled their glasses. Renee picked up a strip of the crispy, light-battered seafood and took a bite. "This is wonderful. The best I've ever tasted. I'm glad you suggested this restaurant."

"I'm pleased you agreed to join me. I've been looking for an excuse to try this place out."

She noticed how his cheeks crinkled when he smiled. The deep blue of his eyes sparkled and matched the shirt beneath his navy blazer. Renee looked away and dipped a spoon into the oil and spread some on a piece of bread.

The soft bread was so tasty, she chewed slowly. So far, the evening was perfect.

They finished the bread and the waiter returned with a fresh basket and refilled their glasses. Then large plates of linguine covered with clam shells, salmon and shrimp were placed before them.

Renee swirled her fork into the pasta and took a bite. The flavors melded together slid across her tongue. She swallowed. "Mmm, it's delicious."

Simon slid a clam out of the shell and popped it into his mouth. He finished it off and took a drink of water. "It is marvelous," he agreed. "The service has been so fast and the food so good, we haven't had much chance to talk."

"I've been enjoying it very much . . . so far," Renee looked into those blue eyes and was glad she'd made the decision to meet him rather than have him pick her up. Everything about this man intrigued her, yet she still knew almost nothing about him.

Dinner finished and plates cleared, the waiter refilled their glasses and brought panna cotta, berry-topped cream custard for dessert.

Renee tasted the first spoonful. "This is heavenly. You're spoiling me."

Her large eyes with their fringe of thick lashes fascinated him. He loved the dimples in her cheeks when she smiled. Everything about this woman captivated him. She was athletic, but not the strained, undernourished bony features of so many women he knew. She had the appealing curvaceous body that was comfortable to hold.

The kind his hands could sink into. His thoughts were drifting into territory he wasn't even close to reaching.

"We've almost finished dinner and you still haven't told me about what you've come up with to help the Mathesons."

Her words broke the silence and brought him out of his reverie. He turned his thoughts from Renee. "No I haven't."

"How long are you going to keep me in suspense?"

"I wanted us to enjoy our dinner before I brought up business. I'm glad I did. It's been good so far."

"You make it sound like you haven't had much success."

"I've been checking on a number of possibilities, but most weren't much help. The best option I've found is a caretaker/groundskeeper job for an elderly woman on an old farm out in Longbranch. It doesn't really pay, but it's a live-in position with a small separate house for the family. I figure with Nick's construction experience, he could fix the place up. It's a win-win situation for both of them." He took a bite of panna cotta.

"That does sound encouraging. I'm sure they'd be overjoyed to have a house to move into."

"I hope so. I don't know the Mathesons very well, but I know Noreen Avery from the Senior Center. She's a sweet old lady and a tough old bird. She's independent and has been doing her best to keep the place up by herself, but she can't do yard work anymore." He swallowed another bite of dessert. "The buildings are in need of repair. I've fixed up a few things in the past, but she could really use someone out there with a carpenter's experience to do the work and keep an eye on the place. It would help her out. I've talked to her about it and explained their situation. She's anxious to meet them."

Renee grinned. "It sounds ideal. Myra would be happy to help any way she can. They're going to be so happy to move out of that tent. Addie's been dreading checking out of the hospital and going back to the campsite. It would be wonderful if they could move her into a real house."

He loved the way her whole face lit up. "That's what I've been thinking."

"When can we talk to them about it?" Renee leaned across the table obviously excited.

"I think it would be best to discuss it with Nick and Myra first just in case they aren't enthusiastic about the idea. I don't want the kids to get upset if their parents turn it down. It's better if they find out after Nick and Myra meet Noreen and have a chance to look the place over."

"They'll never turn down such a deal."

Simon sipped some water. "Probably not, but I've worked with people enough to know that nothing is ever a sure thing."

"You're right." She nodded. "Still, I can't imagine them rejecting this opportunity."

"I can't either." He finished the last bite of his dessert.

"When are you going to tell them?"

"I thought we could do it together. You've spent so much of your time and energy helping them. It's fitting that you be a part of the solution."

Renee touched his hand. "I appreciate that. How about tomorrow? Addie will be getting out of the hospital soon. It would be a terrific going home present."

"Why don't you talk to them and arrange a time for us to get together. You can call me and let me know." He took a business card out of his wallet and wrote down his cell phone number before handing it to her.

She looked at the card before putting it into her purse. "I'll check with Nick in the morning. Myra's been staying at the hospital."

"Maybe tomorrow won't work."

"I'll let you know."

The waiter came back with the bill. "How was everything?"

"Superb." Simon laid down some bills. "Keep the change."

"Thank you." The waiter picked up the money and bill.

"It really was fabulous." Renee added. "The food was scrumptious and the service was excellent."

"I'm glad you enjoyed it. Come back again."

"We will," she said. "And I'll recommend it to my friends."

Simon walked Renee to her car. "I hope you had a good time."

"I did. Thank you for a wonderful evening."

He reached for her hand. "I hope that means you'll go out with me again."

"Yes, I'd like that." She squeezed his hand. "I enjoy your company."

"How about next week? Would you like to go hiking on Saturday? The mushrooms are out. It's a good time to look for them."

"I've never done that." She looked skeptical. "I don't know what ones are edible. Is it safe?"

"Of course, I'd be happy to show you." He let go of her hand.

Renee opened the car door. He touched her hand again and said, "I'll wait for your car to start and make sure you get going okay."

She smiled. "What a gentleman."

"That's me." He closed her door and waved.

Chapter 17

The next morning Renee took Toolie and jogged to the Matheson's camp. Nick was sitting beside the campfire holding a cup of coffee.

"Good morning." Renee came out of the woods and walked across the campsite.

"What are you doing here so early in the morning? Can I get you a cup of coffee?"

"No thanks. I had enough already." She sat down next to Nick and stretched out her legs. "Simon Grayson and I want to talk to you and Myra about options for Addie when she's released from the hospital."

He looked puzzled. "What's it about?"

"I'd prefer to wait until Simon is here. We'd like to speak to you both together, without the kids around. Simon's been trying to come up with some help for you. We think he has a good option, but he wants to run it by you first. I think it's a good idea and I'm quite sure you'll think so too."

"You've certainly aroused my curiosity." He finished his coffee and poured another cup. "Myra's still at the hospital."

"Where's Ethan?"

"Walt's giving him carving lessons on Saturdays. He offered to keep him over there for the day. He's a great influence on the boy and it will keep Ethan occupied while we deal with Addie. I'm going to the hospital shortly."

"I could have Simon meet us over there. What time are you going?"

Toolie perked up her ears and looked at the bushes. A young cottontail emerged and twitched its nose. It paused and looked around. Toolie stood up and whined and moved toward the rabbit. It hopped back and disappeared into the underbrush.

"Toolie, lie down!" The dog returned and laid at her feet.

Nick looked at his watch. "It's almost eight-thirty. I guess I could leave about nine."

"I'll ask Simon to meet us at the hospital sometime around ten." She stood up and Toolie moved to her side.

"I'm sure that will be fine with Myra. See you over there."

Renee pulled back the curtain and entered the hospital room. "How are you doing this morning?" She smiled at Addie then gave Myra a hug.

"I'm okay," Addie said.

"She'll be going home soon." Myra smiled, but her eyes flashed a wary look at Renee.

Renee looked at Nick. "Did you tell Myra about our talk this morning?"

"No. I didn't get a chance yet."

A nurse's aide came in. "My, you've got lots of company this morning. You're looking chipper. Your skin's got a pink glow and your voice sounds good."

"I guess so." Addie shrugged her shoulders.

Rene nodded at Myra. "Why don't we give her some space for a few minutes?" She left the room and Myra followed her out. Renee said, "Simon Grayson will be here shortly. He has something he would like to discuss with you and Nick."

"What about?" Myra's voice sounded apprehensive.

"You'll find out." Renee touched Myra on the shoulder. "I think you'll be pleased. When he gets here, we can go down to the café to discuss it."

"You don't want Addie to hear?"

"Not yet. He wants you and Nick to have a heads up first. Let's go back to the room. He should be here soon."

Addie was sitting up drinking a cup of juice when Simon walked in.

"Hello, a fine morning it is today," he said. He turned toward the bed. "You must be Addie, our long lost explorer." He grinned. "I'm Simon Grayson. You had everyone on the peninsula out looking for you. Gave your family quite a scare. You're one lucky girl."

"I guess." Her cheeks reddened.

A nurse came in and said, "I need to run some checks on Addie, now. It will just take a few minutes."

Renee caught Simon's eye. "Sounds like a good time to go downstairs and have some coffee?"

He winked at Renee. "Good idea. Would you folks like some? I'm buying."

Nick leaned back and rubbed his neck. "I'd love some. How 'bout you, honey?"

"Sure, why not?"

Myra reached over and wrapped her fingers around Addie's hand. "Do you mind if we leave for a while?"

"No. I'm fine."

Myra released her hand. "We'll be right back."

Simon touched Renee's shoulder. "Lead the way. I haven't been here before."

As soon as they were seated at a table, Nick asked, "What do you want to talk to us about?"

Simon stirred some cream into his steaming cup. "I think I found a place for you to live. It's a caretaker job with a private house for your family. But it would be a lot of work. You'd need to fix it up and take care of the buildings and grounds. The elderly woman who lives there can't maintain it by herself. She can't afford to pay a salary, but you'll have a house to live in."

"Where is it?" Myra asked.

"On a farm. In Longbranch."

"That sounds wonderful. We should tell Addie."

"I'd prefer to take you and Nick out there first and introduce you to Noreen. I'm sure you'll like her, but I don't want you to make a decision without seeing the place. It's an old house and bit rundown. Needs paint. Some of the wood's got dry rot."

Myra set down her cup. "After living all these weeks in a tent and going through the ordeal with Addie, anyplace would be an improvement."

Nick blew on his steaming cup. "When do we get to see it?"

"I told Noreen I'd give her a call first."

Nick said, "It sure would be great if we didn't have to take Addie back to the tent."

They drank hurriedly. Simon said, "Let's take a trip out to see Noreen."

"I'll drive," Renee offered.

"You don't mind?" Myra asked.

"Of course not. It'll be fun."

Myra told Addie they had to leave for a while. They followed Renee to the parking lot and all climbed into the Focus.

Simon sat up front with Renee and took out his phone. "Noreen, this is Simon. We'll be there in about forty minutes." After a brief conversation he closed the phone. He turned to face the back. "She can hardly wait to meet you."

Blue-gray water slapped the shore as they drove across the Purdy spit and headed for the Key Peninsula. The tide was out and a crew was harvesting oysters from wire baskets on Burley Lagoon. A silvery sun glinted beneath a pale mask of clouds. A windsurfer skirted across the waves scattering a flock of coots creating a dark flurry of wings as they rose above the waves on Henderson Bay.

Light dimmed as they wound along Highway 302 between towering fir trees. They took the Key Peninsula Highway and paused at the almost town of Key Center while a mother with a toddler and two older children crossed the Key Peninsula Highway from the Credit Union to the library. Sections of forest separated pastures of grazing horses, sheep, goats, llamas, and cattle. Peafowl, chickens, ducks, and geese roamed on a couple of farms.

They crossed the Home bridge passing the food bank at Key Peninsula Community Services and continued south to Longbranch.

"Turn left at the road up ahead," Simon directed. "Just past that pasture with several horses. "Third house on the left." They drove slowly in the shade of large maple trees that lined both sides of the long, deep-rutted dirt driveway. Blossoms brightened lichen-covered fruit trees in an old orchard overgrown with tall grass.

Renee parked out front of the two-story wood-frame house. They crossed grass in need of mowing. Nick ran a finger across the peeling pale yellow paint. The loud bay of a hound dog came from inside when Simon knocked on the door.

A minute later the door opened and a smiling woman with a head full of short white curls greeted them. The red hound howled again.

"Buster, quiet." The woman patted the dog's head.

"Noreen, I'd like you to meet Nick and Myra Matheson."

"Glad to meet you. Come on in." She held the screen door open.

"And this is Renee Stuart, a counselor at the high school."

"It's a pleasure to meet you." Renee smiled.

"Let's sit down in the living room." Noreen leaned on a flowered cane as she hobbled across the hardwood floor and pushed a huge white-footed tabby to the side. "Fremont, you are going to have to move." The cat reluctantly shifted until Noreen got comfortable in the recliner and then crawled onto her lap. The hound circled then curled up on a tattered throw rug next to the chair.

"Noreen, I'm afraid we're kind of short on time," Simon said. "The Matheson's daughter is in the hospital."

"Oh, that's right. How's she doing?"

"Much better, thank you." Myra said.

"That was quite an adventure she had. I read about it in the paper. Even saw it on TV. Everyone was talking about it."

Nick nodded. "I know. We need to put that behind us and move on to a normal existence."

Noreen stroked the purring cat. "I'm hoping we can help each other. I don't want to move out of my home into some retirement place. I grew up on this farm. All my things, Freemont and Buster, I can't bear the thought of leaving this behind. I love the peace and quiet, except for the chickens of course. What farm's complete without hens and a rooster?" Her musical bubbling laughter filled the room.

Myra said, "It's hard to move away from a home at any age."

"Simon, why don't you take them out to see the guest house? Ben and I lived there after we got married. My parents lived in this house."

Simon said, "Good idea. I know where everything is." He rose and led the other three out. Around the side of the house, beyond the chickens, the single story cottage resembled the larger home.

Simon opened the door and they went inside. The floors were the same oak hardwood. Myra entered the kitchen and looked out the window framed with farm-scene curtains. Red barns, cows, horses, chickens and sheep sprawled across rolling hills of green fabric near the large white porcelain sink. Above the maple cabinets, a row of pot holders with various colored chickens wrapped the sunny yellow room in cheerful country color. A small dining room looked out over an overgrown pasture with a faded red barn.

Myra peered down the hall. "Let's see the bedrooms." She opened the first door and looked into a small light blue room with a single bed covered with a multi-colored crocheted afghan. She walked across the floor and slid the closet door open. "This would work for Ethan."

The bathroom was small, but it had a tub with a shower. Nick turned the faucet handle at the sink. Water flowed brown at first, but quickly ran clear. A spider ran across the back of the tub and up across the white tile.

Myra said, "It's going to take some elbow grease to get this place spruced up."

Simon asked, "Think you're up to the task?"

She nodded. "Yep."

Another small bedroom, with pink walls and a single bed with a flowered lace-edged quilt held a large armoire. A full-length mirror hung on the closet door.

"Addie's black clothes and heavy chains are going to look out of place with all those pink flowers and lace." Nick shook his head with a smile.

"Oh, I don't know. After everything she's been through maybe she'll be happy just to have a room." Myra said.

At the end of the hall Nick opened the door and looked at the double bed with a hand-stitched quilt. The walls were a light cream. A strip of wallpaper border with sprays of lavender wisteria trimmed the upper wall. Dingy white lace hung at the window. It wasn't a large room, but was about half again the size of the smaller two.

Myra sat on the edge of the bed. "I can hardly wait to move in. It'll be wonderful to be in a real house again, sleeping in a bed instead of on a cot."

Nick asked, "You're sure you're up to the work and time it'll take to live here? It's a big commitment."

"Absolutely. It will be nice to clean and cook in a real house again. Helping Noreen will be a pleasure. It'll be like a vacation after living in that tent." She allowed herself to fall backwards onto the mattress. A powdery spray of dust particles shot into the air dancing in the filtered light. "Feels heavenly."

Nick flopped down beside her and wrapped her in his arms. "You're right it feels wonderful." He kissed her on the lips.

Blushing, she whispered, "Nick, Renee and Simon are watching."

"I didn't see a thing." Simon looked away with a teasing smile. "You need a room of your own with a bed. I imagine sleeping in a tent with kids has to be difficult."

"You can't imagine," Myra said with a sigh.

"I take it you want to take the job?" Simon grinned.

"For sure." Nick jumped off the bed and reached a hand out to Myra to help her up. "Let's go back to the house and tell Noreen."

Nick knocked on the door.

"Come in."

Noreen had the recliner tilted back. She raised the chair to a sitting position and laid a book on the table beside her. "What do you think?"

Myra squeezed the bony fingers of a frail hand. "We love it already. When can we move in?"

"As soon as you want, but you may not love it quite so much when you realize how much work there is to do around here.

Myra said, "I really don't want to get Addie out of the hospital and bring her back to the tent." She looked at Nick. "Let's surprise her. Not tell her about the move. Just bring her here and welcome her to our new home."

"That's a terrific idea." Renee had a sudden idea. She couldn't wait to tell Simon. "Speaking of Addie, we'd better get you back to the hospital. You all get in the car. I'll be out in a minute." After the door closed, she leaned towards Noreen. "I'd like to get the house ready for them before they come back. I think I can get Simon to help."

"Honey, Simon's a real good man. I'm sure you can get him to do whatever you want. I saw how he looks at you. His wife left him years ago. He needs a nice lady." She winked.

Renee was at a loss for words. Finally, she admitted, "It's been a long time since I've been with a man. I divorced fifteen years ago. I'm used to having my own space. Doing what I want, when I want. Besides, I hardly know him. But, I do like him."

"Take the time. Trust me." She squeezed Renee's hand. "He'll be worth the effort."

Renee left the house and rejoined the others. She slid onto the driver's seat and fastened her seatbelt.

"What did you tell Noreen?" Myra asked.

"Oh . . . it was nothing. I just needed to use the bathroom." She drove silently to the hospital listening to the animated conversation of the passengers.

"I'll drop you off at the front entrance." She pulled in and stopped the car. Myra and Nick got out.

"Thanks for everything," Myra said.

Nick reached for Myra's arm. "Yeah, thanks to both of you."

"You're welcome. I'll see you later." Renee turned to Simon as they closed the doors.

"Simon, I want to do something special for them. I was wondering if you'd like to help?"

"What exactly do you have in mind?"

"Just a little party, hang up a welcome home sign, crepe paper streamers, maybe a few balloons. We could invite Walt and Derek. We could stop and pick up some cake and ice cream and some party decorations."

"That does sound like a good idea, the perfect touch for a special day. I'd be happy to help."

Chapter 18

Nick drove past the road to camp. Addie looked out the window. "Where are we going?" she asked.

Myra said innocently, "We have to stop somewhere else first."

The Explorer turned off the main road and bumped slowly down the driveway.

Addie raised her voice, "Where are we?"

Nick slowed the car. "You'll see in a minute. We're almost there." He pulled up in front of the cottage. The Focus was parked off to the side. "Renee must be here." He turned off the engine.

"We have something to show you. Let's go inside." They got out and Myra put her arm around Addie's waist. Nick opened the front door and waited for Myra and Addie to cross the threshold.

"Surprise!" The cheering group welcomed them inside.

Addie's jaw dropped. She was speechless. Finally, she found the words. "We have a house? We don't have to live in a tent?"

"That's right." Nick laughed. "We have a home."

Myra couldn't hide her surprise. She glanced around the room wide-eyed. Colorful streamers draped from the ceiling. A 'Welcome Home' banner hung from the living room wall. "You went to all this trouble for us?"

Simon grinned. "It was no trouble. Actually, we had a lot of fun doing it."

Addie noticed Renee glance at Simon. Renee said, "He's right. We had a wonderful time."

A silver-haired woman came in and tapped her cane on the hardwood floor. "Why don't you all sit down and have some cake and ice cream?"

Nick moved to stand beside her. "This is our landlady and my new employer Mrs. Avery."

"Noreen." She corrected him.

Nick helped her move to a chair at the head of the table. "Noreen." he said, a wide smile spread across his face.

"Would you like to see your new room, honey?" Myra led Addie down the hall and opened the door.

Addie leaned on the bed and touched the quilt. Then she moved to look out the window. She opened the closet and peered inside. "This is really my room."

"Yes." Myra hugged her.

"Awesome."

"Let's go back and enjoy the party."

Derek handed Addie a plate with cake and ice cream. "I'm glad you're out of the hospital."

"Me, too. Let's sit on the porch." She opened the door.

Myra turned around and called. "Addie, where are you going?"

"Outside."

They sat on the front steps and ate their cake and ice cream in silence. Addie set her plate to the side on the porch and walked into the yard. "Have you been here before?"

"Nope."

They wandered over to the chicken coop. Two hens spotted a beetle walking across the ground and chased the bug. The first bird nipped at the hard shell, the second bird pecked the first as they fought over the insect. The first one swallowed it before the second could take it away. The later arriver pecked the first one on the back.

Addie looked away. "I didn't know chickens were so mean."

"They have a pecking order. Most animals do."

She changed the subject. "I'm glad we don't have to live in that tent anymore. I was dreading that. Maybe I can have friends over."

"I can come and see you sometimes. You're not that far away. Maybe you can come to my house."

"Maybe." She frowned. "I've got so much homework to do to catch up. Don't know how I'm gonna get it all done."

He leaned down and picked up a stone. After rolling it between his fingers, he lobbed it against a tree. "At least you're alive and you've got a good place to study now."

Addie nodded. "You're right. Almost didn't make it."

He looked her in the eye and touched her hand. "You've got a second chance. You were saved for a reason. Make it count for something."

Derek seemed to have a way of looking at things that made sense to her. "Guess I should learn to pay attention to you." She looked towards the house. "We should go back in. Everyone's gonna wonder what we're doing."

They walked across the yard and rejoined the party.

Myra looked up when they walked in, "Where were you?"

Addie said, "Checkin' out the chickens. Didn't know they were so mean, fighting over a bug."

Noreen chuckled. "They're not really so mean. They know who's boss."

Addie followed Renee and Simon into the kitchen. She dropped her paper plate and plastic fork into the trash. She overheard Simon tell Renee they should start winding down the party.

Renee replied, "You're right, but I don't want to leave them with a mess. We should stay and clean up."

Addie interrupted, "I can help."

Simon glanced toward the living room. "I'll pass the word to Noreen. Addie, why don't you come with me?" They left Renee and rejoined the group.

Addie listened as he leaned over Noreen and whispered, "Can I walk you back?"

"What's that?" She touched his arm. "My hearing's not so good."

Simon spoke louder. "Let me take your plate."

Addie blurted, "I'll get it."

"I'm finished. It was delicious, but I can't eat any more." She handed her plate to Addie. "It's been a long day. Past my nap time." She took Simon's arm.

Walt looked at his watch. "We need to take off. My brother's not well. I need to visit him in the hospital."

Nick turned to the weathered face and raised an eyebrow. "I didn't know. Hope it's nothing serious."

Walt frowned. "My brother's had a hard life. Issues from the Vietnam war, PTSD, Agent Orange, alcohol. He has liver cancer."

Myra said, "You've helped us and never hinted at your problems." She laid a hand on his shoulder. "Go spend time with your brother."

"The tribe takes care of our own. His family does what they can. I haven't seen him much lately. Don't get down to the reservation often. I need to see him before it's too late." He turned to his grandson. "Time to go."

Addie followed Derek outside. "When will I see you?"

Derek said, "How about Saturday? Something I want to show you."

"What?"

"Wait and see." He looked over his shoulder. "I'll be here at ten."

She waved. "See ya."

Addie went back in and announced. "I'm gonna take a bath. Been a long time since I've soaked in a tub." She closed the door, stripped off her clothes and left them in a heap on the floor.

Warm water surrounded her. She lay back into the soothing heat, closed her eyes, and drifted off to sleep.

I'm cold, so cold. The rain. It's freezing. She woke with a start, her eyes wildly searching the room. She was lying in a bathtub. The water had cooled. "Thank God it was only a nightmare. I'm not on the island." She got out and wrapped a warm towel around her. Her heart rate slowed and breathing returned to normal.

Chapter 19

Saturday morning the sound of a vehicle pulling into the driveway was accompanied by the baying bark of Buster.

Ethan jumped up and ran to the door. "Walt and Derek are here."

Addie tilted her bowl and swallowed the rest of her breakfast in two gulps.

"That wasn't very ladylike." Myra said.

Walt leaned out of the truck and looked at Ethan. "Ready for your next carving lesson?"

"Sure am." Ethan bolted down the steps and ran to the passenger side.

Derek got out. "We all fit in." He helped Addie get settled on the back seat of the Silverado before he climbed in beside her. Her leg and shoulder felt warm pressed against his body.

Ethan sat up front with Walt. Walt dropped the teens off at Derek's house and they watched him drive away with Ethan.

Addie said, "You don't live far from your Grandpa."

"Nope, just about half a mile," Derek said. "C'mon, follow me." He took off at a brisk walk down a path through the woods.

"Where are we going?" Addie was right behind him.

Damp leaves brushed against her legs as they moved along the path. She fought to suppress negative feelings as they made their way through the woods. They entered a clearing and continued to a huge flat rock.

"*This* is what you wanted to show me? A rock?"

"It's my favorite place. My thinking rock, but it's not where we're going." His arms swung easily at his side as he crossed the field and followed the path into more woods on the far side.

The tree line ended and the trail came to an abrupt stop. They were standing on the edge of a cliff. Gray waves lapped at the beach far below. Visibility was limited by a light drizzle that blotted out the sun and turned the sky gray.

"We aren't going to the beach are we?" Addie peered at the rocks below.

"Shhhh." Derek put his finger to his lips and motioned to the right.

"What is it?" Addie looked skyward.

"Look up in the tree. The big madrona over there." He pointed to a large reddish brown trunk, exposed roots protruding beyond the eroded vertical drop-off. "Up there."

Addie scrutinized the twisted sepia branches. "That's what you brought me to see? A pile of sticks."

"It's an eagle nest. Be quiet and watch." She crouched against the salal and stared at the nest partially concealed by thick dark green leaves.

A few minutes later, widespread black wings glided in and the bald eagle landed atop the nest. Shrieking cries met the parent as the young eaglet opened its beak. The large bird tore off bits of flesh from a fish clutched in its talons and deposited the food into the hungry chick's mouth. Only after the fledgling stopped begging for food, did the parent rip off hunks of meat and consume its own meal. After preening its feathers, the bird stood on the edge of the nest, spread its wings and took off into the air. It soared away and circled north; joining its mate, the pair dipped and danced in the sky.

Addie didn't take her eyes off the duo. "Wow! That was so cool. I've never seen anything like it."

Derek nodded his head.

The eagles circled back and then disappeared behind the trees. Derek stood up and offered a hand to assist Addie. She felt his strong fingers enclose her own and pull her up. She was still weak after her close call with death. His strong arm raised her easily. Her skin tingled in his warm grasp. He released her hand and moved onto the path.

"Let's head back." He didn't look to see if she was behind him. His long black hair tied with a piece of rawhide hung down to the center of his broad shoulders.

Addie followed him silently except for the sound of her legs brushing against the dense undergrowth. He stopped abruptly. She nearly bumped into him.

He turned his head and spoke softly. "Listen."

Taptaptaptaptap

He turned his head, his eyes searching up and down the trunks of trees. "There it is," he whispered pointing, "About halfway up that fir with a broken top. See it?"

"No. I mean I see the tree, but what are you looking at?"

"A pileated woodpecker. He's right underneath that crooked branch. See his red crest?"

Addie stared at the tree.

Taptaptaptap

"I see him. He looks like Woody Woodpecker," she said with a laugh.

"They're not too common, but there's a pair that nest here every year. This area is a great place to come and watch the animals." After a while, the bird flew off and faded into the forest.

Derek advanced and they returned to the meadow. He strode toward the large rock. He put his hands on its level surface and vaulted up. He stood and looked down.

Addie placed her palms on the weathered granite and attempted to heave herself up.

"How'd you get up there?"

"I'll help you." He crouched down and extended his hand. He leaned back and hauled her up. The two of them sprawled across the top laughing. He sat up and crossed his legs.

"I spend a lot of time here. I've never brought anyone here before. Eagles often fly over and deer browse here every day. It's a great place to meditate and gather my thoughts."

The tall grass waved in the gentle breeze. A flash of bright yellow burst from the right and lit on a tall spire of grass. The tiny gold finch plucked seeds from the waving spire, then darted off to harvest another. A chickadee chattered nearby.

Addie breathed in deeply and felt enveloped in a wave of overwhelming peace and euphoria. She planted her hands on the surface behind her and leaned back. "This place is amazing." She took off her shoes and socks and curled and uncurled her toes in the fresh air.

Derek followed her example and stood up, his bare feet flat on the stone. Shoes and socks dropped to the ground and the two of them stood atop the rock, their pinnacle of freedom in a world of their own.

Derek started to chant, his voice soft, clicking guttural sounds unfamiliar to Addie's ears. A tempo that lulled her into a higher level of peace. He began to move his feet. Methodic practiced foot-beats, his head tilted back and his arms reached out as he bent and swayed. Addie's own feet tapped and moved to the age-old sounds. His fluid movements—hypnotic—inviting—swooped around her body and captured her soul. Primitive motions seemed to tell a story. Throaty deep-voiced sounds grew louder, emanating from deep within his throat. Each movement drew her deeper into the field of his powerful emotions.

She was raised to a level of consciousness she had never felt before. She watched, transfixed. Her feet raised and lowered in similar, timid mimicking reactions. Together they moved; he informally teaching, she following his lead.

He threw back his head. A loud whooping wail erupted from his lips. As suddenly as it had begun, the moment ended. He closed his eyes and sucked in air, filling his lungs then exhaled slowly in a long drawn-out sigh.

Something about Derek seemed altered. A new calmness emanated from him. Addie noticed the change and was stunned by the transformation. His physical appearance was still the same, yet something was different. He smiled and touched her hand.

"We should go." His words broke the spell. He jumped off the rock and extended his hand. She took it in hers and allowed him to help her down.

She bent over to slip on her socks and shoes and finished tying her laces. "Aren't you going to put your shoes on?"

"No, I want to feel the earth." He walked barefoot through the field, a path of bent blades in his wake.

Addie passed through the damp field. Somewhere from the trees a robin sang melodiously. Gray clouds opened up and a wide breach of blue appeared in the steel sky. She listened to rustling branches, her thoughts immersed in the setting. The forest, once her foe and a harbinger of anger and frustration was again a comforting friend.

As they emerged from the woods, Derek halted to put his shoes and socks back on. "We'd better get on over to Grandpa's. I wonder how Ethan's doing with his wood carving."

They walked side-by-side in silence as they headed down the road. Addie was surprised how tuned in she was to the sights and sounds coming from the trees as they walked along. The pair turned down the driveway and waved to the old man and boy sitting on the porch.

Ethan jumped up and ran to meet them. "Look what I made!"

Derek examined the wood. It was still a little rough on the surface, but there was no doubt the object in his hand was a frog. "You're doing a good job."

"Thanks." Ethan beamed as he strutted back to the steps with the frog displayed on the palm of his hand.

Walt said, "It looks good, but you still have some finishing to do. You'll be taking it home today."

Ethan sat on the porch, picked up the knife and went back to work.

"So what have you two been up to?" Walt asked.

"I showed her the eagle nest—"

Addie broke in, "It was really cool. The eagles were amazing."

"Thought we'd take the canoe out," Derek said.

Addie's eyes narrowed and she stared at him mouth agape. "In a boat. On the water? I don't—"

"You need to go back out." Derek didn't let her finish. "You'll be fine."

Addie clenched and unclenched her fists as she rocked back and forth on her feet. "You didn't say anything about that."

"No, I didn't." He took her hand. "Come on. I won't let anything happen to you."

She heard Walt's voice.

"Have fun."

Fun. Going out in a boat was the last thing she wanted to do. "I've had enough of boats."

"You need to confront your fears."

"I'm not afraid of boats. I've spent more than enough time at the beach." She tugged against his arm.

He was stronger and pulled her forward. "Come on. Don't be such a chicken."

"I'm not a chicken." She thought about the hens at Noreen's.

He let go of her hand and grabbed two paddles off the rack in the shed. Lips pressed firmly together, she followed him to the canoe. He set the paddles inside and lifted the end closest to the water and pulled forward.

"Can you get the other end?"

He set it into the water and pushed it forward. "Get in."

She did as he asked and moved to the front. He pushed off and jumped in.

Derek asked, "You want to paddle."

"I don't know?"

"Don't worry. There's nothing to it." He handed her his paddle and picked up another one from the back. "You work on one side and I'll take the other."

Addie slapped the paddle into the water on the right side and splashed it back.

Derek said, "Not like that. Watch me." The wood dipped smoothly into the water. His strong arms pulled back to finish his stroke, lifted the paddle above the surface and leaned forward, repeating the process. "Now you try it."

Addie held the paddle out and pushed it vertically into the water with a small splash and pulled back.

Derek nodded. "That was better. Keep it up. I'll take the left side."

He pulled the paddle smoothly, in rhythmic even strokes. Addie plunked hers into the water, splashing them both. Spray erupted as she drew it back. The canoe turned to the left.

"We need to work together. It's a team effort. Watch how I dip the paddle straight in and pull back."

She watched his strokes and did as he said. They headed straight out.

"That's better," he said.

"This is far enough." She didn't want go far from shore. "Let's go parallel to the shoreline." They turned and headed north.

Addie watched the houses as they floated by. A group of people stood on the beach and waved. She waved back.

"Look." She pointed. "There's a heron."

The bird stood in the water, head angled down as it searched for food.

"It's a sign. He's here to guide you." Derek moved them in closer. He spoke softly. "Be quiet. Let's watch him."

They drifted on the waves. The bird eyed them, but did not seem to be alarmed by their presence. It stabbed the water with its beak and swallowed a fish, then moved farther away. A few minutes later the bird flapped its wings and took to the sky.

"Time to head back." Derek picked up his paddle.

Addie thought about the heron. She wondered if it was the same one she'd seen on Raven Island. Was the bird really a messenger sent by some spiritual being to guide her? Her life certainly seemed different since her near-death experience and her connection to Derek. She wasn't sure what it all meant, but she had a strange premonition that her future was altered.

Chapter 20

Nick and Myra entered the food bank and signed up for their basket. Myra looked over the bread and selected a loaf of garlic bread, croissants and two loaves of sliced bread. Nick picked up a box of doughnuts.

A woman came in and set her purse on the counter. "How's it going Stan?"

"Oh, we're still a driver short for the bread truck. Can't seem to get a reliable person to take over after one of the guys had his hip replaced."

"Too bad. Hope you find someone soon." She signed her paperwork and moved to the bread shelves.

Nick stepped over to the counter. "You need a driver? I'm not working. I wouldn't mind doing it."

Stan said, "It's a voluntary position. Doesn't pay any wages. You'd have to be able to drive our box truck to Gig Harbor, weigh and load all the boxes of donations at each store, and then unload them here when you get back. We pick up on Tuesdays and Saturdays. It's a backbreaking job and takes several hours."

"That's okay. We're receiving food from here. Seems like the right thing to do to give back to the organization that's helping our family. I'd be happy to do it."

"Nick?" A volunteer pushed a full cart out.

"Yep, right here." He took the cart and Myra placed their bread and pastry on top and then turned back to the counter. Nick asked, "What do I need to do to sign up to drive the bread truck?"

"Go around the building to the office upstairs and fill out a volunteer application."

"Wait a minute. I'll come with you." Myra said, "I'd like to work in the food bank. I might as well fill out the forms when you do. I'll run the cart in and we'll go up together."

* * *

Nick looked down from the top of the ladder. "I scraped the moss off the roof. Now I'm cleaning out the gutters. They were full of crud. It's a wonder any water drained at all."

Noreen said, "I thought I heard you working up there. I'm sure glad you're here to take care of things."

"It works both ways. We're very grateful to have a place to stay."

"I enjoy the company. It's nice to have young people around again."

Nick climbed down. "I've got to stop working and get cleaned up. I'm making a bread run for the food bank this evening."

"Don't let me keep you." She walked over to the chicken pen, bent down, picked a handful of clover and pushed it through the wire. "Here chick, chick . . ."

The birds scrambled over and scarfed up the leaves.

Nick watched the birds fight over the greens, then he carried the ladder back to the barn.

* * *

Nick came in and flopped down on the sofa in the living room. "Whew, what a job. We went to Costco, Safeway, Albertson's, Fred Meyer, and QFC. They call it a bread run, but we picked up meat, dairy products, vegetables, fruit, and boxes and boxes of bread and pastry. Everything had to be weighed and signed for."

He took off his shoes and rubbed his feet, then lay on his side on the sofa. "I'm beat. Sure will feel good to soak in a hot tub. Boy, am I glad to come home to a real house and hot water."

Myra pushed his legs, "Scoot over and I'll rub your back and feet."

He pulled his knees up and she sat down with his feet on her lap. He closed his eyes. "I sure have missed that. There are a lot of things you can't do very well in a tent."

* * *

Ethan was rolling on the grass, his arms around the red hound. "Buster I got you! I got you!"

The dog twisted out of the boys grip, ran to the driveway. The Silverado pulled up.

Aaaaahhhuuuuu . . . Aaaaahhhuuuuu

"Buster, be quiet." Ethan commanded.

Walt and Derek got out.

Ethan stood up and ran to his friend's side. "Hi, Walt. What are you doing here?"

Nick and Myra came out of the house.

Nick laid his hand on the roof of the truck, "How're you doing?"

Walt took a long breath and sighed. "Not so great. My brother passed away two days ago, Tuesday."

Myra covered her mouth with her hand. "Oh, I'm so sorry."

Nick shook his head, "I don't know what to say."

"I told you he wasn't doing well. It wasn't unexpected. My sister-in-law's having a hard time. I need to help her out this weekend. That's why we came by. I wanted to let you know, I won't be able to have Ethan come over on Saturday."

Ethan looked up at Walt. "I understand. It's okay."

Walt's thick fingers ruffled the flame-red hair. "I'll be able to have you over in a couple of weeks after things settle down.

Myra said, "Don't worry about it. You've helped us so much. Is there anything we can do for you?"

"No, but thank you for offering. Arlene and her family have very strong ties to the tribe. They'll be taken care of.

"That's another thing. I know Derek planned to spend Saturday with Addie, but he has a special duty to perform. My brother was a war hero, a Vietnam vet. He will receive special honors as a warrior. There will be a canoe pull for him. We call it a canoe pull because the paddles are pulled back against the water.

"The ashes of a warrior are placed in a canoe to make the journey around Squaxin Island, our tribal spiritual and cultural center. There will be a ceremony when they return with the ashes. Derek was selected to be one of the canoe pullers."

"Derek—" Walt looked to the other side of the truck for his grandson. "Where'd he go?"

"Addie's in the house." Myra said. "Maybe he went in to look for her. I'll check." She turned and said, "Dinner's almost ready. Would you like to stay and eat?"

"Thanks for offering, but we need to get to Arlene's."

She continued up the steps and opened the door. "Addie?"

The teens were seated at the table.

"Derek's great uncle died," Addie said.

"Yes, I know. Walt told us."

"I was just telling Addie I can't see her on Saturday."

Derek stood up to leave. "I have to go. See you at school tomorrow."

Nick watched the truck drive off. He put his arm around Myra's waist. "Our girl's growing up. Glad she and Derek can't drive yet. It's a little easier to keep an eye on them. He seems like a good kid."

Myra said, "Walt insists he is not using marijuana anymore."

"That's a good thing. But, she'll be sixteen soon. Old enough to date."

"I know."

Chapter 21

Simon picked up Renee for their first mushroom foray together. They left the Key Peninsula and headed west, traveling along the south shore of Hood Canal. Several boats were out on the flat gray water. They left the lowlands, drove up into the wooded foothills in the shadow of the Olympic Mountains. The gravel road wound along the edge of the hillside and continued over a bridge suspended above a deep gorge.

Renee looked down then closed her eyes. "How much farther?"

"We're almost there. Few more miles."

The road got steeper, a narrow cut between tall firs and cedar. Renee grabbed the dashboard as the wheels bounced into a rut and the truck lurched forward. Around a bend the road straightened out and widened. Simon pulled off to the side.

"We'll try our luck here first." He set the parking brake and got out. He opened David Aurora's book, *Mushrooms Demystified* and showed her the pictures. "They look sort of like fir cones, or elk poop. They can be pale gray, brown or black."

"Well that narrows it down." She laughed.

He handed her a mesh bag. "Make sure you stay within sight. It's easy to get turned around out here. You don't want to get lost." He draped a lanyard with a whistle around her neck and handed her a walkie-talkie.

She turned it on and spoke into the microphone. "Don't' worry. I'll be right behind you."

He pushed a sword fern aside and headed down the path. "Let's go."

He climbed over a large moss-covered log, turned and held out his hand. She accepted his help and followed him over. Her fingers tingled after he released his grasp. They continued slowly along the trail, eyes to the ground. "There's one. See it?"

She looked to where he was pointing. "No."

"Right over there next to the trail underneath the big fir." He knelt down and cut the stem with a knife and handed it to her. "Where there's one, keep looking. They grow in patches."

She touched the soft rippled cap. He cut several more and dropped them into his bag. Renee studied the ground but didn't see any. "There's one." She reached down, but instead of a morel, she picked up a fir cone.

He laughed. "They're camouflaged, blend in with the cones. Makes 'em hard to spot sometimes."

She stopped following right behind him and moved farther to the right. She discovered a small clearing and studied the ground. "Aha, I found one." She cut it off and held it up. It's bigger than the ones you got."

"Keep looking all around there." She added two more to her bag. After she stood up, he walked over and found another four nearby.

"You missed a few."

"How'd I miss those?"

"It's easy to spot the big ones. Small morels are tough to see. Search in circles. Look behind you. They don't look the same from different directions."

He stopped. "Look at that."

"What?"

"Boletus edulus, King bolete." He brushed off a large dirt-covered cap, cut into the bulbous stipe and looked inside.

"What are you doing?"

"Checking for worms. This one's good. Got it before the bugs did. Have to get them right as they come out of the ground or it's too late." He put it into a separate bag. "Don't want to get dirt on the morels."

Simon's bag was three quarters full by four o'clock. He had another bag with several boletes. Renee brushed some twigs off a three-foot wide stump and sat down on the soft moss beside a huckleberry bush growing out of the top on one side. "How many have you got?"

"Fifteen." She handed him her bag.

He held them up and looked through the mesh. "You've got some nice ones and they look fresh. I think we should head back. It's been a long day. I don't know about you, but I'd like to get home and get out of these damp clothes." He handed back her bag.

"I'm ready." She stood up. "The mosquitos will be out soon." Renee walked behind him and felt a sense of relief when she finally saw the truck parked on the road.

She leaned against the door, took off her hiking boots, and slid her feet into tennis shoes. "That feels better." She relaxed in the seat. Touched her hand where he'd held it.

His voice interrupted her thoughts. "What do you think about sharing our mushrooms with the Mathesons? I thought we could bring food over for a barbecue tomorrow if they're not busy."

"What a wonderful idea. Let's stop by there before you take me home?" She leaned back, closed her eyes and drifted off to sleep.

Simon hit the brakes. Renee lurched forward against the seatbelt. Her eyes flew open.

"Oh!"

He looked over. "Sorry, didn't mean to wake you."

"I was dreaming."

"A squirrel ran right out in front of me."

She looked back out the window. There was no sign of the squirrel. "You didn't hit it?"

"No. That was one lucky critter."

They turned in at Noreen's and pulled up in front of the guest house. They could hear Buster inside the main house. They walked up and knocked.

Myra opened the door. "This is a surprise. Don't tell me you just happened to be in the neighborhood."

Renee laughed. "No, as a matter of fact we are just back from the Olympic Peninsula. Simon took me on a mushroom foray—"

Simon broke in, "Thought you might like to enjoy eating some of our wild fungi tomorrow. We'll bring all the food. Noreen has a grill. I'll do the cooking."

Myra looked skeptical. "Is it safe? I've never eaten wild mushrooms. Can you be sure they aren't poisonous?"

"Been collecting fungi all my life. It's a family thing. Learned from my parents and grandparents."

Nick joined his wife in the doorway and draped his arm over her shoulder. "I'm sure this man knows his mushrooms. He's not going to poison us. Did I hear you say you're volunteering to do all the cooking, too?"

"Sure am. Another thing Dad taught me. He's one heck-of-a good chef. I make a mean mushroom burger."

Nick raised his eyebrows. "What a guy. Can't pass up a feast like that."

"What time?" Myra asked.

"How about two o'clock?" Simon looked at Renee. "That'll give the sun time to warm things up and we'll have plenty of time to get the grill going and eat before it starts to cool off."

"Would you like to come in?" Myra asked.

"No thanks. Want to get home and put my feet up. It's been a long day." Renee took a step back.

"I'd better get the lady home. See you tomorrow." Simon walked to the truck. "Pass the word on to Noreen."

"Will do." Nick waved.

Renee fastened her seatbelt. "That was very nice of you to offer to bring all the food and do all the cooking tomorrow."

"I'm a nice guy."

She brushed her fingertips across his arm. "You are."

He stopped in front of her house and got out. "You can carry your morels. I'll get your gear." He handed her the bag. Toolie ran back and forth along the fence barking.

Simon carried her pack. "How about a bottle of wine. I just happen to have a nice Riesling. I could sauté some fresh mushrooms."

She said, "That does sound nice."

He worked in the kitchen while she changed her clothes. She returned wearing clean jeans and a sweatshirt. "That smells delicious."

"Have a seat." He served her a plate, poured the wine and sat facing her. They clinked glasses. "Here's to wild mushrooms and a beautiful woman to share them with."

Chapter 22

Nick was cleaning the grill while Myra wiped off the picnic table and benches and adjusted the green plastic tablecloth. She placed a vase of red tulips and bluebells on the table and was heading to the house for the plates and silverware when Simon and Renee drove up.

Renee joined them and set a bowl on the table. "My contribution."

Myra loosened the cover and peeked in. "My, that looks good."

Renee set sliced pickles, onions and tomatoes along with condiments next to the salad.

Half an hour later the coals were ready. Simon laid patties on the grill and stood by as they sizzled over the white-hot orange glow. He set up a single propane burner and melted butter in a frying pan. Herbs and sliced mushrooms went into the pan after the butter melted.

Nick heard the door on the main house close. He hurried over and took Noreen's arm.

"Been a long time since I had a handsome young man as an escort."

He helped her into a chair at the end of the table. "I don't know about the handsome part and I'm not so young. Gonna be thirty-six in a couple of months."

"Honey, compared to me you're just a lad."

Ethan and Buster ran across the orchard. "What's cooking? Smells good." He reached into the ice chest and pulled out a soda.

Myra brushed an ant off the table. "Where have you been?"

"We were out back in the pasture. I found a tree with a hole in it. Climbed up to see if there was anything in it."

Nick asked, "Was there?"

"An old bird nest." Ethan reached for a potato chip.

Myra said, "Let me see your hands."

He held them out.

"Go in the house and wash up. Tell your sister to come out and join us. Dinner's almost ready."

Simon slid a burger onto a bun, ladled some morels over the top and delivered it to Noreen. She sniffed her plate.

"Smells good."

He served up the rest of the table. Addie and Ethan came out and sat down.

Ethan wrapped his mouth around the burger. Cheese dribbled down his chin as he chewed. "This is the best hamburger I ever ate."

Myra swallowed the food in her mouth. "Ethan, wipe your chin."

He rubbed his face with a napkin and took another bite.

"I agree with Ethan," Nick said. "You're one heck of a chef."

Myra licked her lips. "The mushrooms are delicious."

Simon helped himself to fruit salad, "They're one of my favorites. Glad you like them. You'll have to go on a foray sometime. It's relaxing hiking out in the woods. A wonderful way to spend a day.

Addie stared into space. "I've had enough of being in the woods."

Renee said, "I have an idea that might help you appreciate nature again. Would you like to learn to paint?"

"Uhhh . . . I don't know."

"I'd love to learn." Myra broke in. "Could you teach us both at the same time?"

"I'd be happy to. When would you like to start?"

"How about Sunday, eleven o'clock? Is that okay with you, Addie?"

"I guess," she said flatly.

Renee smiled at the girl. "Sunday it is."

They finished eating and the table was cleared. Renee stood in the kitchen washing silverware and glasses.

Myra came in and placed the silverware in the sink. "Simon seems to be quite interested in you."

"Hmm."

"I think he's a very nice man. He certainly has been so far, but I still don't know him very well."

"From the looks of things, I don't think you'll be disappointed."

"I'm not in any hurry. I've been doing just fine on my own."

"I think he might be just what you need."

Renee raised her eyebrows. "Do I act like I need something?"

"Well . . . no, it's not that. You got so involved helping us, caring about Addie. Seems like you have a lot of nurturing and love in you and no one to share it with."

"I had a man once. Fifteen years ago. Got married when I was eighteen. We were high school sweethearts. He was needy and jealous. Didn't have any goals. Don't know what I was thinking." She rinsed a glass and set it in the rack. "I divorced him when I was twenty-three. Put myself through school and never looked back. He's probably working at Wal-Mart somewhere. I wanted more than that. Besides, I have plenty of nurturing to do counseling a high school full of kids."

Myra said, "It's not the same. Maybe you need someone to nurture you." Myra dried a glass and put it into the cupboard. "I think Simon's just that kind of man."

"Hmm. Well . . . we'll see."

Chapter 23

Addie plopped down next to Derek on the school bus. "How did things go with the memorial?"

"We did the canoe pull and ceremony. It was hard for my Great Aunt Arlene and the rest of my family. But they aren't alone. Arlene will get help from the tribe. We're all really like one big family. Glad it's over. Things can get back to normal." He shifted his pack on his lap. "What'd you do?"

"We had a barbecue. Simon and Renee came over. He cooked mushroom burgers. I never ate wild mushrooms before."

"I've been eating wild mushrooms all my life. They're better than store-bought ones."

She nodded. "They were good."

"What are you doing this weekend?"

"Renee's teaching Mom and me to paint on Sunday. I'm not doing anything on Saturday."

"We could go mushrooming. I know some good places close by."

Addie frowned and closed her eyes. "Walking around in the woods? Think I've done enough of that."

"You'll have a good time. I promise. You'll love eating them. I can teach you about lots of edible plants. If you ever get lost in the woods, you'll know what to eat."

She glared at him and frowned. "I'm never gonna end up stuck in the woods again . . . ever."

"You need to go. Face your fear."

"I'm not afraid. I just don't want to. Had enough of the woods. Wish we lived in the city."

The bus stopped and two boys and a girl walked to the front.

"Bye, Addie." One girl waved.

"Bye." Addie whispered to Derek. "I don't even know her. Everybody knows me."

"Yeah, same here. I'm a celebrity ever since I found you."

"I don't like being famous."

"Me either. My stop."

Addie stood up, moved aside to let him out. "See ya Saturday."

"I'll come at ten." He got off the bus.

Addie waved from the window.

* * *

Addie was doing homework at the kitchen table, books and papers spread across the white lace. Myra came in the front door and set a bag of bread on the counter. "We sure were busy today. Gave out thirty-two baskets. Stan said five of those were new sign-ups." She filled a glass of water and sat at the table. "You won't believe what happened over the weekend. Somebody stole the bread truck. Stan was real upset about it. They don't have another big truck to haul that food. Just a van."

Addie looked up in disbelief. "What?"

"Hard to believe isn't it? That someone could steal something that does so much good for so many people." She took off her shoes and rubbed her foot.

The front door creaked as Nick opened it. He swung it back and forth and rubbed his hand on a hinge. "WD40 will take care of that. Been putting roof patch on Noreen's tool shed. That'll have to do for now." He kissed Myra. "Thought I heard you come in."

"I was just telling Addie, someone stole the bread truck over the weekend."

"You're kidding?"

"Wish I was."

"Not the big box truck?"

"That's the one."

"Did Stan call the sheriff?"

"Yes. They were still looking over the video cam tapes when I left."

"What am I going to drive on the bread run later?"

"You'll have to take the van. You won't be able to pick up near as much."

"That's a shame. A lot of people depend on the food in that truck . . . including us."

She pulled a bag of rolls, a loaf of bread and bagels out of the plastic bag on the table. "I know. The food bank doesn't have money to replace the truck. I don't know what they're going to do." She folded the plastic bag and put it in a drawer and set the bread on the counter.

Nick said, "Guess I'd better get on over to the food bank and talk to Stan before I make the bread run. Find out what's going on. Hope they find the creep who took it." He kissed Myra goodbye, "See you later, hon."

Chapter 24

Saturday morning, Derek rode his bike to the Mathesons, knocked and asked for Addie.

"She'll be out in a couple of minutes. You're taking her mushroom hunting today?"

"Yeah. Edible plants, too. We'll stay close by. Just down the road a ways."

Addie came in. "Hi."

"Ready to go?"

Myra asked, "What are you going to put them in?"

Derek pulled a mesh bag out of his pocket. "Here."

He stuffed the bag in this pocket. "Come on, Addie."

Addie walked next to Derek. "Where're we going'?"

"Not far. There's private land not far away. Don't know who owns it. Probably someone in California. They're never here. There's a lot of land like that out here."

They walked along the road for half a mile then turned down a path into the woods. Derek searched the ground.

"See those bright yellow flowers. The pointed leaves look like holly. That's Oregon grape. The berries are a little sour, but edible. Flowers taste pretty good." He picked some and handed them to her. "Try 'em."

She put them in her mouth and chewed. "They're not too bad. A lot better than oysters."

A dead tree stood off to the right. Derek pointed. "Look up there." He forced his way through the brush.

She didn't follow. "What are you doing?"

"Come here."

She pushed branches aside and made her way through the undergrowth.

"See these growing in a column." He pulled out a pocket knife and cut a white fungus off the dead tree and handed it to her.

"They only grow on hardwood—alder."

She turned it over and ran her finger across the gills. "It's edible?"

"Yeah, oyster mushrooms. They're good." He cut the ones he could reach, put them into a bag. "This was a good find. We'll check here again. They'll grow back several times."

"How do you know this stuff?"

"Grandma and Grandpa taught me."

"Where's your Grandma?"

His expression saddened. He looked away. His voice somber, "She died."

"Sorry." Addie touched his arm. "What happened to her?"

"Drunk driver hit her."

"Oh—that's awful."

"It was. Still is. Same accident killed my dad."

Addie stopped and stared. She didn't know what to say. "I'm so sorry."

He shrugged then made his way back to the path and moved on. Addie caught up with him, but didn't say anything.

He stopped beneath a large maple and reached up to grab a branch and pulled it toward him. He broke off a flower. "Try this."

She took a small bite. "It's okay."

He looked to the right. Branches on the undergrowth were broken, bushes trampled. "Check this out."

They clambered through the brush following the mangled wide swath. Derek untangled a trailing blackberry from his shoe and moved ahead, stopped and pointed. "Look at that."

She said, "What's a truck doing here?"

Derek moved closer. "That's the food bank truck." He opened the door. Wires dangled from the smashed dashboard. "That's not good." He opened the hood and shook his head. Disconnected hoses hung loose. "The engine, all the metal's gone."

"Who'd do that?"

"Tweakers. Sold the metal for drug money."

She looked puzzled. "How do you know?"

"Happens all the time." He slammed the hood. "We'll report it when we get back."

He led Addie out of the woods, then walked at her side along the road shoulder. She rushed ahead of him into the house, calling, "Mom." Myra stood at the sink.

The front door banged open. "Mom, you won't believe what we found! The food bank truck."

"What?" A glass slipped from Myra's hand, broke into pieces as it hit the floor. "Oh no. Where did you find it?"

Addie said, "Out in the woods."

Derek set the mushrooms on the table. "About a mile from here."

Myra crouched down and picked up pieces of broken glass. "We'd better call the Sherriff. We can use Noreen's phone."

A Pierce County Sherriff's car showed up an hour and a half later. Derek rode in back with them to give directions. After they drove as far as they could, Derek led the way on foot. He stood back while the deputy walked around the vehicle, looked inside the cab and under the hood.

The deputy kicked a flat tire, looked through the windshield and wrote down the VIN number. "What a shame. The guys who did this didn't get much money for their trouble. The truck's ruined. What a loss for the food bank. Too bad"

Derek shoved his hands deep in his pockets. "Yeah."

"I'll have to impound it."

"Think you'll catch 'em?"

"Wish I could say yes, but it's real tough. Our success rate's pretty low. Thieves recycle the metal and it's gone. We're fighting the system."

"Yeah." He thought about his time doing community service at the food bank and how hard Simon Grayson worked to help out there. The manager, Stan, and all the volunteers, Addie's mom and dad, so many people counted on the food bank for assistance.

His drug experimentation had been a short, dumb episode in his life he had no intention of repeating. He was fortunate he got caught and quit. So many others weren't so lucky. Maybe he could change that. Make a difference. A new thought entered his head.

Chapter 25

Walt drove up to the Matheson's and parked. Derek jumped out of the Silverado, sprinted to the front door and rang the bell.

Derek blurted, "Mrs. Matheson, is Addie here?"

Myra looked beyond him; saw Walt open the tailgate. "Hello, Derek. Yes, she's here. I'll get her." She left him and knocked on Addie's door.

The response was loud, hostile. "What?"

Walt was still unhooking bungee cords when he heard Addie's rude reply. "Hmm, that girl needs an attitude adjustment," he grumbled to himself.

Myra sighed and shook her head. "Derek's here."

Addie appeared and saw Derek grinning ear to ear. "Yo, what's up?"

"Got something for you." He led her to the back of the truck.

Myra followed them. Walt lifted a metallic blue bicycle out of the back and set the kickstand.

Derek said, "It's for you."

Myra looked at Derek, then at Walt. "We can't afford that."

Walt said, "There's no charge. Got a friend who fixes up old bikes. Told him about Addie. This one's a freebee. Didn't cost him any money. Wasn't anything wrong with it.

He cleaned it up some." Walt ran his fingers along the back fender into a small dent. "It's not perfect."

Addie put a leg over, leaned against the handlebars and squeezed the brakes. Her eyes lit up. "It's really mine?"

Walt nodded. "Yep, try it out."

Addie knocked back the kickstand, pedaled down the driveway, switched gears and pumped harder. She returned to the pickup and pushed the handbrakes. Her body lurched forward as the Schwinn came to a sudden stop. "This is awesome. Thank you."

Derek pulled his own Trek out of the back. "Come on. Let's go for a ride."

Myra called out, "When are you coming home?"

Addie shrugged and kept on pedaling.

Walt sat on the tailgate and collected the bungee cords. "Raising teenagers can be difficult. Think they know everything." The creases in his face seemed to deepen as he spoke. "Derek had a very hard time when his dad was killed. It was a bad time for all of us." His mom, Sophie, went through a terrible depression. Lost her husband and her mother. She spent a lot of time on the reservation. She got a lot of support there. Derek turned to drugs . . ."

Myra's eyes teared up. "I had no idea."

He rubbed his chin. "It's getting better. Working with his hands has been good for Derek. I've tried to work with him. He's a skilled carver. Follows direction well. Simon Grayson has been a big help. Derek really looks up to him."

Myra said, "I don't know what to do about Addie. I thought moving into a house with her own room would change everything, but she's still moody and short-tempered. I lose my patience. Say things I shouldn't. Regret it later. It's so frustrating."

Walt said, "I know it's hard to do, but maybe she needs a little space. She and Derek seem to be good for each other. I know they're too young for a real relationship, but right now I think what they both need is a friend. A confidant."

Myra tilted her head back and rubbed her neck. "Oh, I suppose you're right, but they're still so young. Think they're invincible. Addie seems to find trouble. I hope she can manage to get her life on track. It's so hard to preach to her when our own situation is so precarious."

"It'll get better."

"I certainly hope so. The sooner the better."

Addie followed Derek down the road. Two miles away, Derek turned off and pulled into his driveway. They parked the bikes.

Addie put her feet on the ground. She recognized the path to his favorite place and followed him on foot. They crossed the field. He vaulted up onto the rock and extended a hand. She sat cross legged facing him on the flat surface.

"We need to talk. Didn't want anyone to hear us."

"About what?"

"Got a plan. That's why I got you the bike. Too hard and slow to walk. Since we can't drive, a bike was the best solution."

Addie looked puzzled, "What are we gonna do?"

Derek looked up at the blue sky, white billowing clouds drifted east toward Carr Inlet. His gaze shifted down to the tall grass, seed heads waving in the light breeze. "I've been thinking about the thieves who stole the food bank truck. Don't think cops are gonna bust 'em. They hid their faces from the cameras."

Addie planted her hands behind her and leaned back. "What's that got to do with us?"

"We can go places cops can't. Go undercover. No one will suspect us—"

She broke in. "You *gotta* be kidding."

"Nope." He reached down, plucked a grass stem, stuck it between his teeth and chewed.

Mouth agape, her eyes squinted as she looked at him sitting in in the sunlight. His expression was serious.

"How are we gonna do it?"

"We'll go at night. That's when the creeps come out."

"My parents won't let me do that—"

"We'll have to sneak out. Wait 'till they're asleep."

She shook her head slowly. "I don't know?"

He leaned forward and rubbed his knee. "Got it figured out. You can climb out your window. They won't even know you're gone."

"What'll we do if we catch 'em?"

"Call the cops. All we gotta do is find out who they are. See what they're up to." He untied the rawhide strip behind his head, shook out the mane of long black hair, raked it back with his fingers and retied it.

"What if they catch us?"

"They won't. I promise."

"How can you be so sure?"

"These guys all live in the woods. It'll be easy to sneak up on 'em."

A hint of a smile crossed her lips. "Does sound kinda swag."

"It'll be fun, an adventure. Besides, we'll be helping the community."

A Steller's jay called nearby. Derek looked away, focused on a big leaf maple behind him. The raucous voice interrupted again. The bird flew out of the tree, a flash of blue. It swooped across the field and landed on a fir branch at the edge of the woods on the other side.

Derek smiled, jumped down, reached for her hand. "We'd better get back. Don't want you getting into trouble."

She took his hand, jumped down. "When are we gonna do it?"

"Thought we'd go next Saturday night. I'll tap on your window."

"Okay. What time?"

"Eleven o'clock. Your family goes to bed early, right?"

"Yeah."

"Good." He let go of her hand and walked beside her through the grass.

Chapter 26

Addie lay under the covers, eyes wide open. The lamp was off and the house was quiet. A full moon glowed dimly through lace curtains casting eerie shadows on the bed and walls. Finally, she heard a quiet tap on the window. Even though she was expecting it, the sound startled her. She pulled back the covers and rolled out of bed. She felt for her shoes and slipped them onto her feet then tiptoed to the window. She'd unlatched it earlier, loosened it with a screwdriver and checked to make sure it would open easily. She climbed out and bent her knees as her feet hit the ground.

Derek pulled the window closed. She followed right behind him. When they reached the bushes next to the road, Derek finally spoke, "I brought two flashlights." He handed her one. "Here, put this in your pocket."

"Gotta tie my shoes."

He aimed a beam of light at her feet. "Hurry up."

"Where are we going?"

"About three miles. That's why we needed the bikes."

He pulled her bicycle out from behind a bush and switched on the headlight. Then he wheeled out his Trek mountain bike and put a leg over. After the headlight was on he turned off the flashlight and shoved it inside his jacket pocket. He pedaled and looked back. Addie's light glowed golden. Twenty minutes later Derek slowed down, stopped and placed his left foot on the ground.

Addie pulled up. "Are we there?"

"Shhhh." He spoke softly, "Turn off your light and use your flashlight." He rolled his bike down a path and leaned it against a large madrona. He took the Schwinn and parked it next to his. "This way. Stay close."

He kept his light pointed at the ground. Branches crunched beneath their feet as he forced his way along a narrow path through the underbrush. A coyote yipped somewhere in the distance. A dog barked in response. He stopped in his tracks.

Addie still moving, bumped into him. "What are you doing?"

"Shhh."

Leaves rustled in the trees above them. A dim light glowed beyond the edge of the woods. A car engine rumbled and wheels crunched on gravel. Bright headlights lit the clearing fifty feet away. Derek laid a hand on Addie's shoulder and shoved her down. He crouched beside her. He pushed the button on his flashlight to turn it off, reached for hers and did the same. The dog barked again.

The car door opened, someone got out and walked to the house. A motion-sensor light lit up the driveway. A man came out of the house, took something from the visitor and handed him a small package. The driver returned to the car, backed around and drove off. The light switched off.

Derek and Addie didn't move. Addie's leg started to cramp. She rubbed her calf, kneaded the muscle with her fingers. She moaned softly.

"Shhhh." He waited a few minutes, then whispered, "Let's move closer." He crept forward, extended his arms to push aside branches as he led the way. He stopped in the cover of salal and huckleberry bordering the driveway with a direct view of the front door.

They hunkered down a few minutes later as headlights penetrated the darkness, illuminating the open space a few feet away. They couldn't see the dog, but it started barking again. The driver of the dark-colored small pickup left the engine running, the muffler rumbling loudly as he got out.

Derek could see the interior of the house when the front door opened. A pungent smell emanated from the house and permeated the air. Derek could see the man inside.

A surprisingly high-pitched voice came from the tall, clean shaven, bald man. "Got the money?"

"Yep." A rail-thin man handed over a wad.

Baldy counted the bills and slid them into a pocket before releasing a baggy into the hand of the buyer. He stepped back inside and closed the door as soon as the thin man turned away. Derek could just make out the hollow cheeks, he recognized the uncombed dark hair that straggled around the man's shoulders; he'd seen him at the food bank. The truck lights flashed on the bushes right in front of them as the truck backed out and turned around.

Derek held his breath and looked down at the ground. He hoped the driver wasn't looking in their direction. Red tail lights faded into the darkness.

Addie exhaled loudly. "That was scary."

The dog barked louder. The door opened. Baldy stepped out and stalked into the driveway.

Addie shut her mouth and grabbed Derek's arm. She listened to her heart pounding in her ears. She couldn't breathe.

Baldy peered towards the road and looked around. The dog continued to bark. The coyote yipped again. The dog barked louder. The shrill voice called out. "Shut up, Harley!"

The barking ceased.

The man looked around one more time then disappeared into the house.

Addie's voice was shaking, her voice barely audible, "Let's get outta here."

"Not yet, let's see if anyone else shows up."

Addie closed her eyes and exhaled. She shifted her legs and crouched lower. She let go of his arm.

Two more vehicles pulled in. Money and drugs exchanged hands. They watched the last vehicle pull away and waited.

Finally, Derek whispered, "Let's go." He inched backwards, pulled a branch out of the way and held it aside for Addie. They were almost back to the bikes when they heard a car coming. Derek stopped and reached back, his hand on Addie's shoulder. "Wait."

The car drove past, but they didn't move. As soon as the tail lights disappeared around a curve, they pushed forward. He lifted his bike over the underbrush and rolled it to the side of the road, then went back for Addie's. He mounted his bike and said, "Don't turn the light on until we get past the driveway. Don't want anyone to see us."

As soon as he turned his light on, Addie did the same. He sped away. She tried to keep up, but his light dimmed as he pulled ahead. She gulped air gasping for breath, her legs ached. Derek turned and looked back. She had fallen behind. He stopped to let her catch up.

She halted behind him. "Don't go so fast." Her chest heaved as she sucked air.

"We're almost there."

Addie's breathing slowed and returned to normal. "Okay."

He led the way and they rode up the driveway. They didn't want to make noise opening the barn so Addie parked her bike behind the house. Derek opened her bedroom window, laced his fingers together and squatted below. He spoke softly, "I'll help you up."

Addie grabbed the window sill and put her left foot in his hands. She started to pull herself up while he pushed from below. She went up and over and flopped onto the floor with a thud. "Ummph." She sat for a minute, held her breath and listened. The house was quiet.

Derek stood up and leaned in. He spoke in a soft voice, "Are you all right?"

Addie got up off the floor. "Yeah. I'm fine."

"I'm taking off."

"See ya."

Addie closed the window and looked at the clock, 3:30. She got undressed, slipped on a nightgown and pulled the covers up to her chin. She closed her eyes and tried to sleep, but thoughts of the night kept running through her mind. What if they'd been caught? Would he have killed them? She knew lots of people got murdered because of drugs. How dangerous was this? She felt lucky to be alive. Perhaps she was pushing her luck. She was no cat, but she was beginning to feel like she was running through more lives than a person should expect.

At last, exhausted, she yawned, rolled over and fell asleep.

Chapter 27

"Addie." Myra knocked on the door again. "Addie, time to get up."

"Unhhhh." Addie rolled over and buried her head under the pillow.

Myra opened the door and walked in. "You slept in late this morning. Are you sick?"

"No—just tired."

Myra pulled the pillow off Addie's head. "Remember, Renee's giving us a painting lesson today. We're supposed to be there at eleven. It's ten o'clock. You need to get dressed and have breakfast."

"Unhhhh. I don't wanna go." Addie rolled over and pulled the quilt over her head.

"You were looking forward to it." Myra peeled back the covers. "It'll be fun."

Addie sat up on the edge of the bed, a scowl on her face. She rubbed her eyes and headed for the bathroom.

Forty-five minutes later, she stared out the car window. Toolie was running along the fence line barking when they pulled into the driveway. She got out and leaned down to pet the dog. The muscles in her legs ached from their workout the night before.

Renee met them at the door. A few minutes later all three were seated at the dining room table, Renee sat at the head of the table between the other two. She squeezed some paint onto a pallet, three colors: alizarin crimson, pthalo blue and cadmium yellow. She placed the pallet next to a heavy block of paper in front of Addie along with an inch wide brush. Myra had a similar set of materials in front of her.

"The first thing we're going to do is a flat wash." She dipped her brush into the blue and mixed in a bit of water. She ran the brush across a square on the page. When she was done, she had a solid color square. "Now you do the same."

Addie frowned at the square on her paper. It was a bit blotchy, the color not as even as the one Renee painted. "It's not very good."

Renee smiled. "It takes practice."

Myra looked at her attempt and laughed. "Guess I'm going to need a lot of practice."

They painted a square in each color. Renee examined their work. "Now let's do a graded wash. You're going to dilute the paint three times in three wells." She painted a red square. "Each brush stroke across the page will be lighter than the one above it."

Addie painted a square then leaned back and groaned. "Why are we doing this? Why can't we just paint a picture?"

Renee looked at Addie's square. "It's important to learn basic techniques first. You've got too much water in the bottom line. Take a paper towel and blot up a little." She dabbed the paper. "Be patient. You'll be painting pictures before you know it."

Renee showed them how to mix the primary colors to make shades of green, purple and orange. They painted wet on wet. Brushed water across the paper and used a wet bush full of paint to spread color across the page. Then a dry brush on wet paper. A wet brush on dry and finally a dry brush on dry paper. They practiced brush strokes and learned how to create texture and lift off paint.

Addie yawned. "I'm tired."

Myra looked at Renee. "She slept in late. I think she got too much sleep."

Addie rolled her eyes.

Renee said, "We've done enough for one day. We'll meet again next week if you like."

Myra rinsed out her brush. "That'll be fun."

Renee handed them each a folder. "Save your work and bring it back each time. We want to keep track of your progress."

Nick met them at the door. "How was your first art lesson?"

Myra opened her folder and pulled out a few sheets of paper. "It was just basic. We'll do more next week."

Addie walked straight to her room dropped the folder on the dresser and flopped onto the bed.

* * *

The bell rang; school was out for the day and Derek waited for Addie. "Did your parents say anything about Saturday night?"

"Nope, I was wiped out Sunday." She stopped at her locker and grabbed her backpack. She snickered. "Mom didn't suspect a thing. She thought I got too much sleep. Funny, huh?"

Derek raised an eye brow and gave a slight nod. "Not bad. Better than knowing you snuck out."

"True."

Derek stood aside and waited for Addie to board the bus. She chose a seat near the back. They discussed her painting and his woodwork, carving the canoe at his grandfather's.

Before he got off, Derek said, "We'll go out again next Saturday night. Just like last time."

* * *

They rode to Baldy's and stashed their bikes in the brush. The stars and moon were hidden behind a thick layer of clouds. Addie clung to Derek's arm. "It's so dark. I can't see anything."

Derek paused and directed his flashlight behind him. Addie's lips were pressed tight together. A car turned down the driveway. Headlights penetrated the darkness, illuminating the edge of the woods.

He switched off his flashlight, and whispered. "Get down."

They hunched over, unmoving until the car turned around and drove away. Then they crept forward and took their position hidden in the salal and huckleberry bushes across the driveway from the front door. They didn't have to wait long. A car pulled in. Derek pulled a pen and notepad from his pocket. A woman got out and rang the doorbell.

Baldy appeared, and the now familiar exchange played out. As the car backed around, Derek wrote down the license number.

A fine drizzle started to fall. The moist air settled on the salal and Addie's hoodie. Addie's damp hair and clothes clung to her shivering skin. She closed her eyes and fought the memories that flooded back. April, barely two months ago, stranded on the island. She clung to Derek.

Wheels ground on the crushed rock on the driveway. Another set of headlights gleamed in their direction. The motion sensor lights flashed on. A man got out. Derek recognized the voice. When the buyer turned to leave, Derek saw his face. He wrote the name, Buck Jameson, beside the license number.

Addie brushed her sleeve across her running nose. She cupped her mouth and nose while Buck drove off. Baldy turned his back and was about to close the door. Addie sneezed. The dog barked. Derek grabbed Addie and hunkered down.

Baldy turned back. "What the hell was that? Who's out there?" The dog barked louder. Baldy pulled a gun from a clip on his belt and stepped off the porch. He crept along the perimeter of the driveway, stopping every few feet to peer into the bushes.

Derek and Addie were frozen in place, too afraid to breath.

Another truck pulled in. The driver rolled down the window. "What's going on?"

"Heard something out here. Checking it out."

"Hey man, I'll come back another time." His tires squealed as he peeled onto the main road.

Addie lost her balance, and grabbed Derek's wrist.

Baldy turned back and squinted into the salal, then disappeared around the side of the house. The front lights turned off. A few minutes later, the lights flashed on as Baldy came back into view.

Addie's legs ached. She closed her eyes and held her breath, fearing they would be found and shot.

Baldy walked up the steps and stood looking from the doorway, but didn't go inside. When he stepped over the threshold he didn't close the door, but pulled up a chair and sat on the porch. Addie rubbed her aching knees.

Another car pulled in. Baldy stood up. The driver got out and lit a cigarette. "Hey man, whatcha doin' out here?

"Watching."

"For what?"

"Don't know. Thought I heard someone, but I haven't seen anything." Baldy clipped the gun onto his belt and went inside. "Be back in a minute." He left the door open and came back with something in his hand. The buyer handed some bills. Baldy counted the money, stuffed it in his pocket, and handed over the bag.

"See ya."

The car left, but Baldy remained in the light for a minute that felt like an hour. When he moved inside, Derek whispered. "Let's work our way back. Stay down."

They moved slowly, pausing after each step. A branch crackled. Addie's fingernails dug into Derek's arm. Baldy stepped outside. He reached for the gun again. They were hidden in the dark. He stood out against the bright lights.

Addie looked toward the road. They had another hundred feet to go. She took a deep breath and exhaled quietly through her nose.

Baldy looked the other way and walked to the other end of the driveway.

Derek tugged her hand and whispered, "Run!" He lurched forward pulling Addie behind him.

Baldy turned around. A gunshot sounded in the bushes and a bullet slammed into a tree.

Derek reached Addie's bike, yanked it out and pushed her forward into the darkness. "Keep your light off."

He got ahead of her, turned into a driveway, and laid the bikes down. They took cover in the salal, huckleberries and ferns. Derek looked back. A pair of headlights emerged from the driveway a ways behind them. Someone got out and stood briefly in the light, then the car turned north and the tail lights dimmed as it drove away.

They stayed where they were too afraid to move. About ten minutes later, headlights came slowly towards them. Their eyes followed the lights as the car idled forward, passed close by and disappeared into the darkness. Finally, it returned, moved on, and turned down the driveway it came from. They waited until it was silent except for their breathing, then they took off, pedaling fast.

Addie parked her bike behind the house and Derek helped her climb through the window. She watched him pedal away before she pulled the window closed. She climbed into bed, but her heart was still racing.

Addie kept hearing Baldy's voice, *"Who's out there?"* She lay wide awake for a long time before her lids felt heavy and she felt herself drifting off.

A series of gunshots awakened her. She bolted upright in bed gasping for breath.

The door eased open to frame her mother. "Addie, are you awake? Honey, it's time to get up."

Chapter 28

Addie sat, legs dangling over the edge of the thinking rock. She closed her eyes and listened to the sounds of birds chirping unseen in the surrounding trees.

Derek was lying on his back staring at banks of clouds as they rolled in darkening the sky. "Whatcha thinkin'?"

"Can't get over how lucky we were. That dealer could have killed us. Two near death experiences in two months." A soft whistle escaped between her teeth. "Pushing my luck, don't you think?"

"Yeah," Derek bit his lip. "Guess we'd better let the cops deal with the creeps. It's too dangerous. They arrested that jerk anyway. We helped get one bad guy put out of business."

"Did our good deed. I'm done with that."

"How's painting going?"

She turned her head and smiled. "Going good. Renee says I'm a budding artist. Don't know about that. I'm working on a painting of a heron. I'll show you when it's done."

He fingered the amulet hanging by a rawhide thong around his neck. "Your totem."

She nodded. "Yeah."

His brow furrowed. "I've been thinking. What are we gonna do now that we're not solving crimes?"

"I don't know."

"We could go canoeing, again"

She scowled. "No way."

"Sure. Why not?"

He sat up and laid his fingers on her hand. "I'll be there. It'll be fun. You'll see. You need to get back out on the water. Confront your fears. Besides, your totem, the heron, will watch over you. You were fine last time."

"I don't know. We'll see."

A drop of rain plopped on his hand. Another landed beside him, a dark spot spreading across gray stone.

He jumped down and reached for her hand. "It's starting to rain. We better get back."

They ran across the field as rain pummeled in a sudden drenching downpour. Their feet pounded the path as they threaded their way through the trees. Derek tore across the clearing beside his house and ran for the veranda out front. Water bypassed the overfilled gutter and poured off the roof in a drenching curtain that caught them as they passed through to the porch.

Addie vaulted up the steps behind Derek, bent over, hands on her knees, gasping for air in deep breaths between loud bursts of laughter.

Derek's mom opened the door. "What's going on out here?"

She looked at her son. The rawhide thong tying his hair was twisted to one side. Wet tendrils of hair pulled out, dripping down his face. His gray T-shirt and jeans clung to his wet skin.

Addie raked her hand through her hair to pull it away from her eyes, catching her fingers on a fir twig woven into the tangle. She stood straight and looked down at her shirt, twisted the bottom, wringing drops of water from the black cloth onto the porch. More water plopped onto her tennis shoes from the hem of her black jeans. "Sorry, Mrs. Tilton."

Sophie shook her head, a smile in her eyes belying the stern look on her face. "Come on in. I'll fix some hot chocolate. You two better get dried off before you catch cold."

Addie sat at the kitchen table, a heavy hand-woven robe draped across her shoulders. She sipped from the mug and eyed a shelf hung on the wall. "What are those baskets made of?"

Sophie lifted a basket off the shelf and set it on the table in front of Addie. "Cedar bark, I make them myself. Mother and Grandmother taught me."

"Wow. That's really cool." Addie set down her mug, picked up the basket and ran her fingers across the fiber. "How'd it get so smooth?"

"It's a long process. Not many know how anymore. I teach a few girls over in Shelton, at the cultural center on the reservation." She sighed and her voice lowered, sounded sad. "Not many want to learn the old ways."

Addie studied the fine close-knit light and dark pattern interwoven in intricate detail. "It's beautiful." She handed it back to Sophie.

"Thank you."

"How long does it take you to make one?"

Sophie replaced the basket and removed a larger one. "Oh, that one took a couple of months. This one almost six months. Takes time to prepare the bark."

Addie looked at the wider strands and ran her fingertips along the soft, glossy smooth golden fiber.

Sophie said, "That's yellow cedar, a little harder to find than red cedar, grows higher in the mountains, it has a lovely color."

Addie looked around the room. Her eyes focused on a hand-carved eagle, wings outspread, hanging from the ceiling, a salmon clutched in sharp talons.

"You're all so talented. I don't know how to do anything."

Derek slurped a swallow of chocolate. "You're learning to paint."

"Yeah."

Sophie smiled and pointed to a framed picture on the wall. A young girl sat at a table beside an old woman. An unfinished basket was in front of the woman, fingers holding the unthreaded fiber. "I was taught at a very young age. That's me with my grandmother.

"I helped my mother and grandmother gather bark. It's soaked and pounded to split and soften the fibers. Different plants, fungi and lichens are used to dye different colors. There's much to learn besides the weaving. I've been doing it my whole life." She picked up the basket and put it back on the shelf. "I'd better check on your clothes in the dryer."

Addie and Derek finished the cocoa and put on their warm dry clothes.

Sophie said, "I'll drive you home."

Chapter 29

The sun was high, an orange ball in an almost cloudless midday sky on Saturday, a perfect day to be out on the water, much different than their soak in the rain the week before. Addie sat in the front of the canoe and stared ahead. The quiet swish of paddles dipping into the water and waves slapping against the sides were the only sounds. They cut neatly through the murky surface creating a rippling path in their wake. The canoe surged ahead with each pull. They rounded a point and followed the shoreline.

"If you get tired, we'll switch sides."

They hung along the shore. A steep sandy cliff rose above the beach. They heard the familiar call before the eagle appeared above the trees and soared above the water. They stopped paddling and watched as the bird circled a few times then dove, feet extended, into the water. Great wings flapped as the bird lifted into the air, a flailing salmon clutched in sharp talons. The bird grew smaller until it disappeared over the cliff, beyond the trees.

"That was awesome." Addie turned to look back. "But the poor fish."

Derek shrugged his shoulders. "That's life. Every creature has to eat." He resumed paddling.

After a couple of hours he said, "We'd better head back. Don't want your parents freakin' out."

"Yeah, they're totally paranoid now. Always thinking something's gonna happen to me."

"Well, you did almost die on Raven Island."

"Believe me, I'll never forget. I'm *not* gonna do anything like that again."

Derek said, "Good thing they didn't find out about our run-in with that drug dealer."

"Yeah. They would have killed me."

He leaned forward and looked into her eyes. "I do have something I want to show you, but it means taking the canoe at night. We have to go out after dark. We'll sneak out like before, but instead of going after drug dealers we're just gonna take the canoe and paddle around."

"I . . . don't know."

"It'll be fun . . . no danger . . . piece of cake."

"All right. Promise me nothing bad's gonna happen."

"No problem. I promise."

They paddled back and brought the canoe to the beach at Walt's. Derek pulled the canoe ashore and they carried it up beside the shed.

Derek said, "Grandpa's had this canoe most of his life. He and his dad, my great grandpa, made it together. Someday it will be mine."

Addie looked at the canoe. "Gee, it's really old."

"Yeah, about fifty years."

Addie walked beside Derek around the side of the house.

Ethan and Walt were sitting on the steps carving.

"Grandpa, we're back."

Walt turned the piece of antler in his hands. "How was your excursion?"

Derek laid a hand on the shoulder of the carved bear beside the porch. "It was great. Saw an eagle."

Addie said, "Yeah, it swooped out of the sky and caught a fish. It was amazing."

Ethan jumped up, leaped off the steps and walked over to Derek. He held out his latest project. "What do you think of my bear?"

Derek took the wood and turned it around in his hands, scrutinizing the workmanship. He grinned. "Looks like you're getting the hang of it, but still have a long ways to go."

Ethan nodded. "I know."

Derek smiled and handed it back. "It takes time and lots of practice. Grandpa's an excellent teacher."

Walt said, "Ethan's a fast learner. How 'bout some lemonade?"

Derek said, "Yes, please."

Addie pulled up a chair beside him. "Sounds good."

Ethan returned to his perch on the step. Walt returned bearing a tray with four glasses. He handed a glass to Ethan and sat next to Derek. They finished their drinks.

Walt got up to clear the table. "Would you like a ride home, Addie? I have to drive Ethan."

"Sure."

"See ya," she called to Derek.

Chapter 30

A few pinpoints of light, sparse stars, punctuated the black emptiness of the calm moonless night.

Derek whispered, "Get in."

Addie felt her way along the canoe and sat down. She hugged herself, fighting waves of fear. Derek shoved off and jumped in.

He picked up a paddle and handed it to her. "Here."

She dipped the paddle into the water. "Where are we going?"

"You'll see."

"I can't see anything. It's pitch dark."

Dim lights faded into the distance as they left the shoreline and headed into deep water. They paddled silently for what seemed like hours, but was only about thirty minutes.

Derek said, "Stop paddling."

The canoe slowed as they drifted forward. "What's out here?"

"I'll show you. Look at the water." He lowered his paddle and swirled it deep into the water. Tiny sparkling lights glowed beneath the surface.

"What is that?" Addie leaned over and dipped her fingers into the water.

"Plankton."

"Plank what?"

"Plankton. Tiny creatures that bioluminesce. That means they give off light."

Addie stirred the water again, laughing as minute stars glittered in the wake of her fingertips.

"They're common in the warm months. Young fish and other animals eat them. They're important in the food chain of marine life."

Addie squinted, struggling to see his face in the darkness. She was amazed by his knowledge of the world around them. "Where do you learn this stuff?"

"I grew up with the teachings. My ancestors have always been dependent on the creatures of the water for food, especially salmon. Even clams and oysters eat 'em. We're taught about all forms of life in our world as soon as we are old enough to understand. I was curious . . . wanted to learn more, so I Googled plankton on the internet."

"Hmm." Addie inhaled deeply, then wrinkled her nose. "What's that smell? Fuel?"

Derek turned to face the wind and breathed in. "Diesel. Must be a boat out here. Don't see any running lights. You hear an engine?"

"Nope."

"Stay quiet." He lowered his paddle quietly into the water.

A dark shadow loomed in the distance blotting lights from the far shore. Derek smelled the unmistakable indications of an engine. He lifted his paddle and listened. The silence of a quiet night, and a dim constant hum, not normal to the nighttime sea. He whispered, "Someone's there. Don't want to be seen."

"What?"

"Shhh."

He dipped his paddle silently into the water and stroked forward.

A boat hull loomed ahead. Derek stopped in mid-stroke. Bubbles rose to the surface from the depths not too far off to their right. Derek reached over and shoved Addie down onto the floor of the canoe.

He crouched low and whispered into her ear, "Geoduck poachers."

Her voice was a sharp whisper. "What?"

He reached out and put his hand across her mouth. His lips brushed her ear. "Poachers."

Addie gasped as her heart raced. "Get me outta here."

Derek focused on the boat.

Faint footsteps echoed across the water. The silhouette of a man stood out against the cabin of the boat. A diver surfaced. The hum of the engine shut down. The deckhand reached over and helped a diver into the boat.

The canoe drifted closer.

Addie nestled against Derek. He could feel her heart beating against his chest.

The boatman stopped moving. "Who's out there?"

The canoe continued ahead, drifting slightly, both kids huddled low. Derek squinted, looking for the boat name or number.

A loud gun report and a splash nearby.

A gruff masculine voice hollered, "I've got you in my sights. Get over here."

Addie groaned and sat up as Derek paddled toward the boat.

Derek touched her shoulder. "I'm sorry."

The canoe rocked against the boat's stern. Fingers reached down and twisted into Addie's hair and a strong arm yanked her up out of the craft by her shirt and hair.

"Ouch! Shit!" Her arms flailed out and she grasped the ladder on the back of the boat. The man hauled her up and flung her down into the boat. Her face hit the metal deck, splitting her lip. Addie sniffed, wiped her sleeve across her lip and drew her knees up against her chest.

"Now, you get up here." The man waved a pistol and pointed the barrel at Derek.

Derek dropped his paddle into the canoe and stepped onto the drop transom. He started to climb aboard. The poacher grabbed him by the back of his shirt and hauled him over. Derek sprawled on the deck and rolled against Addie.

Derek lay gasping, the wind knocked out of him. Finally, he muttered, "What about my canoe?"

"I wouldn't worry about that right now if I was you."

Their abductor unwound a roll of line and tied Derek's hands behind his back, then wrapped another line around his ankles. The man felt the bulge in Derek's pocket and pulled out the pocket knife.

"You won't be needing this."

Addie choked back sobs, "Where are you taking us?"

"Shut up, bitch."

The poacher jerked her arms behind her and trussed her up as he'd done to Derek. They were blindfolded with rags that smelled of brine and shellfish, first Derek, then Addie.

The teens leaned against each other on the deck. The motor chugged and turned over. The engine noise grew louder as they sped away.

Addie's lip hurt. Her nose ran as silent tears flowed down her cheeks. She tried to brush her nose across her shoulder, but couldn't reach that far with her wrists bound. She could feel the rhythmic rise and fall of Derek's chest against her side . . . small comfort.

The engine slowed then stopped as they edged against a dock. The boat rocked as someone climbed over the side. Soft soled shoes padded away. Rough hands wrapped a cloth around her face and tied the gag behind her head. The knot of fear tightened in her gut and she fought to keep the bile in her throat. She felt Derek squirm next to her, heard him grunt, then silence. She leaned closer against him, felt the movement of his chest, and said a silent prayer.

Footsteps crossed the deck.

"You unload our product and get it squared away," the now familiar voice ordered. "I'll take care of our guests."

"Sure thing boss."

The line around Addie's legs was untied then a hand grasped her bicep in a vice-grip and yanked her to her feet.

"C'mon, you're coming with me. Make a sound and you and your boyfriend are fish bait."

Addie stumbled across the deck. Her kidnapper hauled her over the side. She tripped as the dock inclined. She cursed as her elbow wrenched painfully against the constraint of her captor. A minute later the hollow sound of her steps on the dock changed as they reached solid asphalt footing. She was jerked to a stop. Sounds of keys jingling and a lock turning were followed by the creak of metal hinges. Hands grabbed her by the shoulders and flung her down onto rough carpet.

"Wait here." The line wrapped around her ankles again. "I'll be back with your friend."

The door slammed shut.

Addie struggled to breathe through nostrils pressed against carpet that smelled of salt water and fuel. She tried to roll onto her side. She worked her way over and felt the cold steel of the wheel well against her back. She sucked in deep breaths.

Her heart raced with the sound of the key in the lock and the door opening. A thud was followed by a groan. She felt Derek's warm body slammed in beside her. The door slammed again. The driver's door of the van opened. The engine started and they were moving.

New terror crept into her thoughts. Where were they going? It seemed like ages since they were laughing together in the canoe.

The van turned and came to a stop. A metal garage door hummed open, the van moved forward, stopped and the door closed behind them. The van door opened and Derek was yanked away.

"I'll be back for you," the voice sneered.

Addie felt nauseous, hoped she didn't puke.

A few minutes later, the rope binding her ankles loosened and someone lifted her out.

"Let's go."

The sound of their footsteps echoed on concrete. Heavy metal hinges clanged open and damp cool air chilled her skin. The gag was removed from her mouth.

Addie inhaled a deep breath relishing the free intake of air. Goosebumps rose on her arms as she shivered in the cold. "Where are we?"

"You're in a warehouse. No one can hear you or find you in here."

"Why are you doing this to us?" Addie asked with a sob. "We didn't do anything."

"You were snooping around. Following us."

Derek said, "We went for a canoe ride. Just wanted to look at plankton."

"You should have stayed away."

Derek countered, "It was dark. We didn't see you. Wasn't our fault. You weren't supposed to be there."

"That's tough luck for you now, isn't it?"

Addie's voice cracked, "What are you going to do to us?"

"Well, the two of you have put me in a bad position. You're gonna stay here 'till I get things sorted out."

Addie shivered. "It's cold. We'll freeze to death."

"That might not be such a bad way to go," their kidnapper said.

Addie sobbed loudly.

"I'll get blankets." They heard the door lock latch.

Addie started to cry.

Derek leaned against her. "This is my fault."

Addie sniffed, "No, you would never have taken me there if you'd known this would happen. I don't blame you. How could you know these creeps would be there?"

"I should have stayed away."

She leaned against him. Her voice was soft. "It wasn't your fault."

"Don't know how we're gonna get out of this. I promised nothing bad would happen to you. Didn't keep my word."

Addie remembered the day he rescued her off the island. Had he saved her then just so they could die together now? She twisted her wrists against the rope, chafing her skin.

They sat on the floor, huddled together against the wall. Sometime later their captor returned. Addie said, "I need to use the bathroom."

Derek nodded his head, "Me, too."

"Okay. One at a time." He grabbed Addie's shoulder. "You first."

Addie struggled to her feet. He led her out of the room and into a room some distance from where they were being held.

"I need to be able to use my hands."

He loosened the knot. Addie rubbed her wrists. "I can't see."

"It's a small room. Figure it out. I'll be right outside."

The poacher left them bound and blindfolded. Addie's lip was swollen and sore. She was cold. Not as cold as on Raven Island, but terror was just as real. There was one consolation. She wasn't alone. She snuggled against Derek. Her tears dampened his cheek.

Chapter 31

Myra knocked on the door. "Addie, it's time to get up." There was no response. She knocked again, harder. "Addie." She opened the door, walked in and stared at the empty bed. She hurried into the kitchen. "Addie's not in her room."

Nick swallowed a spoonful of cereal. "She must have gotten up early. Maybe she went out to collect the eggs." He finished eating breakfast and drank the rest of his coffee. He set his dishes in the sink and walked to the door. "I'll have a look."

A few minutes later Nick returned. "She's not there. Her bike's gone."

Myra frowned. "Dammit, she knows we're supposed to go to Renee's for our art lesson. I thought she was starting to enjoy painting." She picked up the phone and speed-dialed Derek's number.

A few minutes later Myra hit the off button. "Derek's not home either. Sophie said he must have left early this morning." She looked at Nick, shook her head and exhaled in a loud moan. "Where the hell is she!"

"Let's not panic yet," Nick said.

"Remember the last time!" Myra shrieked.

He wrapped her in his arms. "How can I forget?"

"I know you haven't forgotten. I'm sorry."

He said, "She's only been gone a few hours and she's with Derek. I'm sure she's fine. It's too soon to hit the panic button."

"You're right. But she's in trouble when she gets home."

Myra called Rene and told her the kids were missing. There was still no sign of Addie by the time Walt drove up with Ethan a little past three.

Myra asked, "Have you seen Derek and Addie?"

Walt shook his head. "No, but their bikes are in my back yard and my canoe is gone."

"They went canoeing?"

"Apparently so." He smiled and placed his hand on the hood of the truck. "Don't worry. Derek knows the water. He'll take good care of her."

Ethan had a big grin on his face. He held out his hand. "Look at my bear."

Myra took the wood and turned it around in her hand. She held it close to her face and ran a finger across the muzzle.

Ethan blurted, "It's not done."

Myra handed it back. "You're doing a fine job. I'm proud of you."

Ethan grinned from ear to ear. He shoved it into his pants pocket. "Thanks Walt. See ya." He took the steps two at a time and disappeared as the screen door slammed.

Myra turned to Walt. "Please send Addie home as soon as they get back."

"I will."

Myra was peeling potatoes when Nick walked in at 5:00. He bent over and kissed her cheek. "What's for dinner?"

"Chicken and mashed potatoes."

"Sounds good." He pulled up a chair at the table.

"Addie still hasn't come home." She dropped a potato into the sink.

"Walt said she and Derek took his canoe. He said he'd make sure she comes right home."

"Well, at least we know who she's with. Derek seems like a good kid."

"But he's done drugs in the past. How do we know he's still clean? What if he's in some kind of trouble? He could drag her into it."

Nick stroked the side of her face. "Honey, we don't have any reason to think he's involved in anything illegal.

"She didn't tell us where she was going." Myra waved the potato peeler in her hand. "We need to put her on restriction after this. She has to follow our rules."

"I agree. I'll have a talk with her when she gets here."

Nick looked at the clock. "It's after six. Dinner's getting cold. We can't keep waiting for Addie."

Ethan said, "Yeah, I'm starving."

Myra picked up the phone. "I'll call Walt. Maybe they're on their way." The conversation was brief. She frowned as she set down the phone. "They haven't shown up. Walt didn't say too much, but I could tell from the sound of his voice he's concerned."

Nick served up dinner. Ethan finished his plate and helped himself to seconds. Myra swirled a spoonful of gravy around the potatoes. She finally scooped up a bite and tried to swallow. They stuck in her throat and she drank a mouthful of water. She put down her spoon. "I'm not hungry." She got up and carried her plate to the counter.

Nick stood in front of her. He placed his fingers under her chin and lifted her face to look into her eyes. "Honey, I'm sure she's fine. Try not to worry."

"I can't help it. Remember the last time . . ."

"How can I forget? But, she is with Derek. Walt seems confident they'll be fine."

"Maybe he's done something to her. We don't know what he's capable of."

"Don't go jumping to conclusions. He's never done anything to give you that impression. They've both been doing better than ever in school with this blooming friendship."

"They're teenagers. How do we know what they're up to? You know what trouble kids get into these days. Remember he got mixed up with drugs. Maybe he's getting her involved in something like that."

Nick put dish soap in the sink and turned on the water. "Addie's too smart for that."

"You don't know that. Sometimes I think we don't know her at all. Ever since we lost our house . . ." Myra started to cry and ran down the hall.

Nick turned off the water and went after her.

The next morning they still weren't back. Myra didn't sleep at all. She closed her bloodshot eyes and rubbed a puffy red eyelid. How could this be happening again? Just two months after getting Addie back, she was missing again. It was incomprehensible.

The phone rang. She rushed to pick it up. "Hello." She looked at Nick while she listened then spoke into the phone. "Just a minute." She moved the phone away and spoke to Nick. "It's Walt. He has a friend with a boat. They're going out to look for the kids."

Nick grabbed the phone out of her hand. "Walt, I'm going with you. When are you leaving?"

Myra yelled into the phone. "I'm going, too!"

She stripped out of her nightgown and pulled on her clothes.

Nick ended the call and stroked her hair. "Honey, I think you'd better stay here with Ethan. We'll let you know when we find them."

Myra pounded her hand against his chest. "I'm going. Ethan will be in school all day. I'll call Renee and ask her to come and get him when he gets home. I'm sure she won't mind."

Chapter 32

Nick and Myra were waiting in the Explorer when Walt showed up. Myra shifted to the back and Walt climbed in up front. He barely had time to fasten his seatbelt before the SUV lurched forward. They drove in silence south to the Longbranch Marina.

Walt led them down the dock to an aged wooden-hulled boat, Sea Wolf. "Mitch, we're here."

A silver-haired, scrawny man leaned out of the cabin and hollered, "You two climb aboard and sit down. Walt, you get the lines then we'll be off." He took the seat at the helm and turned the key. The engine turned over and revved up.

Walt tossed in the line at the bow then went to the stern. He climbed aboard and they pulled away from the dock, heading out of Filucy Bay.

They scanned the water and shoreline as the boat slowly plowed through Drayton Passage along Anderson Island. The tide was out and a group of people with buckets, rakes and shovels were harvesting clams on the rocky shoreline. Mitch powered down and headed close to the beach so they could take a closer look.

Myra leaned over the side and squinted at the clam diggers.

They continued slowly down the west side of
Anderson Island. Mitch said, "I'm going to head back up
to the Key Peninsula. We'll stay away from shore so we
won't be backtracking."

Nick nodded. "Sounds good."

The blue green water was glass smooth as they
scanned the surface. A boat speeding in their direction
turned away and headed south toward Nisqually. Mitch
maneuvered the Sea Wolf to head into the wake. They
rocked across the waves and then steered back on course
moving close to the shore at Devil's Head. The isolated
beach was barren. A wide sandy coastline on the west side
strewn with driftwood logs caught their attention. They
pulled in for a closer look. They were almost touching
bottom as they approached the shore. A lone sea gull left
tracks in the damp sand as it prodded a seaweed-covered
rock. Mitch shut off the engine and the boat slowed to a
stop.

Myra stared glumly at the bird on the deserted stretch
of land. "They aren't here."

Walt nodded. "Let's try Raven Island where Addie
was stranded. Maybe they went there." Mitch restarted the
motor and they headed north. They circled the small
island, but there was no sign of the canoe or the two
teens.

Walt had a sudden thought. "Maybe he took her to
Squaxin Island. He wouldn't take her on shore. Only
Squaxin members are allowed on our tribal ceremonial
site. But maybe . . ."

Mitch moved the throttle and they lurched forward.
Harstine Island loomed ahead and they followed the

coastline, slowing as they neared Dana Passage. Rounding the narrow southern tip of Harstine Island, they veered north and the strip of land belonging to the Squaxin Island tribe came into view. Mitch slowed and the craft hugged the shoreline, veering around a floating oyster platform. Mesh baskets suspended along pontoons were filled with maturing oysters. After passing a second raft of shellfish, they slipped closer to the beach.

Walt said, "No one lives here anymore. We meet on the island once a year."

Nick and Myra kept their eyes focused on the beaches and forest beyond as they scrutinized the land. No sign of the canoe or missing teens was evident. A blue heron wading in the shallows turned its head in their direction as they passed by. They left Peale Passage and headed south on the west side of the island. They cruised around the tiny island of Hope and continued southeast following Squaxin Island back to Dana Passage. They hugged the coastline of Mason County then turned south between lower Pierce County and the Key Peninsula.

It was late afternoon. Sunlight glared on the glassy surface. Myra shaded her eyes with her hand against the glare. Something caught her eye. She pointed northwest. "What's that?"

Walt looked in the direction of her line of sight. "Mitch, head over there." He motioned.

Mitch throttled down and turned toward the object floating in the water. As they pulled closer, Myra gasped, her hands drawn in to her chest.

A canoe floated on the surface, paddles lying inside, one across the seat. There was no sign of Addie or Derek.

A primal scream escaped from Myra's throat. She lurched to her feet, rocking the boat. Nick stood and clutched his wife. She buried her face in his chest.

Walt's chest heaved with a deep sigh. He closed his eyes and chanted quietly.

Mitch maneuvered alongside the canoe and shut down the motor. He left the helm and attached a line to the canoe.

Walt stopped chanting and looked over the water. "Maybe they went ashore and the canoe floated away. Remember what happened to Addie."

Nick looked the older man in the eye. "I thought Derek knows these waters so well. You said he's been on them his whole life."

Walt looked away, his gaze resting on the canoe. He nodded, shoulders slumped. He had no words.

Nick scanned the distant shorelines, most of which they had already passed with no sign of Derek or Addie. His eyes glared into the gray green water beside the boat. The murky sound gave no hint what lay in the depths.

The cry of an eagle broke the silence as the great bird soared in the distance and then circled above. Walt's eyes followed the bird until it grew smaller, vanishing in the distance beyond Devil's Head.

Mitch said, "We have to call 9-1-1 and file a missing person's report." He made the call and told the details including the location of the canoe to the dispatcher. He ended the call and faced the other three. "They'll meet us here to write up the report. Coast Guard, police boats and fire department rescue teams are on the way. They'll start a search."

The sun was bright in the blue sky. Goosebumps rose on Myra's clammy skin as she shivered in the afternoon warmth. Arms pressed against her belly, she fought to suppress nausea that brought the gorge to her throat. She'd eaten nothing since dinner the evening before. She leaned over the water as her empty stomach disgorged phlegm and bile.

The Coast Guard arrived in half an hour followed a few minutes later by the Pierce County Sheriff Department. A gray pontoon boat pulled up accompanied by a pair of jet skis: Key Peninsula water rescue joined the effort. Another boat cruised towards them and slowed as it approached. The aluminum-hulled fireboat was sent from nearby Anderson Island. A crewman from the Coast Guard worked out a grid search pattern and assigned areas to the men. Before they headed out, a Coast Guard helicopter came in low and hovered above, then it turned south heading toward Nisqually Flats.

After a brief discussion of the search plan the suited-up dive teams pulled on fins and masks, entered the water and disappeared beneath the surface. Trails of bubbles broke the surface and radiated away from the boats. White water rooster tails trailed the jet skis as they took off for Case Inlet on the west side of the Key Peninsula.

Intent on the paths of bubbles, Walt, Nick, and Myra kept their eyes glued on the water. Myra's fingers clenched and rubbed against each other until blisters rose on raw, red skin. Finally aware of the pain, she raised a hand to her face and bit down on a fingernail.

A deputy sheriff wrote down information from the families while two others examined the canoe. With nothing appearing amiss in the craft it was puzzling that the teens were missing. Forty-five minutes later the divers resurfaced. There was no sign of the missing pair.

The captain of the Coastguard vessel said, "We'll keep searching. We need to study the currents to have a better idea where to search. We'll rotate divers in short shifts."

The deputy said, "We'll have teams looking from shore, but we're talking about a wide area with no clue which direction to look. I'll have Mason and Thurston Counties notified to widen the search area. The word will go out on the news media to notify the public to be on the lookout for them. I'm sorry. We'll do everything we can."

Myra burst into tears and collapsed onto the deck of the boat. Nick dug his fingers into his wife's shoulders. Eyes closed, his lips moved in silent prayer.

Walt kept his gaze on the water. A familiar shrill cry caught his attention as once again an eagle soared into sight and circled above. Instead of returning back to the Key Peninsula it soared higher and headed toward Anderson Island.

Mitch interrupted their thoughts. "We better head back. It's getting late. I'm running low on fuel and we have to tow the canoe."

Nick's voice was barely above a whisper, "Yes, of course."

Myra slumped sobbing against his chest as they pressed back into the seat.

Walt was silent, eyes on the water as the engine revved and they headed back.

Half an hour later they pulled into the marina. Walt stepped off the boat and tied the lines to the cleats. Nick joined him on the dock and they hauled out the canoe. Nick gave Myra a hand as she got off the boat. She leaned against his shoulder as they headed to the parking lot.

Mitch grabbed some line off the boat and helped Walt carry the canoe. They tied it to the rack on top of the Explorer and loaded the paddles into the back.

Mitch touched Walt on the shoulder. "Sorry things didn't turn out better, but maybe . . ."

Walt looked up to the sky. "There's still hope. They didn't find any bodies."

Myra blurted, "She's not dead. She can't be dead. I'd know it."

Nick helped her into the back seat. She fastened her seatbelt and closed her eyes. Nick sat behind the wheel and turned the key. Walt sat in the passenger seat and watched as Mitch and the marina disappeared from view.

Chapter 33

After three days of searching, there was still no sign of the missing teens. Mitch steered the boat close to shore. Myra and Nick stared at the beach while Walt and Sophie focused on the water.

Sophie leaned over the side and stared into a mass of floating kelp. "I just can't believe this . . . Derek's spent his whole life on the water. It doesn't make sense. How could . . ."

"What was he doing with Addie?" Myra shrieked angrily at Sophie.

Sophie choked back a sob, struggling to speak.

Nick wrapped his fingers around Myra's bicep. "Honey, we don't know what happened."

"It's his fault. He brought her out here. She wouldn't be gone if it weren't for him."

Nick spoke softly, "We can't blame Derek. He's missing, too. It's certainly not Sophie's fault. She's just as upset as we are. That's why she's here. Remember, Addie took a boat before she met Derek and we got her back thanks to him. We *never* would have found her if it weren't for him. If he's with her, I'm sure she's safe. We can't give up."

Myra slumped against the seat. Her eyes turned to the vacant beach. "Now, he's taken her away."

The lines etching Walt's face had grown deeper, sunken into folds of his sagging cheeks. His lips pressed together in a firm line. He spoke no words.

A Pierce County Search and Rescue boat had a team out in deeper water off Devil's Head. The dive team resurfaced and climbed back aboard. They pulled up the dive flag, the engine started up and the boat cruised a few hundred feet farther south. The divers dropped the flag overboard and followed it back into the water.

The Key Peninsula Fire and Rescue team traversed the water on jet skis in Drayton Passage on the east side of Devil's Head within sight of the Key's rescue boat and dive team. They planned to search the land and west coast of McNeil Island and even tiny, poison oak-infested Pitt Island.

The fireboat covered the north side of Anderson Island and Balch Passage including the south side of McNeil Island and Eagle Island.

Numerous small craft traversed lower Puget Sound between Shelton, Tacoma, Olympia, and the inlets surrounding the Key Peninsula and Gig Harbor. All eyes searched the water and beaches for any sign of Derek and Addie.

The sun was low in the sky when the Coast Guard vessel approached and the captain called out. "We are suspending the search. We've done all we can and there really isn't any more we can do. This is no longer a rescue mission. We'll be pulling out along with the rest of the teams. I'm sorry." He turned back to his crew and the vessel cruised off leaving the Sea Wolf rocking in its wake.

The sun was setting over the Olympic Mountains, a flaming blaze of color illuminating sky and water in a splendor of glory unappreciated by the five mentally and physically exhausted members of the search party aboard the Sea Wolf as it turned for home, heading back to the Longbranch Marina.

Nick held the door for Myra and helped her onto the sofa when they got home. He filled a teapot with water and turned on the burner. As soon as the kettle whistled he prepared two mugs of tea and sat beside her.

Myra took a sip and closed her eyes, mouthed a silent prayer as the tea soothed her parched throat. Lack of sleep and hours sitting in the summer sun were taking a toll. She ran her tongue across her dry cracked lips. "Nick, what are we going to do? How can we keep going like this? What if we never find her?"

"We'll find her. I know we will." Nick's voice sounded hollow, betraying the fear he failed to conceal.

He reached down, removed her shoes and socks and placed her feet on his lap. He massaged her toes, worked up to her arches and ankles, his strong fingers soothing muscles and joints. The action of his fingers provided small comfort to feelings of helplessness overwhelming him . . . failing Addie . . . his family . . . again.

They remained on the sofa enveloped in silence.

A knock on the door jolted their unshared pain. Myra looked at her watch. "It's after ten. Who can that be?" She shuddered. Her heart raced and her stomach clenched in a knot. She fought to control feelings of fear and dread coursing through her body.

"I'll get it." Nick stood up and went to the door.

"I know it's late." Renee entered, followed by Simon. "I just had to come by and see how you're doing."

The chill that ran down Myra's core warmed at the sound of her friend's voice as the brief look of terror that crossed her face was replaced by a sad smile. "I was afraid you were the Sheriff's Department coming to tell me they'd found their bodies."

Renee walked over and hugged Myra. "I'm sorry. We didn't mean to frighten you. It was inconsiderate of us to drop in on you like this . . ."

"No," Myra shook her head. "I'm glad you're here. Please sit down."

Simon said, "We've been out looking for them all day. We borrowed a boat from a friend of mine. Checked out Eagle and Anderson Islands. No sign of them anywhere."

"I heated some water," Nick said. "Care for some tea?"

Renee sat in an easy chair across the room. "I'd love some."

Simon took a seat in a rocker beside her. "Sure, sounds good."

Nick poured two more cups and joined them in the living-room.

Myra looked at Renee. "I'm so angry. I know it's not right. Derek's missing, too. Sophie and Walt are just as upset as we are. But . . ."

"Don't feel guilty," Renee said. "Anger is a normal emotion. It's natural to want to blame someone. We don't know what's happened to them yet. They could be hiding out somewhere, maybe from some of the shadier characters. Someone on the wrong side of the law."

Myra's voice was angry, "If they had a problem, why wouldn't they tell us? Why would they just take off?"

Nick cupped his face in his hands and rubbed his eyes. "I don't know. When we find them they're going to have to face some serious consequences. They'll need very close supervision."

"What if we never find them?" Myra blurted, her voice cracking as she broke down into a loud sob.

Renee looked her in the eye. "Don't say that. She came back last time. Let's pray we find them both soon."

They finished their tea. Renee stood up. "We'd better get going."

Simon carried their cups to the sink then walked over and opened the door and held it for Renee. "We'll keep searching. They've got to turn up somewhere."

Myra nodded silently.

Nick locked the door behind them.

Chapter 34

Addie shifted her weight and bumped against Derek. "My butt's killing me. I'm sick of this crap. Their never gonna let us go. No one's gonna find us here."

"Yeah. They haven't tried to ransom us."

"Huh! Lotta good that'd do. Our families don't have money." She twisted her wrists against the zip ties that had replaced the rope that fastened them together. The skin beneath the plastic was raw from the effort and she was no closer to escape. They were too tight. "We don't have time to get loose."

"I know. Been trying. Need a plan."

"Yeah. We don't even know how big this room is or what's in it."

"Being trussed up like an animal and blindfolded doesn't help."

"We don't even know how long we've been here." Addie's stomach rumbled loudly. "I'm starving."

Noises came from the other side of the door, the faint hum of the motor, voices.

Addie whispered, "Hope they brought us something to eat."

The door latch clinked and hinges creaked. "Brought you food." Footsteps crossed the floor.

Addie said, "I need to use the bathroom."

Derek added, "Me, too."

"You know the drill. One at a time." He grabbed Addie's ankle and clipped off the tie. "You first." He hauled her to her feet and shoved her out the door. Her hands were freed from behind her, and rebound in front. Her feet shuffled across the now familiar smooth concrete. After she finished, he returned her to the room. He pushed her back down to the floor, and refastened her ankles.

A gasp escaped as she landed with a loud thump against the hard surface. "Ouch! What are you going to do to us?"

He didn't bother to answer, cut Derek's ankle tie and yanked him up. Derek's wrists were clipped free and rebound in front. "C'mon."

Addie's mouth watered as she smelled the aroma of burgers and fries. Her stomach was growling as Derek and their captor returned. She heard a grunt as Derek landed against her. A paper bag was thrust into her hands and a plastic bottle landed on her lap. She opened the bag and unfolded the foil around the cold hamburger. Reaching into the bag and removing her meal with bound hands was a bit of an ordeal. She took a bite and chewed slowly. She heard Derek digging into the bag, then the sound of his teeth crunching a crisp french fry.

They ate their meal in silence listening to the sounds of chewing and voices and various thuds, rumbles and whishing coming from behind the door.

Funny how you notice sounds and smells when you can't see anything, she thought.

She finished the burger and started on the fries. After the last bite, she stuck her hands into the paper bag and felt a few more fries lying on the bottom. She polished them off and wiped her mouth before drinking a few sips of water. She sighed before speaking, "I don't want to drink too much. They don't let us use the bathroom enough."

"I know."

Addie whispered, "What are we gonna do?"

Derek twisted his wrists against the tie. "I haven't figured that out yet, but if we can get the ties off, we'll have to jump the guy when he comes through the door."

"We'd better not wait too long. They can't keep us forever."

"Yeah, they might decide to kill us."

Addie tried to reach an itchy spot on her back but gave up She pressed against the wall and rubbed back and forth. That helped a little. "Sometimes, it's real quiet in there. They must be gone then. That's gotta be the best time. We need to pay attention to what they're doing."

"Okay. We can't tell what time it is, but we should be able to have some idea how long they're gone."

The door knob rattled. "Shhhh." Addie whispered.

The door creaked open. Footsteps came closer. Addie's wrists were clipped free, her arms twisted back behind her and the plastic bit into her skin tighter than before.

"Ouch, butthead, you're hurting me. Get your hands off me."

"Shut up, bitch." He shoved her.

Her head cracked against the wall. A loud groan escaped as pain radiated from the throbbing welt.

"Whadja do to her? Leave her alone!" Derek yelled.

Addie heard a loud slap followed by a grunt. Footsteps thudded across the floor. Hinges creaked as the door slammed shut. The key turned in the lock. Addie listened to the sounds in the other room. The voices stopped and the motor revved. Then it was quiet except for the normal background hum.

"Are you all right?" Derek's voice sounded concerned.

She spoke slowly, dragged the words out. "Sorta. Hit my head. It's killing me. What a jerk. How about you?"

"Yeah, I'm alright, but we gotta get out a here. If I can get up onto my knees, maybe I can work my way around the room. Find something I can use." Derek twisted his body and tucked his legs behind him. Turning sideways against the wall, he leaned his shoulder and used the friction against his body to push himself up onto his knees. His weight pressing his knees against the hard concrete hurt. He forced the pain from his mind and inched his way forward.

Addie whispered, "What are you doing?"

He stopped moving. Took a deep breath. "Checking things out." He moved forward again. Thud. "Unhh."

"What happened?"

"Bumped into a table." He leaned up and rubbed his cheek against the rim and top. "Think it's a bench." He managed to work his way along the edge. His chin brushed against the rough wood surface and a concave hard object. He recognized the shape of a geoduck shell. The large shell would have a sharp edge. He worked the shell forward with his face. It slid off the top and clattered onto the floor.

Addie's voice was muted, the words tumbling quickly on each other, "What was that?"

"Found a shell. Think I can use it." He crouched down and worked his knuckles against the floor, felt the rough, finely grooved surface and managed to slide it up between his fingers. "Make some noise so I can find my way back."

Addie started humming. Derek rocked forward until he felt her leg. He moved closer and brushed his shoulder against hers then he turned and touched the back of his hand against her fingertips. "Here." He pushed the shell against her. "Take this and hold onto it. I'm gonna see what else I can find." He twisted away, forced his burning knees and aching legs to cooperate.

By the time he finished working his way around the room he was exhausted and his legs were on fire. "We're in a closet. It's kinda small. Found a couple of brooms, a dust pan, small garbage can, buckets, hoses, some cardboard boxes full of rags, and a few pieces of wood."

Chapter 35

A loud rumble and then a quieter motor stopped. Then it was silent except for the now familiar background hum.

Addie spoke in a rush of words, "I think they're gone. Let's go for it."

"Where's the shell?"

"Shoved it under my shirt. Lean over. I'll put it in your hand."

Derek twisted sideways and moved his fingers against Addie's side.

"Lower, and farther back." She leaned towards him.

He brushed his hand across the hard surface and then curled his fingers around the shell. "Got it." His thumb circled the rim and he turned it so the sharpest edge faced out. "Okay, I'm ready. Hold still."

"Try not to cut me."

His fingertips felt around the tie for the clear spot between her wrists. He pressed the edge against the plastic, sawing back and forth.

"Ahhhg!"

"Sorry, trying to be careful."

"I know."

A few minutes later, the tie snapped.

"Got it!"

Addie leaned forward and rubbed her fingers around her sore wrists. Then she pushed the blindfold off her head. "It's pitch black in here. Must be a light switch somewhere."

Derek said, "Worry about that later. Get my wrists loose."

She turned to face him and felt for his hands. He put the shell into her palm and rotated it so the sharp edge pointed toward him.

He felt the vibration against his skin, bit his lip when her hand slipped and cut his hand.

"Sorry."

"It's okay."

A few more times, his wrists burst free.

"Give me the shell. I'll get my legs." Minutes later, he was on his feet feeling for the light switch. They squinted, adjusting to the bright light. Derek said, "I'll get your feet, then we'll get ready for the next step."

Before long she was free, rubbing her ankles. "Glad to get those off."

They spent some time going through objects in the closet. Derek spotted a large jar of zip ties; same size as those used to bind them. "These'll come in handy." He formulated a plan and they prepared for their escape.

Derek said, "We need to turn the light off. Don't want them to get suspicious. Get back on the floor and rest up. We'll get up and get ready when we hear them coming."

The motor rumbled, engine shut off. A car door slammed.

Derek whispered, "Get ready."

Addie grasped a broom handle and Derek picked up a four-foot length of 2 x 4. Derek stood next to the wall near the edge of the door. Addie took her place right beside him. They waited.

Addie's breath came in deep gasps. Goosebumps rose on her clammy skin. She was too scared to move. She reached out for Derek. Her hand gripped his biceps.

He squeezed her hand and whispered softly, "Don't worry."

They heard footsteps on the other side of the door. Addie lowered her hand. The lock clicked. A cone of light widened as the door opened. Addie inhaled loudly, the man turned; she swung the broom, connecting the handle with his throat. The kidnapper's eyes bulged as his hands flew up to his neck. Derek swung the 2x4. It cracked against the man's skull. Blood oozed from beneath his dark hair, ran down the side of his face and dripped onto the floor. He collapsed to his knees with a loud grunt. Addie bent down and punched him in the nose. Blood spattered onto her shirt. He fell against her legs. She jumped back. He careened forward.

"What's going on!" a voice yelled from beyond the door.

"Quick,!" Derek whispered. "Get his hands." He pulled the man's arms behind his back.

Addie wrapped a zip tie around the unconscious man's wrists. Her trembling fingers missed the eyelet. She tried again. The tip threaded through the hole and she pulled the tie until it was snug, secured his ankles.

"Good job." Derek pulled the man further inside the closet and stuffed a rag in his mouth.

Footsteps coming at a fast pace rounded a corner and approached quickly.

"What the . . . !"

The board swung and collided with the man's forehead. His eyes rolled back and he fell unconscious to the floor. Addie fastened the ties and they tugged the second kidnapper into the closet and left him lying beside his cohort.

Addie looked at the two men. Her voice sounded weak. She stammered, "Think we . . . ki . . . killed them."

The second man moaned.

Derek shook his head. "No, come on. Let's get outta here."

Addie stepped around the pair. Derek closed the door behind them and locked it.

Addie blurted, "Gotta pee."

Derek looked across the room filled with tanks, tubs, and refrigeration units. He pointed. "Bathroom must be over there." He ran across the room.

Addie finished, and paused at the sink. She looked in the mirror, horrified by what she saw. Her hair was in tangles. Blood, mixed with dirt, was spattered across her cheeks and clothes. She washed her hands and rushed out.

Derek grabbed her hand. "Let's go."

They ran for the door and burst outside. It was dark.

Addie looked around. "Where are we?"

"Don't know." Bright lights were shining to the left in the distance. They ran toward the lights.

Several blocks later Addie stopped. She dropped his hand and bent over grasping her knees. She was gasping. "Wait . . . gotta . . . catch . . . my . . . breath."

Her breathing returned to a slower rate and they were off at a run again.

The lights grew brighter, closer, a pink glow. The "Poodle Dog."

Addie recognized the restaurant. "We're in Fife."

They hurried across the parking lot and disappeared inside.

A trio of bearded, scruffy-looking middle-aged men seated at a booth, peered from under the brims of their baseball caps and frowned.

The scowl on the hostess's face disclosed her shock as she walked toward them menus in hand. "Two?"

Derek said, "We need to call the police."

The frown vanished from the woman's face, replaced by a look of concern. "Follow me."

* * *

Nick answered the phone on the first ring. "Addie? Oh, my God."

Myra was on her feet, running across the room. "Addie's alive?" Tears flooded down her cheeks. She grabbed the phone out of Nick's hand. "Addie . . . Addie . . . you're safe?"

"Yeah."

"We're coming to get you. Where are you?"

"The Police Station in Fife."

"We're on our way."

Chapter 36

Ethan ran up the driveway, his arms waving wildly, Buster at his side, "They're here."

The Silverado rolled up, and came to a stop. The Tiltons got out and walked across the grass. Walt carried a foil-covered tray to the picnic table.

Sophie set a pie next to the tray. "Huckleberry and salal."

Myra moved to stand beside her and said, "I'm glad you came. I feel terrible about the way I treated you when the kids were missing."

"Don't worry about it. I don't blame you. You were hurting."

"That's no excuse. You were hurting, too."

Sophie shrugged her shoulders. "It's done. That was two weeks ago. We're fine, now." She looked across the yard where Derek and Addie were standing beside the chicken coop. "Derek hasn't talked about it much."

"Neither has Addie though she's doing better than I would have expected. It's been such a hard year. Derek's been good for her. I'm grateful for that. She managed to catch up on all her schoolwork and passed all her finals with good grades. I don't know how she did it."

"Derek did well, too. Better than ever," Sophie said beaming.

Myra's eyes roamed across the farm: Noreen's home, the orchard, Ethan romping with Buster in the field. She was grinning ear to ear. "Our whole family's doing better, thanks to Noreen. Simon changed our lives, connecting us with her. Now that school's out, Addie's going to have more responsibilities at home. She's helping Noreen, doing some dusting, making the bed. And, she's promised not to take off without permission."

The wind changed direction and the smell of burning charcoal filled their nostrils. Nick put some patties on the grill. "I'm real proud of Addie. That girl's got spunk. Those kids were damn lucky. It could have turned out real bad."

Walt nodded. "Yep." He turned and looked up at the sound of wheels on the drive. "Renee and Simon."

Nick raised a spatula in a wave. "Hey, you're right on time. The burgers will be done in a few minutes." Renee held Simon's left arm while he carried a large covered bowl cradled in the other.

Toolie leaped out of the Focus and bounded across the yard tumbling with Ethan onto the grass. Buster bayed loudly as the pair rolled on the ground.

Myra opened her arms, welcoming Renee and Simon. Renee seemed almost reluctant to let go of Simon, but then she wrapped Myra in a tight hug. "Lot's to celebrate today."

Myra glowed. "True."

Simon set the bowl beside the pie. "Those kids are real heroes. Everybody's talking about it. Quite a news story. It's in all the papers, talk radio, on TV and not just local. Receiving quite a bit of national coverage.

"Detectives with Washington State Department of Fish and Wildlife have been trying to catch those poachers for years. No one even knows what long-term effect this will have on the species. Puget Sound is the mother lode of geoduck production. Those big clams can live for a hundred years. This could exterminate them. Now, they put the kingpin out of business and he and his cronies are behind bars."

Nick slapped his side. "Quite a coup for two kids."

Myra groaned and frowned, "I wish the state had caught them sooner on their own."

Simon scooped dip onto a potato chip and crunched. "Poachers have the best surveillance equipment their illegal profits can buy. The state has limited resources and only a few guys to try to stop them. With Asian markets paying millions of dollars for geoducks, over a hundred bucks per pound, too many crooks are willing to destroy the environment and threaten the species. Each diver can make from $500 – $2000 a night. Geoducks sell for a hundred bucks a pound illegally."

Myra crossed her arms. "This wasn't just about clams. Who knows what they would have done to Addie and Derek."

Nick flipped the burgers. "Honey, let's forget about what didn't happen and be glad everything turned out alright."

Myra moved beside him and put an arm around his waist. "I am happy."

He bent down and kissed her. "I know you are." He pressed the spatula against the meat. "Burgers are done." He whistled loudly and called, "Hey kids, dinner's ready."

Ethan ran across the field, both dogs at his side. Derek and Addie walked slowly and sat down quietly next to each other at the table.

Myra looked at her son. "Ethan, please tell Noreen that dinner's ready, then go wash your hands."

Simon said, "You go wash up. I'll get Noreen." A few minutes later, he escorted her on his arm and helped her settle into a comfortable seat at the head of the table.

"That's a beautiful bright skirt you're wearing," Myra said.

Noreen looked at all the smiling faces. "I thought this occasion was a perfect time to wear pretty flowers."

Myra agreed, "It certainly is."

Sophie peeled back the foil on a tray of smoked salmon. "Walt caught and smoked this fish himself in the traditional way. It's very good."

Noreen focused on the array of foods. "Well, we're certainly eating well aren't we? No geoduck?"

Walt said, "Not today. I have some smoked at home, but didn't think to bring any."

Nick served up the burgers, then helped himself to a large piece of fish. He popped a bite into his mouth. "Mmmm." He licked his lips, "That is good."

Walt said, "The Squaxin Island Tribe will be holding the First Salmon Ceremony. You might like to come and see how we celebrate the tradition of releasing the spirit of the first-caught salmon to the water. We have a big salmon feast. It's coming up in August. The ceremony is open to the public."

Renee said, "That sounds interesting. I've always wanted to go."

Myra swallowed a mouthful of hamburger and wiped a drip of catsup off her chin. "That would be an honor and it sounds like fun."

Ethan blurted with a mouthful of food, "I wanna go."

Nick laughed. "We'll all go."

Sophie picked up a forkful of salmon, paused before putting it into her mouth and said, "Did Derek tell you he is participating in the Canoe Journey this year?"

Addie looked at Derek. "What's that?"

Walt said, "Coastal tribes meet and travel by canoe, ending at the host tribe's site. The Sqauxin Island tribe's hosting it this year, so we are the ones holding the ceremony. Derek will be one of the pullers paddling the canoe. He has to practice with the other members to be part of the crew. He had to get special permission from the Tribal Council since we don't live on the reservation."

All eyes turned to Derek. He shrugged his shoulders and continued eating.

After dinner, Derek apologized, "Grandpa, sorry I took your canoe without permission."

"You know I don't mind if you use it, but I need to know when you're going out."

"I know." He turned to face Myra and Nick. "Mr. and Mrs. Matheson, I never meant to put Addie's life in danger."

Addie said, "Derek kept his cool. I was scared, but he figured out how to get away."

They repeated the tale of their harrowing experience at the hands of the kidnappers, answering the many questions.

Finally, Derek asked, "May I be excused?"

Sophie nodded, "Yes."

Addie said, "Me, too." She stood up and followed Derek before anyone had a chance to respond.

Myra watched them walk away. "Those two have become good friends. We'll have to keep an eye on them. They've had too much freedom. I want to know exactly where they're going."

Sophie nodded. "I can't be home all the time. It's hard being a single mom."

Walt laid his hand on hers. "I'll pay more attention to Derek. Keep my eye on him."

"Thank you."

Nick said, "Maybe we should take Addie's bike away for a while."

"No." Myra replaced the foil over the salmon. "Living out here in the country, it's too far to walk anywhere. She's still too young to drive and with the price of gas, we can't afford to take her anywhere. I don't want to resort to that."

* * *

Derek walked over to the chicken coop, stooped down and pushed a handful of clover through the wire. The birds rushed over and grabbed up the leaves.

Addie punched him on the shoulder. "How come you didn't tell me about the canoe journey?"

"Didn't come up."

"It's not like you didn't have time."

His eyes narrowed. "Wasn't sure I'd be alive."

"Oh." Addie looked down at the ground. "Yeah."

Derek stood up and brushed his hands together wiping off the remains of the leaves. "You're not gonna see me much for a while. Gonna be practicing for the 'Paddle to Sqauxin'."

"How long's it gonna take?"

"Um . . . a few weeks. Some tribes have to start the journey the beginning of July. They come from all over the Northwest. Farthest tribes take three weeks to get here."

Addie raised her eyebrows. "Three weeks. In a canoe? Yuck!"

"We'll be on the water for about a week. We'll stop every night."

Addie frowned and looked away. He reached over and touched her hand. "Maybe your family can come see us. We start in Port Angeles, but have stops along the way, and end up in Olympia." He rubbed his chin. "I'll get you a schedule."

Addie bit her lower lip. "I don't know . . ."

"The ceremonies are open to the public. Lots of people will be there. Maybe you can come with Grandpa and Mom."

Addie rubbed her wrist, almost healed from being bound. She made a pnnff sound. "We'll see."

Derek said, "This is a very big deal. It's a tradition that was started in 1989 as part of the Washington State Centennial celebration. That was the Paddle to Seattle. They didn't have another one until it was revived in 1993. Since then, there's been one every year. This year is very special for me. Squaxin Island tribe, People of the Water, are hosting it, a huge responsibility. I will miss you while I'm gone, but I'm honored to be part of the crew. I would be proud to have you be there to see us land. The journey will make the final landing in Olympia, the end of July.

"After it's over we'll have a week of potlatch. All the other tribes will be our guests, feasting, dancing, singing, giving gifts. It's a time to follow the traditions of our ancestors."

Chapter 37

Addie stopped pedaling and coasted to a stop. Beads of salty sweat rolled into her burning eyes. She brushed her arm across her damp brow.

Derek halted behind her and planted his feet on the ground. "What's up?"

She grabbed the front of her T-shirt, and rubbed her face with the damp fabric. "Gotta stop. I'm roasting."

He looked up, squinting in the bright light of the sun blazing high in the cloudless azure sky. "It's only about quarter mile to the store. It'll be cool in there and we can get our ice cream. My treat."

Addie groaned. "Wish Mom had driven us. She said she couldn't afford the gas."

"At least she gave you permission to come."

"It seemed like a good idea."

"Yeah. Come on, let's get going."

A few minutes later they rolled across the Home bridge and turned into the Country Store parking lot. Addie led the way and the door closed behind them. She bent forward, hands on her knees, inhaling deep breaths in the air conditioned building. "Why'd we ride this far today?"

"Didn't think it'd be so hot."

"Yeah." She straightened up, walked over to the freezer and slid open the lid. "What'cha want?"

He reached in and pulled out a Rainbow Pop. "This."

Addie looked over the selections and finally made her decision. Grinning, she reached for a Fudgesicle. "Been a long time since I had one of these."

Derek paid the cashier and started for the door.

Addie stopped. "Let's eat 'em in here where it's cool."

"Sure." Derek peeled the wrapper off his Popsicle and tossed the paper into the garbage.

Addie slid her tongue over cold, satiny chocolate and licked her lips. "Mmmm, this is so good." She looked around, but Derek had wandered down an aisle on the other side of the store and disappeared. She headed for the cool drink cabinet.

The door chimed as another customer walked in.

Addie found the refrigerated drinks and studied the variety of bottles and cans behind the glass. She took a bite of fudge and sucked on the icy chocolate before swallowing slowly.

A tall lanky man exuding a stench of cigarette smoke brushed past her and grabbed a six pack of Bud out of the beer case. The stubble-faced hollow cheeks turned left around the snacks and headed back to the counter. Tufts of unkempt hair were visible beyond the shelves. Addie tip-toed toward the back corner to find Derek.

"Give me your money," a voice barked.

The cashier stammered that she couldn't open the register without ringing up a sale.

The man had a gun pointed at her chest. He shoved the beer across the counter. "Use this."

The cashier slid the pack across the counter. Nothing happened.

"Open the register," he commanded.

Her hand was shaking. "The bar code didn't work."

"Run something else."

Addie moved around the end of a row of shelves and peered down the aisle. Her fingers tightened on the ice cream bar as thick sticky liquid dribbled and ran across her fingers.

The man picked a pack of candy from a snack rack and tossed it on the counter. "Here."

The cashier picked up the candy and ran it across the glass. The bar code beeped and she opened the register. She took out the money and set it on the counter.

The guy picked through the bills. "Is this all?"

"We don't keep a lot of cash."

Now the guy's hands shook as he waved the gun, shoving the money into his pocket. The revolver went off.

The cashier screamed and fell to the floor behind the counter.

Addie slunk back crouching into a ball behind shelves of canned goods. She watched him in the fisheye mirror in the back.

The man looked behind him and Addie caught his wild-eyed glare. "C'mon bitch. You're coming with me."

Derek was just around the end of the shelf. She reached for his hand. Too late.

A strong grip yanked Addie by the arm. The gun barrel pressed against her side. She dropped her ice cream and stared into ice cold blue eyes with dilated pupils. She couldn't see the clerk, but heard moans coming from behind the counter as the man drug her towards the front of the shop. "Let go of me!"

He didn't answer, but shoved her around the end of the shelf and dragged her across the floor. The door chimed as they got to the entranceway. Her high-pitched shriek, "Where are we going?" was answered by a slap on the cheek.

Addie looked across the counter and saw the cashier lying on the floor, her shirt soaked with blood.

Derek launched himself from behind a shelf of crackers. He slammed a can of chili into the side of the man's head, grabbed and twisted the man's gun arm behind his back and knocked the gun loose. It skittered out of reach. He wrestled the man to the floor taking Addie down with him.

Addie squirmed out of the man's grasp, and slammed her balled fist into his crooked nose as hard as she could. His head whipped back. He groaned as blood spurted across Addie's shirt.

Derek sat on the gasping gunman's back. Addie threw herself across his legs.

Derek wheezed. "Addie, find something to tie his hands."

Addie got to her feet, heart pounding, and searched rows of shelves for something that would work. She spotted a section at the end of a shelf with hardware and outdoor supplies. Fishing line. "This'll work." She ripped open the package, unwound the reel, and then sprawled across the man's legs. He twisted and thrashed while she wound the clear filament as tight as she could get it around his bony wrists.

Derek reached for the spool. "Here, give me that." He pulled it down behind the man's legs and wrapped it around the guy's ankles, making sure the line bit into surrounding skin.

Addie finished knotting the ends at his feet and stood up. She moved behind the checkout counter and crouched beside the cashier. "She's still alive. Shot in the shoulder." She gagged for a moment at the sight and smell of blood splattered across the woman's white T-shirt and blue shorts pooling on the floor. "Gotta call 9-1-1." She stood up and looked for a phone.

The clerk's voice was barely above a whisper. "There." She raised her good arm and tried to point.

Addie found the handset under on the counter and punched in the numbers. Between breaths she said, "Shooting at Country Store . . . in Home on the Key Peninsula . . . need an ambulance . . . police . . . suspect's tied up." She answered questions about the victim and repeated what she heard to Derek.

The clerk mumbled, "Call owner . . . back of phone."

Key Peninsula Fire and Rescue showed up on the scene barely two minutes later. One said, "Good thing we just got back to the Home station." The two paramedics were astonished to see the perpetrator lying bound on the floor apprehended by the skinny teenage girl they remembered from the news after her near death experience on Raven Island and her companion from the geoduck kidnapping just a month ago.

"Where's your wound?" one asked.

Addie looked down at her bloody shirt. "It's not me."

"Where's the victim?"

"There." Addie looked down. "On the floor." She noticed the shocked look on his face when he saw the victim.

"Marianne, hang in there. We'll get you to the hospital. You'll be fine."

He wrapped a blood pressure cuff around her biceps and inflated it. A slight puff of air escaped between his pursed lips when as he read the numbers on the gauge.

Marianne's voice was faint, "How'm I doing, Brian?"

"Fine . . . just fine."

Addie noticed the look of concern on his face as he hooked her up to an IV.

The team loaded her onto a gurney and began to prepare her for the half hour ride to St. Anthony. A siren blared in the distance.

The EMTs had stopped the flow of blood and were monitoring Marianne's heart rate when the Pierce County Sheriff roared in. Deputy Rollins rushed in. "Sorry, I caught a call in Purdy."

Brian told Rollins, "You're going to have to wait for a statement from the victim. She took a bullet. Gotta get her to St. Anthony. Talk to the kids. They know all the facts."

Rollins looked at Derek and then over at Addie. "Not you two again?"

Derek shrugged his shoulders. "Yep."

"You kids keep looking for trouble and one of these days you're going to wind up dead."

Addie frowned. "We didn't do anything wrong. Just came in for some ice cream."

"Yeah," Derek nodded at the bound man on the floor. "He shot the cashier. Then grabbed Addie and was gonna kidnap her. Held a gun to her side. I had to do something. He'd a killed her—"

Addie blurted, "Yeah. The lady behind the counter gave him the money. The creep shot her anyway."

Another deputy, Taylor, walked in and eyed the man on the floor. "Addie and Derek. Now what? You two have a habit keeping us busy."

The ambulance drove off with siren blaring, lights flashing.

An Asian man came roaring in. "What happened?" Addie saw him blanch when he saw the blood behind the counter. He asked, "Where's Marianne?"

Rollins said, "Sorry, Mr. Kim, she was shot. Shoulder wound. She'll be okay. They just took her to St. Anthony. We're going to have to close you down for a while. Need to get the team up for the investigation."

Mr. Kim asked, "Who did this?"

Addie pointed at the trussed up man on the floor. "He did."

Taylor said, "The kids are heroes. They managed to subdue and apprehend the perpetrator. It's going to take some time to get this sorted out."

Mr. Kim stared at the blood on Addie's shirt. "Who are these kids?"

Addie looked out the door as more sirens blasted from the north. She said, "We came in to buy ice cream."

Derek nodded, "He came in to rob the place while we were here."

A third Sheriff's Department SUV pulled up, followed by a fourth. The parking lot was soon full of Pierce County vehicles.

Addie couldn't take her eyes off the handcuffed man who glared at her before he was taken outside, sandwiched between Rollins and another burly deputy, and deposited into the back of a county car.

Taylor gestured to Derek and Addie. "I'll have to take your statements. We'd better call your parents. Let them know where you are and tell them what's happened."

Addie rolled her eyes. "Oh crap."

Chapter 38

Derek took his place in the canoe and held his raised paddle along with other pullers. He yawned and turned his head to look east. The Cascade Range loomed dark in the distance, framed by the pink light of dawn. The white cap of Mount Rainier rose high in the sky disappearing into a heavy silver mist.

At the command from the skipper, paddles dipped into the water. They pulled in unison and the canoe left the shallows by the shoreline and headed into the swift current of the Tacoma Narrows. They passed beneath the double suspension bridges connecting Gig Harbor to the city of Tacoma. The sound of traffic on the bridge faded away as they passed the southern tip of Gig Harbor and Fox Island came into view.

Derek pulled on the paddle, each stroke in sync with the rhythm of the chanter's voice and beat of the drum. Distant sounds of the Puyallup crew a couple of hundred feet ahead mingled with the support boat's engine. The line of canoes stretched far ahead moving steadily towards Nisqually. Diamonds glittered across the water as the sun rose higher above the Cascades lighting a clear blue sky. Crowds of people were gathered on the beach waving as each canoe passed. Numerous small craft hung back, onlookers following their progress.

Derek saw the orcas from the corner of his eye; tall dorsal fins protruding above the water, dark flat bodies dwarfed by the distance, then submerging out of sight. They reappeared, rising as one—closer—bigger—dark fins marking their progress as the whales closed in. A few minutes later, a black and white head broke the surface off to the right, spraying water as the orca exhaled. The enormous male halted, sank and disappeared, then burst up vertically thrusting the top half of his body out of the water. Large white teeth glistened, exposed as water cascaded off gaping jaws. The pullers raised their paddles as chanting ceased, all eyes focused on the lone cetacean as he plunged creating a splashing spiraling surge that rocked the canoe. He resurfaced—closer, and was joined by a second smaller whale. Several more rose and dipped narrowing the gap between them and the canoe.

The pod circled and paused, raising their heads above the surface, curious eyes focused on the canoe and the crew. The chanter spoke to the whales, not the loud pulsing rhythm to the now silent drum, but a soothing tone.

The whales welcomed the company of the native canoes. A mother approached the Squaxin canoe, a young calf pressed against her side. The curious pair moved in near enough to brush the fiberglass hull. Derek reached down and stroked the smooth skin of the calf's white and black back. The whales rose higher exposing more of their bodies above the surface, inviting fingers to touch their silken skin. The mother permitted gentle hands to stroke her and her baby for a few minutes before the pair dipped beneath the surface and rejoined other members of the pod that had started to move on.

The mammals swam a couple hundred feet away and then dove and rose, leaping, spiraling, fluking, breaching, and blowing, splashing water in surges that heaved the canoe. The orcas entertained the Squaxin Island crew for several minutes before they stopped their performance and turned north up Puget Sound toward Seattle.

Derek waited for the whales to leave before he dared to speak. "Wow! That was awesome! They've never come that close before. I'd never touched one."

The skipper nodded. "That was a sign from our ancestor's blessing our journey. They are pleased. We are the people of the water. Do not forget the teachings of our ancestors. That is the theme of this journey. The ancestors sent the spirits of the whales to remind us."

He removed his woven cedar hat and swept it through the air in front of him, the trailing eagle feather twisted and twirled as it caught the breeze. He replaced the hat on his head. "Time to go. We've got to work to catch up."

Paddles dipped into the water. The drum beat at a quicker pace than before, accompanied by the renewed voice of the chanter. The canoe glided across the surface, closing the distance between them and the Puyallup crew, now far ahead.

* * *

Addie stared at the line of women and girls. Many wore cedar bark hats, and were dressed in red and black native costumes of their tribes. They were standing on the grass just behind the rock wall breakwater.

Addie wiped her damp brow, and brushed a strand of hair from her eyes. She whined, "When are they gonna get here?"

Walt tipped up the brim of his cedar hat and squinted at the guide boats in the distance. "Shouldn't be long."

Rhythmic chants and drumbeats emanating from the small ring of traditional-garbed tribal members were interrupted by the announcer. Cedar bark strips swayed from his waist as he spoke into the microphone. "They're on the way in. The first canoe should be rounding the point in just a minute."

Ethan jumped up and pointed excitedly. "I see 'em!"

Myra laid her hand on his shoulder. "Ethan, sit down and be quiet. You're blocking people behind you."

Ethan turned and looked behind him. Hundreds of people filled the bleachers. "Oh. Sorry." He took his seat and looked out over the crowd below, many seated on lawn chairs all along the beach in cordoned off sections reserved for various tribal family members.

The announcer said, "There are almost one hundred canoes. Some of these crews have been on the journey for up to twenty-one days. They have come from as far away as the north end of British Columbia or the northeast coast of Vancouver Island. They are tired and sore from their journey. Let us welcome them. Osweecum. Welcome."

The black and white eagle stitched to the back of Sophie's red cape dipped and rose in the breeze with Sophie's movements as she welcomed the canoes, along with the other women, hands and arms motioning fluidly to the arriving crews.

The first canoe paddled closer, soon followed by another. Before long, several more rounded the point and stretched in a line coming towards the port. Many bore the carved and painted native designs of spirits and totems. Each tribal canoe was announced and paddled parallel to the shore, welcomed by the cheering crowd, then turned away and circled offshore to tie up in a roped-in enclosure to await the remaining tribes. The volume of noise from the crowd died down as the latest canoe tied up and everyone waited for the next arrival. At a break in the formation everyone settled down until the next canoe appeared.

All eyes focused on the point far out it the channel. The next tribe pulled into view. The expectant cheering crowd left their seats with a roar welcoming the crew, accompanied by chants and drumbeats. A line of canoes was strung out closing in on the finish. Crews took their places patiently awaiting the final pullers. Three hours later, the Squaxin Island canoe was finally announced. The crowd went wild as the sleek plain-sided gray fiberglass hull pulled into view.

Derek could hear the roar of the crowd, and drum beats as they rounded the point and the Port of Olympia came into view. Chanting voices grew louder along with the beating drums. He could see the line of welcoming women, dressed in red and black ceremonial costume, hands motioning together in the traditional welcoming ceremony. The waterfront was crowded with people who lined the beach and filled the bleachers. The crew pulled into the last spot in line. Derek relaxed his arms and forgot about his aching muscles as he and the eleven other members of the Squaxin crew took their place at the end of the line of one hundred canoes. They watched the final step of the journey unfold.

Tribe by tribe, in order of longest distance traveled, the canoes paddled to the shore where each crew was welcomed by their tribe. After they were welcomed and invited to come ashore, they pushed off and paddled away to the dock. The crews tied up and left their canoes for the last time, eager for rest and food.

The Squaxin Island tribe was the last to take their turn and be welcomed ashore, eager to rest, eat, and celebrate. Derek looked forward to a good night's sleep and the week of potlatch ceremonies awaiting them.

* * *

The Mathesons, Simon, Renee, Walt and Derek gathered on the beach at Arcadia Point with hundreds of other people, tribal members and non-members alike. Everyone listened quietly to the Squaxin singers.

The First Salmon Ceremony commenced with tribal members drumming and singing ancient Salish songs welcoming the first harvested Chinook salmon. It arrived on a canoe with cedar boughs adorning the bow. When it reached shore, the salmon was carried up the beach on a fern-draped cedar plate. It was honored, blessed and sliced open to release its spirit. After it was filleted, the carcass, with head, tail, fins, and skeleton intact was returned as it arrived, on the same plate back to the canoe. It was paddled out and carefully returned to the water.

Walt explained, "According to tradition, if the first salmon caught each season is treated with honor and respect, his spirit will return to the salmon village under the sea where he will gather his relatives, tell them of the respect he was given and lead them back to their home stream. This is done so fishing the next season will be good."

Cedar skewers secured butterflied salmon on long stakes over flaming wood coals.

Sophie was serving food, clams, fry bread, potato salad, baked beans, and salmon. Elders were served first.

Renee took a plate from Sophie and joined the others. She scooped a clam out of the shell and swallowed it slowly. "It's wonderful how everyone takes such good care of the older people. They're treated with such respect."

Walt cut into his fish with his fork. "That is the way of our people. It has always been."

Addie looked at the paper bowl of clams on her plate. "I'm not eating clams."

Derek said, "Cooked, they're good. Try one."

"Uhn uhn. You want 'em?"

"Sure." He took the cup and made room on his plate.

They finished their meal and headed back to their cars.

Derek was standing beside Walt in the parking lot.

Simon shook Walt's hand. "Thank you for inviting us. It was quite an experience."

"You're welcome."

Derek watched Simon kiss Renee before helping her into the car.

He touched Addie's hand. "Thank you for coming."

She smiled. "Thank you for inviting me. I had a good time."

He chuckled. "Except for the clams."

She cuffed him on the arm. "Yeah."

Chapter 39

Simon turned into the gravel lot on the grounds of the Longbranch Improvement Club and backed in beside the Community Services van. "How's it going, Stan?"

The food bank manager finished loading boxes onto a dolly. "Weather's nice, should be a big turnout for Old Timer's Day."

"Where's the YMCA booth?"

"Right behind Community Services." Stan wheeled the boxes to the large canopy in front.

Simon looked over the array of games, camping equipment, cookware, clothing, plants, books, artwork, and pet supplies stacked on and underneath the tables. He examined a boxed lantern. "Looks like you got a lot of donations for the silent auction and sale this year."

Key Peninsula Community Services Director, Kim Seger, stuck a price tag on a child's tea set. "Yes, hope we make a lot of money. Sure can use it."

"Stan said my space is right behind you."

"Right next to the children's fishing game. Geraldine will be running that as soon as she finishes helping Stan and me set up here." KPCS Assistant, Geraldine Ferari, was taping down bid sheets for auction.

Derek joined them. Simon looked at his watch. "Eight-thirty, right on time." They erected the canopy, and set up a table.

Derek held a birdhouse in each hand. "Where do you want these?"

Simon set a wooden planter on the grass. "Put 'em on the table."

Derek finished unloading the truck while Simon arranged the assortment of birdfeeders, birdhouses, and planter boxes.

Simon hung the YMCA sign from the front of the canopy, stood back and studied the display. "Looks good." He walked back behind the table and sat down. "Thanks for helping out."

Derek peeked inside the hole in front of a birdhouse. "No problem."

"You guys did a great job building all these. Your hard work will help support the Troubled Youth Program."

"Yeah. You taught us. It was fun."

"I had a great time working with all of you. It was time well spent getting you to do something that helped the Y and helped yourselves. That program gets a lot of kids straightened out and on the right track. They get a chance to have a decent life. Look what it did for you. You're off drugs, doing well at school. Now that your Community Service time is finished, I hope you learned something from the experience."

Derek shrugged his shoulders and mumbled. "Yeah, I guess."

Simon looked him in the eye. "Derek, don't sell yourself short. You've come a long way this year. I couldn't be prouder of you than if you were my own son. You've been a remarkable influence on Addie. Not only did you save her life, not just once, but twice, possibly even three times. You're a friend she can count on when she really needs one."

"Well . . . I . . ." Derek bent down, and tied a shoelace.

After a long pause Simon said, "Son, you have showed a maturity beyond your years. Plenty of men wouldn't have had the guts to do what you did."

"Mom was freakin' out. She says I'm reckless."

"Your mother's afraid for you. Can't say I blame her."

"I can take care of myself."

"You've been lucky. Very lucky."

Derek sighed and admitted, "I know."

Derek heard Nick's familiar deep voice and turned to see Addie walking beside her family. Nick reached across the table and grasped Simon's hand. "The booth looks terrific."

"Yeah, the kids were very productive."

Chainsaws roared as preparations for the logging contest geared up across the field. An announcer blared introducing a competitor.

Ethan tugged on Nick's hand. "Dad, I wanna see the logging competition."

Nick grinned and put an arm around Myra's waist. "Honey, let's go."

Addie looked at Derek. "I don't care about that."

Derek said, "It's a tradition at Old Timer's Day. The Longbranch Improvement Club has it every year, sponsored by the Community Center. Local loggers have fun showing off their skill. It's cool."

"All right." Addie followed him to the seats.

Renee walked up to the YMCA booth.

Simon flashed her a smile. "Hi gorgeous."

She moved around the table and gave him a hug, then pulled a folded Key Peninsula News out of her handbag and poked a finger at the front page. "Have you seen this?"

He looked at the paper. "Yes. It was all over the TV, too."

"Those two kids are always in the headlines for something." Renee inhaled a deep breath and exhaled loudly. "What are we going to do with them?"

Simon laughed and shook his head. "I don't know. What do you want me to do? They aren't my kids. Even if they were, what could I do?"

"I don't know. I just can't help worrying about them."

"You spend too much time worrying about everyone else's children. Maybe if you had a couple of your own you'd be too busy to worry about other people's kids."

She raised an eyebrow. "What are you saying? Surely you can't be thinking . . ."

"Oh, I have been thinking." He gave her a quick kiss on the cheek.

Renee stood there, mouth open, but for once, she was speechless. She'd given up on the idea of having children a long time ago, after she'd given up on marriage. Her life was devoted to other people's children. Simon's comment rekindled a memory of a long lost hope.

Chapter 40

Addie sat across from Myra in Renee's dining room. Renee sat at the end of the table. Addie loaded her wet brush with pigment and transferred gray color onto the paper. A few minutes later she paused and stared at the image taking shape before her eyes. "How am I doing?"

Renee set her brush down, and got up to stand beside Addie. "Marvelous. You'll want to sign that one."

Myra sighed as color from her sap green tree ran and pooled into blue water on the painting in front of her. She pushed back her chair and joined Renee behind Addie. "Honey, that's beautiful. You're the artist in the family. I certainly am not."

Renee patted Myra on the shoulder. "It just takes practice. You'll get better." She lifted Addie's painting off the table and leaned it up on the desk against the wall several feet away. "We'll have to get it matted and framed." She turned and smiled at Addie. "You really do have a natural artistic talent. Such a good eye for detail and the ability to bring your paintings to life. You may be able to turn this hobby into a real money maker. Possibly even a career."

Addie beamed. "You think so?"

Myra looked doubtful. "Renee, I don't know about that. Artists don't really earn a living. I don't think it's a good idea to put that idea into her head."

Addie's smile faded.

Renee said, "I don't normally recommend art as a career, but I think Addie does display a rare ability. There is more to art than selling your work. Teaching is a possibility. Addie, even if you don't make art a career choice, it certainly has the possibility of at least bringing in some extra income. Even without income, the sense of accomplishment and personal pleasure is worth the practice." She handed the painting back to Addie.

Addie replaced the picture on the table, sat back down and picked up a fine brush.

Myra dampened drying paper and starting blotting up green color to repair her blue water.

Addie added vegetation to her painting. She paused and stared at the bird on the page. Thoughts about the heron on Raven Island and her nightmare came back to life. Her eyes closed and she shuddered involuntarily at the unwanted vision. Am I ever going to forget about that? She rinsed her brush and laid it aside. "This is finished. I'm gonna give it to Derek."

Myra glanced over at Addie's work and then looked down at her unfinished painting. "I'm going to quit for today. Think I need to let this one rest for a while."

Renee stopped working on the hummingbird feeding from fuchsias. "Derek's going to love it, Addie."

"Can I come back and do another one?"

"You sure can. We'll continue to paint every week just like we have been . . . except . . . um . . . except . . . ." Renee paused and a sly smile flashed across her face. "I have something to tell you."

Myra looked concerned. "Is something wrong? Are you alright?"

"Oh, I'm fine." Her smile lit up her eyes. "Simon and I are getting married."

Myra jumped up, rushed around the table and hugged her friend. "Renee, that's wonderful news. When did he ask you?"

"Last week—"

Myra broke in, "And you waited 'till now to tell me?"

"I know. I should have told you sooner, but I wanted to adjust to the idea myself before I told anyone. You're the first to know."

Myra looked at Renee's left hand. "Where's the ring?"

Simon's taking me shopping next weekend to choose the one I want. We'll find a wedding band for him, too."

"Do you have a date set?"

"No. Not yet, but it will be very soon. We decided not to wait. We want to start a family and my biological clock is ticking. We're going to have it outside at Weddings in the Vineyard." She sighed. "Never thought I'd get married again, but Simon convinced me I needed to rethink that position. He does seem to be the perfect man. I can't visualize my life without him."

Myra held up her left hand and twisted the ring on her finger. "I'm so happy for you. I'm sure you both will be very happy."

"When I see you and Nick, how much you love each other in spite of having to overcome so much adversity, I am envious."

"You . . . envious of me?" Myra's mouth dropped. She shook her head.

"Yes, I know you'll get past the hard times and be stronger than ever. I want what you have. The relationship. I didn't think it was possible for me, but now that it is, I can hardly wait."

"Do you need any help?"

"Yes. I really do. If I expect to get this planned in just a few weeks. I'll need all the help I can get."

"Well, we'd better get started. Let's get these paints put away." Myra picked up her brushes and water containers and headed to the sink.

Renee said, "Myra, I'd like you to be my matron of honor."

"What about your sister?"

"She doesn't live here. We're not close. Simon and I both feel connected to you." She dumped her water down the drain. "Addie, will you be a bridesmaid? Simon and I would never have met if we hadn't been searching for you. Without you, there wouldn't be a wedding. We wouldn't think of holding our wedding ceremony without including you."

Addie stared wide-eyed at Renee. She fingered the row of silver rings in her ears. "Didn't know I mattered."

Renee wrapped the girl in her arms. "Of course you matter. Addie, you and your whole family are very important to Simon and me. I'm sure the Tiltons feel the same way, especially Derek."

Addie's cheeks flushed deep pink. She bit her lip and ran her fingers along the silver chain dangling from her black jeans. "I don't know . . ."

Myra laid her arm across Addie's shoulder. "I know."

Addie looked down at the floor. "Okay. I'll do it."

Renee slid the brushes into a ceramic holder. "Good."

Chapter 41

Renee was lying awake in the dark, thoughts of the past three weeks replaying again and again. She flipped the switch on the lamp and looked at the clock: 2:36 a.m. She'd be a wreck today if she didn't get some sleep. She pulled the covers aside and sat on the edge of the bed. Toolie came to her side and licked her hand. She put her hands on the dog's head, leaned down and buried her face in the thick coat.

"Well old girl, our lives are going to change today."

The dog whined and twisted around to lick Renee's face. Renee went to the closet, took out the gown she'd wear to pledge her love to Simon and thought about her good luck in finding him. She held it to her chest. Eyes closed, memories surfaced: meeting him for the first time at the search for Addie, Addie and Derek, how much Simon's influence had on Derek's life. She and Simon had such a strong connection to kids and community. She smiled, hung up the dress, crawled into bed and turned out the light.

Rows of grapes spread out on both sides of the covered patio. Sheep grazed in a pasture beyond the vineyard, sharing the pasture with a large flock of chickens, ducks, and geese.

Chairs were lined up beneath the canopy that provided shade in the late summer sun. Grape vines and flowers looped along the lower edges. A string quartet seated beside a row of grapes beneath another canopy played music. Derek rubbed the back of his damp neck beneath the tight braid. "I hate having to wear a suit. I'm too hot."

Walt pursed his lips and nodded. "I know. Glad I don't have to do this often, 'specially the tie."

Derek said, "Me, too."

Sophie walked between her son and father-in-law, taking each by the arm. "Think it's time we sat down."

A lanky teenage boy with blond hair wearing a dark blue suit led them to seats near the front.

Ethan walked ahead of Nick who escorted Noreen. They took seats behind the Tiltons. Ethan sat behind Derek and thumped the older boy on the shoulder. "You look good man."

Derek looked at Ethan's pressed, blue button down shirt. "You, too."

Seats filled soon. Renee's sister sat up front, Simon's mother on the other side. Before long Simon walked to the front, a bright blue carnation that matched his eyes pinned to the lapel of his navy blue suit.

Everyone turned to watch as the young usher led Addie by the arm. Derek gasped and his mouth gaped when he saw her. Her dark hair cascaded in soft curls, blue and white carnations woven into the locks. Delicate blue fabric flowed around her as she walked. He couldn't take his eyes off her as she stood up front.

Myra came next on the arm of Simon's brother, Alex. Nick grinned from ear to ear.

The wedding march began and all eyes turned to the back. Renee clung to the arm of Grant Cleary, the tall, dark-haired local Battalion Fire Chief. Pearl beads reflected rays of sunlight and glowed against the champagne-colored satin. Renee took her place beside Simon. Grant released her arm, and stepped aside. The music finished.

Before the minister could speak, the silence was broken by a chorus of bleating sheep. Laughter broke out. Even Simon and Renee had to laugh. Simon looked toward the waiting crowd, threw up his hands with a grin, and then motioned to the pastor to begin.

As soon as the minister started speaking, the sheep were silent and stood watching from behind the wire fence, all eyes on the people beyond the rows of grapes.

The ceremony continued with vows said, rings exchanged, and ended with a long kiss. The music started, and the couple walked down the aisle.

Renee and Simon greeted their guests and then cut the cake. Derek left his mother and grandfather and went to stand beside Addie.

Addie groaned and said, "My feet are killing me. I hate these shoes."

He motioned to a table and chairs. "Go sit down. I'll bring you a piece of cake."

Addie sat and took off her shoes. She was rubbing her feet when Derek set two plates on the table. "I'll be right back." He returned with cups of punch and sat beside her.

Addie finished her cake and swallowed a sip of punch. "I hate high heels. You're lucky you never have to wear 'em . . . and this dress." She rolled her eyes. "Ugh."

He grimaced and loosened his tie. "At least you're not choking." He looked into her eyes. "I think you look pretty."

"Hmm . . . well . . . thank you, but I can't wait to get out of these clothes."

"Me, either." He squeezed her hand.

Everyone milled around chatting for a while until Simon made an announcement. "We are going to be leaving here and heading for the big reception at the Civic Center in Vaughn. There will be food, drinks, live music, and dancing. Many more people will be joining us. Renee and I will see you there at three o'clock."

Renee added, "I'm going to throw my bouquet. All you unmarried ladies and girls need to line up."

Addie pried her feet into her shoes and lined up with the others. Renee tossed the bouquet. It flew straight into Addie's hands.

Nick hollered out. "Good catch, girl."

"I wasn't even trying."

Everyone cheered and laughed. Addie clutched the flowers to her breast. She limped up to Myra and begged her to stop by home and let her change before the reception.

"Of course. Let's go."

Addie waved to Derek. "Going home to change."

Derek said, "See you there."

* * *

Nick stood in the hall. "What's taking you all so long?"

Ethan came out of his room carrying a gift-wrapped box and slammed the door with his foot. "I'm ready."

Nick said, "What's that?"

"A sign. 'The Graysons'. Made it myself," he said proudly. "Walt helped me."

"That's real nice of you, son." He yelled down the hall, "Myra, what's keeping you? Thought you were right behind me."

Myra came out and patted her head. "Had to touch up my hair."

"You look beautiful."

She threw her arms around him and said, "You always say that."

"Well, it's true. You always look fabulous to me. Even more so today."

Ethan screwed up his face and said impatiently, "Can we go?"

Nick rapped on Addie's door. "Come on, girl."

"Coming." She opened the door. She still had the flowers in her hair, but she was wearing a pair of black jeans and a blue T-shirt.

Myra's smile turned to a stern frown. "Can't you put on something nicer than that?"

"Nope."

Chapter 42

Half an hour later they arrived at the Civic Center. Ethan bolted up the ramp, present in hand. Nick and Myra followed arm in arm. Addie trailed behind, eyes searching for Derek. She finally found him standing downstairs not far from the punch bowl talking to some boys she recognized from school. She caught his attention and he moved away from them and came toward her. She could hear them speaking her name as she walked off.

"What'd they want?"

"They saw us on the news over the summer. Remember, the shooting at the store and then when we were kidnapped."

"Oh, everyone's gonna know about us. Why can't people just leave us alone?"

He shrugged his shoulders and shook his head. "Don't know. I don't wanna be famous."

"Me either." She headed in the direction of a food-laden table. "Come on. Let's get something to eat. No clams."

He chuckled. "No clams."

They loaded up their plates and sat at the far end of the building away from everyone else. Addie was swallowing a bite of potato salad when Renee came over carrying a large gift-wrapped box.

"There you are. I've been looking all over for you. I have a present for you." Renee set the large box beside Addie on the table.

Addie looked puzzled. "For me? Why?"

"To thank you for being in my wedding party."

Addie ran her fingers along the ribbon and looked at Renee. "You didn't have to get me anything."

"I wanted to."

Simon joined them, Nick and Myra in tow. Renee said, "I'd like you to open it, now."

Addie slipped off the ribbons and tore the paper. "I can't get the tape off."

Derek produced a pocket knife and sliced through the tape. She opened the box and removed the packing paper. Her eyes lit up when she looked inside.

"Oh, my, gosh." She lifted out a pallet, brushes, tubes of paint, a traveling brush holder, a drawing book, and a block of watercolor paper. She was grinning from ear to ear. "I don't know what to say. Thank you."

"You're welcome. That's high grade cotton cold-pressed paper from France."

Addie lifted the paper and studied the front of the cover. She set it down, jumped up and threw her arms around Renee. Tears ran down her cheeks. "Thank you so much. That's the best present I ever got."

Renee kissed her on the cheek. "I know you'll do me proud. I can't think of a more deserving person. I'm certain you'll be a wonderful artist. I want to be sure you have the opportunity to work toward that goal."

She put her arm around Simon, "Now, I need to get back to my other guests. Have a good time."

"Thank you, again . . . and congratulations." Addie watched as Renee took Simon's arm and they walked away. She repacked her new art supplies along with the ribbon and bow back in the box.

Nick said, "Would you like me to lock those in the car for you?"

"Yes." She handed him the package.

Myra grabbed up the paper. "I'll put that in the trash."

They went out leaving Addie shaking her head. "I can't believe Renee did that for me."

Derek reached across the table and touched her hand. "You're a good person. She likes you."

Addie didn't say anything. Finally, she picked up her fork and scooped up a bite of baked beans.

A few minutes later a band walked on stage and started tuning instruments. Then the music started up and the bride and groom took to the dance floor. Before long space on the floor was becoming crowded. Derek asked, "You wanna dance?"

"I don't know."

"Come on." He stood and came around the table and took her by the hand. They squeezed onto the dance floor near Nick and Myra.

After the last song, Simon announced, "Renee and I will be leaving. We're going camping in the Olympic Mountains. We'll be heading out early in the morning on our honeymoon."

Addie looked aghast at Derek. "They're going camping on their honeymoon. Ugh. That sounds horrible. Why would they wanna do that?"

Renee heard her comment and laughed. "She took the mike and said, "We're just going for a few days. School will be starting and I don't want to take time off. We'll take a longer trip during vacation."

Addie exhaled loudly and rolled her eyes. "I can't think of anything worse."

Walt maneuvered through the crowd and cornered Simon and Renee as they left the stage. He said, "I have something for you in the back of my truck. It's kind of big. Need to deliver it to your house.

Renee asked, "What is it?"

"You'll see."

Renee held Simon's hand as they passed between the throng of well-wishers amidst a shower of rice. She stopped and put her hands on her hips when she saw the car. "Oh my, I hope we can see out the windows."

Ethan still held a can of shaving cream. A boy standing beside him said, "That looks swag."

Renee laughed. "Not sure what that means, but it's hard to miss."

Simon looked at the strings of cans tied to the back bumper. "Hope we aren't littering on the way home."

He helped her in and they drove off, cans clanging loudly against the pavement.

Toolie ran in circles behind the fence barking at all the people gathered in the driveway.

Renee looked puzzled. "What are you bringing us?"

No one answered. Walt started to unfasten bungee cords holding a tarp down across the bed of the truck. Ethan ran to the other side and worked to help Walt. They pulled the tarp aside revealing a long cylindrical object wrapped in burlap.

Walt wrapped his arms around the end of it and heaved backwards. Nick moved quickly to help. Derek joined the two men.

Nick said, "Let me take this end. It's heavier."

Simon said, "Let me give you a hand." He stood by to grab the end that was last out of the truck. He grunted under the weight of the burden. "Renee. Get the gate. Keep the dog out of the way."

Renee unfastened the latch, grabbed Toolie's collar, and held her aside. "What in the world are you bringing us?"

Myra pushed the gate open wider and stood back next to Sophie.

Walt called out to Renee, "Where would you like it?"

"Well, I'll have a better idea when I know what it is."

Walt grunted, his voice strained, "Let's set it down here." He untied the twine and unwound the sacking, revealing a totem pole.

Sophie closed the gate and Renee turned the dog loose.

Renee's eyes opened wide. "Walt, it's too valuable. I can't accept that."

He said, "It's a gift for both of you. A token of our thanks. Simon helped straighten out Derek and get him off drugs. We owe you a great debt—"

Simon broke in, "I was just doing my job."

"You both do much more than your jobs. You change kids' lives. Who knows what would have happened to Derek if it weren't for you."

Renee raised her eyebrows. "But this had to have taken a long time. "How'd you manage to get it done? You couldn't have made it for us."

Walt nodded and said, "Um, true. I'd been working on it for quite a while. I needed something to do. Besides, I didn't do it alone. Derek did a lot of the work."

Ethan blurted, "I helped, too."

Walt smiled and laid his hand on the boy's shoulder. "Yep, it was a training project. We all worked on it. And, you're right. It wasn't originally meant for you. I wasn't sure where it was going to end up, but when you announced your wedding, I knew this was exactly where it belonged."

Renee turned away and looked at her house. She pointed to a spot beside the porch next to a rose bush. "Right there will be perfect."

They carried the heavy pole and erected in its new home making sure it was level.

Toolie ran up and sniffed the painted wood. Renee stood back and looked up and down the new addition to her yard. She came closer and ran her hands across the mother bear holding the cub at the base. Tears pooled in her eyes. "I can't believe you're giving this to us. What a treasure." She touched the salmon above the bear. She hugged Walt. "I love it. It's extraordinary. What's the bird on the top?"

"Raven," Sophie said. "He's magical and gives courage and knowledge."

Myra looked at Renee, who was leaning against Simon. "Honey, we need to get home and leave these two alone. I'm sure they have a lot to do before tomorrow."

Renee said, "We're pretty well packed, but there are some last minute details to take care of. It's been a long day and I really am tired."

Sophie said, "Before we go, I have something for you, too." She went back to the truck and returned with a wrapped package.

Renee opened the box and lifted out a cedar basket. She caressed the smooth bark. "It's exquisite."

"I made it especially for you." Sophie smiled.

Renee kissed her on the cheek. "The quality is superb. I know you put a lot of hours into it. What an amazing skill. Not many women are capable of making anything like this."

Myra took the basket and held it up. The golden satiny fibers glowed in the sun's rays. "It really is beautiful."

Sophie sighed and nodded. "My grandmother taught me. Not many want to learn the old ways anymore. A few young ones still want to carry on the traditions of our ancestors."

Ethan handed Simon a package. "I have one."

Simon peeled off the wrapping. "The Graysons. This will be perfect beside the front door."

"I made it myself," Ethan said proudly. "Just had a little help."

Simon shook his hand. "Great job."

Nick said, "It's another tradition to give a newly married couple some privacy."

Renee blew a kiss to this crowd of friends who were now such an important part of her life.

Chapter 43

Simon shut the door on the canopy. "Truck's loaded." He wrapped his arms around Renee's neck and kissed her deeply. Toolie jumped in and Renee climbed beside her. Two hours later they parked at the trailhead at Mt. Ellinor. "I want to find a spot to camp first. I have a place in mind." He showed her a clearing nearby. They hauled out their gear and set up the tent. Renee rolled out their new double sleeping bag.

He peeked in. "Okay." He wrapped his arms around her and gave her a long kiss. "We could hike later."

She stepped back. "I think we should get started. There's plenty of time for that when we get back down."

"You're right, Mrs. Grayson, but I'm going to hold you to that." He patted her on the butt, before he took her hand.

They started out walking between stands of scrub pine and mountain hemlock. Toolie trotted ahead at the end of a thirty foot leash. The incline increased and they followed the well-worn switchbacks traversing the steep hillside, pausing to sit on a bench and take a drink. Renee poured water into a collapsible dish for Toolie. They shared a package of trail mix, tossing bits to several chipmunks that scurried away after stuffing their cheek pouches. A gray camp robber flew down and gobbled up some snacks before the chipmunks could reach them. Renee took a number of pictures of the animals before they continued, stopping frequently so Renee could get more photos.

"Future painting material," she explained. I need lots of scenes to work from." She worked Simon into a few of the shots.

A hoary marmot watched them from atop a large basalt rock. Renee managed to click a couple of pictures before Toolie saw it. The critter scurried away and disappeared into a hole in the ground.

"Toolie! No!" Renee commanded. The dog turned away and trotted back to where they were standing.

A blacktail doe with twins nibbled strawberries and wild roses in a nearby meadow. A hummingbird buzzed near Renee's shoulder then flitted off to sip nectar.

They paused beside a clump of huckleberries and sampled some of the purple fruit before moving on. A trio of young men passed them, waving as they passed. The tree line was left behind as they paralleled the ridge following the steep path beyond sloping meadows below.

A mountain goat with two kids leaped from rock to rock in the distance. Renee snapped picture after picture. "They're beautiful. Isn't it amazing how they can get around on those cliffs?"

"Yes. Be glad they're way over there. Mount Ellinor was closed earlier this year. They were attacking people. Killed a man."

"I heard about that. They don't look mean."

"Used to be you couldn't get close. People started feeding them. Some became aggressive, especially bucks during rutting season. Rangers yelled at them and threw stones to scare 'em off. They opened the trail again. If a goat comes close, wave your arms and shout."

Renee took more pictures. "It's so beautiful here. I can't believe the view today." She pointed east. "I can even see the Space Needle."

He took the camera out of her hand and slung it around his neck. "Let's get to the summit. Mt. Ellinor's 5,951 feet at the top. The view's even more spectacular from there."

They climbed across the steep ridge to the base of the vertical rocky pinnacle. Toolie barked from below as Simon hauled himself to the very top of the crest. He called down. "Come on up. The view is breathtaking."

"No. I can see it quite well from here, thank you. But please take pictures for me."

He held up the camera and snapped shots in a 360 degree radius, then finished up with a few of her.

She said, "Let me get a couple of you up there."

He climbed down far enough to pass the camera to her then he returned to his perch at the top. She took several pics of him standing on the edge. He descended and she took more shots of him with Mount Rainier and the southern hook of Hood Canal in the background. She looked below to Lake Cushman. Charred remains of a forest fire from a month ago scarred the landscape.

He took a drink and said, "We'd better head back. Want to get to bed early." He winked and swept his arm down in royal gesture. "After you, my lady."

Renee laughed. "I'm coming, kind sir."

They hadn't gone far, just left the top ridge, when a pair of mountain goats, mother and kid bolted across the trail in front of them. Toolie barked and ran after the pair.

"Toolie. Noooo!" Renee screamed.

The dog disappeared over the edge behind the goats. Renee tried to hold onto the leash, but it slipped out of her grasp. They heard a yelp. Then silence.

Renee clamored to the rim and peered over. The goats worked their way agilely along the side of the almost vertical drop. Renee scanned the jagged edge. There was no sign of Toolie. She sank to her knees and keened.

Simon clasped her in his arms and pressed her face to his chest.

"We have to find her," Renee sobbed. "I can't leave her on this mountain."

A young man and woman ran up the trail. "What happened?" the man asked. "We heard a scream."

Renee tried to talk, but her garbled words broke up in choking gasps.

Simon's chest heaved as his breath escaped in a long sigh. "It's our dog, an Australian shepherd. She went over the edge."

"Oh, my God," the young woman grabbed her companion's arm. "Jerry, do something."

He walked to the edge and looked over. He extended his arms, palms up. "What? Can't even take one step down. It's too steep. Sorry. I don't see anything. Did you hear her?"

Simon said, "Just when she went over, after that, nothing."

Jerry said, "We can call Olympic Mountain Rescue. They might be able to find her. I can't imagine she'd still be alive, but maybe . . ."

Renee wiped her eyes on her shirt sleeve. "Call them now."

Simon made the call. He explained the situation, then disconnected. "They said to give it a night. She may walk out on her own."

Renee shook her head. "Simon, you can't believe that."

The young woman said, "You've got to have hope. Maybe he's right."

Jerry said, "I suppose it's possible."

Simon kissed Renee's cheek. "Honey, lets hike to camp and wait for her there. Maybe she'll show up. If she's still gone in the morning we'll call in a rescue team."

They made their way down the slope. At the bottom they posted a sign asking hikers to be on the lookout for the tricolor shepherd. Simon prepared a thick stew for dinner on the camp stove.

Renee took a bite and tried to swallow. "I'm sorry. I can't eat." She left him seated eating alone while she paced the area calling for Toolie.

Simon cleaned up the remains of dinner and then held her hand while they searched the woods until it got too dark to see without a flashlight.

"Honey, let's go to bed. We'll see what happens in the morning."

He opened the tent flap and held it aside, shining the flashlight while she went in. He got undressed and slid into the sleeping bag and held it open waiting for her. She shivered in the cool mountain air and cuddled against him. His warm body pressed against her. He kissed her salty tears as she lay beside him. His hopes for a romantic night together vanished, swallowed into the cool night wind.

Renee was lying awake listening to sounds of Simon snoring, when she heard something rustling outside the tent. Maybe it was Toolie. She didn't want to wake Simon. She grabbed a flashlight, crawled out of the sleeping bag and unzipped the tent flap, then crept across the ground calling softly, "Toolie."

Instead of the dog, four pairs of eyes glowed in the beam of light. A mother raccoon turned away and rambled across the campsite leading three half-grown kits. They vanished into the darkness.

Renee returned to the tent and snuggled against Simon, warming her chilled hands against his warm body. Silent tears rolled down her cheeks as she listened to yipping coyotes.

She got up at dawn after the long sleepless night. Simon felt the unwelcome blast of cool air as she climbed out of the sack and opened the tent. He blinked and rubbed his temple. "You're getting up already?"

"Yes. I'll put the water on for coffee."

He got dressed and joined her outside. She handed him a steaming mug.

She blew on the hot liquid before taking a sip. "I want to go back up. See if we can find her."

"Okay, it shouldn't take long if we're not taking pictures along the way."

"I won't be stopping. If there's no sign of her when we get there, I'm calling for help."

"That's a good plan. We should know in a few hours."

This time Simon followed behind as she powered up the slope. They were the first ones on the trail. She stopped at the now familiar location. "This is the place." She called out, "Toolie!"

There was no response other than the wind howling between the rocks. The beauty of the surroundings was wasted on Renee who felt nothing but the shock and worry about her missing pet. She pulled her cell phone out of her pocket. "I'm calling again."

Chapter 44

Six members of Olympic Mountain Rescue hiked in at 11:30 in the morning. Renee jumped up from where she had been sitting on a rock and rushed up to greet them. "You're here to find my dog?"

One of the men set down his pack. "Have you seen or heard any sign her?"

Renee shook her head. "No." She wiped tears off her cheek and pointed. "That's where she went over. I had her on a leash. I couldn't hold on."

Simon wrapped his arms around her shoulders. She buried her face against his chest. He said, "It happened so fast. Sorry we had to call you."

"Don't apologize. We're all volunteers. "

The men took off their packs and set down a litter. They laid out lines and prepared equipment, then sent a member rappelling over the edge. Team members above fed out line as he dropped lower.

Renee watched him push away from the cliff, swing out and drop down. She held her breath as he descended in space. Only a rope and harness prevented him from plummeting onto the sharp rocks far below.

Her throat caught at the horrifying thought. What if he died trying to save her dog?

After what seemed like hours a voice called up. "I see her. She's on a ledge."

Renee clutched Simon's wrist and held her breath.

"She's alive."

Renee closed her eyes and threw back her head "Ohhh. Thank God."

Members above prepared for the second part of the search and rescue mission. A litter was attached to lines and lowered to the man below.

Renee watched, holding her breath. Toolie was muzzled, wrapped, loaded, and tied onto the litter. Then the man guided the litter above him as they were hauled up.

Renee crouched beside the dog and cradled her head. She could hardly look at the blood, torn flesh and protruding bone on the shepherd's front leg. The dog whined feebly while one of the team wrapped a splint and bandage around her leg.

The rescuer unclipped the rope, and removed his harness. "She'll have to be carried out."

Simon frowned. "Over three miles."

"No problem. We rotate in short shifts. That way no one gets too fatigued. Soon as we get our gear together we'll start out."

Renee removed the dog's muzzle and filled the portable dish with water. Toolie slurped without pause to breath. Harnesses and coiled ropes were packed away. The team posed for photos before two men hoisted the litter between them and the procession started down.

Renee mustered up a smile as the group reached the upper parking lot. "I'll sit on the jump seat in back. Toolie can stretch out on the bench seat up front." She watched as the harness and lines were removed from the litter and the dog was lifted out and shifted onto a blanket laid on the seat. Toolie yelped as they moved her.

"Sorry, girl." The man turned to Renee. "The vet's gonna have quite a job saving that leg."

Renee wrapped the blanket around the dog and turned to the crew. "I can't thank you enough. I would have lost her if it weren't for you."

"You're welcome."

Simon reached out and shook the hands of each of the members of the team. "You guys do a great job. I'm really impressed. You made it look easy."

"Hey, that's why we're here."

"No offense," Simon tapped the man on the arm, "but I hope I never have to call you again."

The man removed his helmet and rested it against his knee. "Hope you don't either, but I'm glad things turned out good this time."

Simon waved and helped Renee climb into the back of the cab. He reached for her seatbelt.

He drove slowly trying to avoid the worst of the ruts in the road as they bumped along. When they reached the campsite he said, "I'll break down the tent. You stay with Toolie."

She phoned the veterinary clinic as soon as they reached a place where they had service.

Less than three hours later a vet technician helped lift Toolie onto a litter and they carried her into the clinic. Dr. Burgess was waiting for them in an examination room. "Put her on the table."

The vet unwrapped the leg and frowned. "This doesn't look good. I'm going to have to take her right into surgery. We'll have to keep her at least overnight, possibly longer. She may have internal injuries. I'll call you after I get that leg taken care of and finish analyzing her then I'll have a better idea what we're facing."

Simon opened the door and held it while Renee walked into the waiting room. Renee stopped at the desk. "I'll be home waiting for Dr. Burgess to call." She picked a business card off of the desk, wrote a number on the back and handed it to the receptionist. "Here are my numbers."

The receptionist said, "The doctor will call you as soon as he knows the extent of the injuries."

Renee said, "I'll be waiting." Simon curved his arm around her lower back, escorted her out and onto the truck seat where Toolie had ridden.

Renee said, "I want to stop and see Myra before we go home."

"Sure. We can do that."

Half an hour later, they pulled into the Matheson's driveway. Myra met them on the steps. "Why are you back already?"

Renee walked up the steps and hugged Myra. "It's a long story."

Myra said, "Come in and tell me all about it." She filled three glasses with iced tea and then joined her friends at the table.

Renee sipped while explaining the details of their trip. Myra refilled the empty glasses. "Well, that wasn't the honeymoon you'd planned."

"Nope," Simon laid his hand on Renee's thigh, "but she'll make it up to me."

Renee clicked her tongue and spoke with a twinge of irritation, "Simon."

Myra nodded. "After spending a couple months in a tent with two kids, Nick and I almost feel like we're on our second honeymoon."

Simon raised his glass. "Where is Nick?"

Myra's brow furrowed. "He's at the fire station. It's been a weird couple of days. We had a few fires while you were gone; the library and a couple of wildfires. He saw the sign posted asking for volunteers, so he signed up."

Renee said, "Thought I smelled smoke on the way home. I was so concerned about Toolie, I didn't think much about it. What happened at the library?"

"Not much damage, something in a closet. They got it out, but the fire department was stretched to the limit. They had to call in outside crews. Now, Nick's determined to become a fireman," her voice sounded concerned.

Renee touched Myra's arm. "It's normal to worry about our loved ones." She pushed back her chair and stood. "We'd better get going. I need to soak in the tub. I'm pretty grubby."

Simon sniffed his arm pit. "Yep, need a shower." He brushed a smudge of dirt on her cheek with his index finger. "But you, my dear, look lovely."

They were just walking in the front door when the phone rang. Renee rushed to pick it up.

"This is Dr. Burgess."

Renee fought the lump in her throat. "How is she?"

"Not as bad as we thought. I put some screws in her leg and she'll have to have a splint for a couple of months, but there weren't any internal injuries."

"That's great news."

"I'm going to keep her overnight. You can pick her up in the morning. Any time after nine."

"Thank you so much."

"She's one lucky dog."

"We'll be there at nine."

"We?"

"Yes. I got married. I'm Mrs. Simon Grayson, now. We were on our honeymoon when it happened."

"Congratulations. But this certainly didn't get you off to a good start."

"No. It didn't. But, things will be fine, now. Thank you."

She replaced the phone on the charger and threw her arms around Simon. "We can pick her up in the morning."

He kissed her deeply on the mouth. "Good. Now, you can forget about that bath. We're going to take a shower. I'll wash your back."

Chapter 45

One week into their junior year, Addie and Derek met in the hall after the bell. They'd made a pact not to talk to anyone about the events they'd been involved in. Neither one wanted the notoriety that plagued them the year before. They crossed the parking lot and followed the well-worn path into the woods in front of the school to avoid the other students until it was almost time for the bus to leave.

A gangna stepped from behind a tree and blocked the way.

A lean kid with muddy brown dreads taunted, "Hey, Tonto, you and your bitch keep outta our way. You got no business stickin' your noses where they don't belong."

"Yeah, bitch," a pimple-faced girl with fuchsia-dyed locks kicked Addie in the shin and shoved her.

Addie crumpled in pain and started to fall. Derek grabbed her arm and held her up. The group encircled them, punching and kicking their intended victims. A clenched fist connected with Derek's belly. His grasp on Addie loosened as he collapsed and lay gasping on the dirt, the wind knocked out of him.

"Derek," Addie shrieked. She grabbed the girl's hair and twisted her head around. The girl's arms wind-milled as she backed off.

A scrawny forearm with a snake tattoo twining beyond the elbow wrapped around Addie's neck and tightened. She clawed the skin, drawing blood from the flexing snake. His grip loosened and Addie bit him. He released his grasp, and the snake moved away. She sucked in air, fighting to catch her breath.

Derek rolled, got to his knees and started to rise. A hand reached out and grabbed the rawhide strip binding his hair. His hair released and hung below his shoulders. He tried to kick the leg of his attacker. Missed.

A man's voice called out, "What's going on here?"

The bullies dissolved into the woods, then vanished among kids boarding school buses. Derek took Addie's hand and they straggled together to the bus.

* * *

Myra was unloading the dish rack when Nick came in the front door. She paused with forks in her hand. "How'd it go?"

"Turned in my resume and application packet." He walked over and kissed her "Got signed up to take the written test."

"When are you doing that?"

"In a couple of weeks. My background check should be complete by then."

She finished putting away the dishes and closed the cupboards. "I wish you'd get more construction work, I'm not thrilled about this career change. You won't even be getting paid—"

He interrupted, "I know. I've heard it before. You know the job situation. If I do this as a volunteer, chances are I can eventually work up to a paid position."

She frowned. "You'll have to spend so much time away from home."

He wrapped his arms around her. "That just means we'll have to make the most of our nights together."

"What about the kids? Addie's gotten into so many scrapes lately."

"True, but I haven't been able to stop any of that. Hopefully, my making some positive life changes will send a clear message."

She leaned against him. "Hope your right."

The door flew open and Addie blew past them.

Nick called out, "Hi, Addie."

Addie headed down the hall and disappeared into her room without a word and slammed the door behind her.

Nick followed her and opened the door. Addie was sprawled on the bed. "Hey, why so rude? What's going on?"

Addie shrugged. "Nothing."

Nick sat on the bed. "Tell me what's wrong."

Addie screwed up her face and looked away. "I can handle it."

Nick's voice took on a tone of concern. "Handle what?"

"This dumb bitch at school posted some crap on Facebook. She and some other kids are treating Derek and me like trash."

"What are they doing?"

"Those bitches use drugs. Now, they're pissed about that dealer we turned in. They're calling us names and shoving us around."

Nick reached down and pulled her up to face him. He looked her in the eye. "Did you report them?"

"Like that would do any good."

"I'll go to the school and have a talk with your principal."

"That'll just make things worse."

"No it won't. Trust me."

Addie placed her hands on her hips. "Yeah. Right."

He put his hands on her shoulders. "Look, you aren't the first kids to be bullied and you won't be the last. We have to stop the bullies. Schools are equipped to handle these kids."

She sighed loudly and looked away. "I'm gonna do my homework."

"Okay. This isn't over. I'll talk to your principal on Monday."

Nick left her and returned to the kitchen. Myra looked at him. "What's the deal?"

He explained the situation about the bullying. Myra turned and started for Addie's room. Nick reached out and caught her wrist. She said, "Let go. I need to speak to her."

"Give her some space." He steered her to a chair. "I told her I'd take care of it."

Chapter 46

Nick and Myra paused at the top of the stairs to gaze at the woods in front of the school where Addie said the bullying had taken place. The tall firs appeared serene, a peaceful sanctuary to the right of Henderson Bay in the distance. They passed through the heavy metal door and headed directly to the principal's office and were sent right in.

Mrs. Ringwold sat up straight behind a large oak laminate desk, dark short hair silvering at the temples. "Mr. Matheson, you said your daughter is having an issue with our school." She pulled her chair closer to her desk and reached for a pen and notepad. "You weren't specific over the phone. What seems to be the problem?"

Nick placed his hands on the desk. "She's being bullied."

Mrs. Ringwold's dark eyes narrowed and she set down her pen. "Are you sure?"

"Of course, we're sure," Myra said. "Our daughter wouldn't make this up."

"I wasn't implying that—"

Myra broke in, "She didn't even want to tell us. It's like pulling teeth to get her to talk about it. She's more upset by the slurs directed towards her friend, Derek Tilton, than she's concerned for herself."

"What slurs?"

Myra clasped her hands and squared her shoulders. "They made insults about him being an Indian. Called him Tonto."

"We have a zero tolerance policy for discrimination and bullying in our school. Do you know the names of the students doing the bullying?"

Nick blew a loud breath. "No. She doesn't know. Or, wouldn't say."

"I'll make sure we get to the bottom of this and put a stop to it. I appreciate you coming by. I'll keep you informed."

Nick said, "Thanks for fitting us in."

"That's my job. If there are any more problems, let me know."

He held the door for Myra. "Will do."

Renee almost bumped into them in the hall. "Hello. What are you doing here?"

"Addie and Derek were bullied." Myra raked her fingers through her hair. "We came to talk to the principal."

"I hadn't heard anything about it."

Nick responded, "We just found out about it the other day."

Renee said, "I'm sure Mrs. Ringwold will put an end to it. She's very good at cracking down on troublemakers. She involves the entire staff in awareness of these issues."

Myra said, "I hope so." Her expression changed to a smile. "How's Simon?"

"We're getting along very well. Just a few minor adjustments getting used to sharing the same space."

Nick nodded. "How's Toolie doing?"

"Better. She's still having a tough time getting around, but her leg's healing. The vet's optimistic."

Nick said, "That's good news."

Renee looked at her watch. "Sorry. I've got to run."

"Stop by soon." Myra reached out and touched her hand. Bring Simon."

"I will."

* * *

Addie met Derek in the hall on their way to the lunch line. They found seats in the far corner. She started to eat.

He drank some milk. "How's your pizza?"

"It's okay. Crap, here come the gangnas."

Dreadlocks shuffled behind Derek and yanked his hair lifting him out of his seat. "Hey asshole. Who let you off the reservation?"

Derek shoved an elbow into his attacker's gut. Dreads stepped back, but hung on. Addie swung her foot out and caught him in the knee. He buckled, lost his grip and slumped to the floor. Snake-arm moved in and caught her by the forearm. He yanked her back and up and then slammed her to the floor. He pinned her down with his boot against the back of her neck. Fuchsia-hair kicked Addie in the leg while two more male attackers rushed in and grabbed Derek's arms. A crowd gathered surrounding the brawlers.

Mrs. Ringwold and the vice principal appeared accompanied by a security guard and several teachers. Her voice was stern, "Everyone into my office. Now."

The guard grabbed the tattooed arms and held them behind the teen's back. "Come on." He frog-marched the subdued brawler ahead of him.

Mrs. Ringwold reached out a hand and helped Addie up. "You and Derek need to come with me, too."

Addie scowled and grumbled, "We didn't do anything. They attacked us."

"I know. We have to get this sorted out and take statements. Police are on the way."

The group had just made it into the office when three large uniformed deputies appeared. "What's going on here?"

Addie said, "We were just eating lunch. Not bothering anyone. They came up and attacked us."

A deputy narrowed his gaze on Snake-arm. "Is that true?"

Snake-arm shrugged and remained silent.

"How about you?" the deputy turned his attention to Dreads.

The teen stood stone-faced, speechless.

Two more deputies entered the crowded office. Deputy Rollings noticed Addie and Derek standing together flanked by the principal and vice principal. "Not you two, *again*?"

Addie pressed her lips together and nodded.

He shook his head.

A deputy said, "We're going for a ride."

Six handcuffed suspects were removed from the school and deposited in three waiting Pierce County Sheriff Department cars. Their parents were notified.

Addie and Derek were questioned and statements were taken. It took just a little over an hour.

Derek stretched and rubbed the back of his neck "What's going to happen to them?"

Rollings said, "The three who attacked you will be arrested and charged with assault. The others will probably be suspended from school."

Mrs. Ringwold was told about the charges against the three students still being held.

She said, "I have suspended the three who didn't instigate the attack for one week. The other three have been expelled. They will not be permitted to return to this school."

Addie smiled. "Good."

Derek turned to Deputy Rollings. "Thanks man."

Rollings nodded. "Glad I could be of service. Think it'll be the last time?"

Derek looked at Addie. "Hope so."

The bell rang while they stood in the office.

Students who hadn't been in the cafeteria when the confrontation took place heard about it and wanted to know the details. The school bus was abuzz with chatter from curious students. Voices called out.

"Who were the creeps?"

"What happened to 'em?"

"What'd Ringwold do?"

"Derek. Did you get hurt?"

Addie and Derek were the center of attention, again.

As soon as Addie walked into the house Myra rushed up and hugged her. "Your principal called and told me what happened. Are you alright? How's Derek? Were these the same kids?"

"Mom. Slow down. I'm fine. So's Derek. She set her backpack on the table, opened the refrigerator and removed a gallon of milk. "The creeps were the same. They won't be back. Got expelled."

"Mrs. Ringwold told me."

"I'm starving. Didn't get to finish my lunch."

Chapter 47

Nick nursed a cup of coffee. Words were beginning to blur on the page. He yawned and rubbed his eyes then closed the book, got up and dumped the rest of the cup down the drain.

He stripped his clothes off and crawled quietly into bed. Myra rolled over and put her arm around him.

He wrapped her in his arms. "Sorry, didn't mean to wake you."

"That's okay, I was just dozing. What time is it?"

"Two o'clock."

"Oh, you are up late."

"Yeah, who'd have thought there'd be so much information you have to know just to be a fireman."

"Think you're ready for the test?"

He fluffed up his pillow and turned onto his back. "I sure hope so. Spent enough time studying that blasted book."

"I'm sure you'll do fine."

There was no response. He was already starting to snore.

* * *

Simon drove up to the Mathesons and parked. He opened the car door for Renee and then lifted Toolie off the back seat and set her on the ground.

Addie squatted and hugged the dog. "How is she?"

Renee smiled. "Much better. Since the cast came off last week, she's able to get around pretty well. The vet said it'll take six months for her to be fully recovered. She'll always have a limp, but she'll have a good life."

Simon patted the dog on the head. "Her goat chasing days are over." He started for the house. "Where's your dad?"

"He's out back of Noreen's house. Something about the porch."

Renee said, "I'll go find Myra while you track down Nick."

Simon heard the skill saw before he spotted Nick.

Just about done. Could use a hand setting a couple of new supports in. Hope you don't mind?"

"Not at all. That's why I'm here."

"Hang on a minute." Nick made the last cut and shoved out the old wood.

"The new posts are leaning against the house. I just need help to put 'em up." Nick hoisted the end of a 6 x 6. They lifted it onto the porch.

Nick measured the post and cut off an end. "Okay, that should do it." They positioned it and Nick screwed in some brackets. "Next one." He moved to the other side and cut the second post out. It was replaced with no trouble.

They finished the job and Simon helped pick up the tools. "How's firefighting training coming?"

"I love the physical part of the job. The most fun was 'the viper' they call it—an impossible task. Simulates a broken 2 ½" hose line. Normally two people can control it, higher pressures, take three people. You have to get it kinked over to stop it. When they make you do it by yourself it's a bitch. Everyone comes out soaked."

Nick coiled the electrical cord. "Classwork can be boring sometimes, HazMat's the worst, especially Federal info and laws, and the chemicals, but I'm getting through it. Be glad when it's over and I can get down to the business of fighting fires for real."

They set the rotted posts aside. Nick said, "I'll cut these up later. Noreen can use them for firewood."

They carried the tools to the shed. Nick stashed the drill in a drawer and hung the cord on a hook. "How's married life treating you?"

"Wonderful, except for the dog going off the cliff right off the bat. It couldn't go anywhere but better after that. Just a few minor differences to work out. You know. Where to hang my stuff in her overstuffed closet. Making room for my tools. Letting me hang a few pictures on the walls. Renee's a talented artist. I just wanted a little bit of space on the wall to make it feel like home."

Nick laughed. "Wait till you have kids. Then you'll see how little space you have for yourself. Not to mention time."

Simon handed Nick the saw. "Give us a little bit of time to get used to living together first. At least have a real honeymoon. Then we'll start working on that."

Nick locked the door behind them and they walked back to the house.

The women were sitting in the living room on the sofa. Toolie lay on the floor beside them.

"Finished?" Renee asked.

Simon paused before heading down the hall. "Just have to wash up. Then we'd better take off. Have some chores to do at home."

Addie pedaled her bike down the driveway, and turned north.

They passed her about half a mile down the road. Renee said, "She's sure in a hurry. Must be headed for Derek's house."

Simon caught her eye. "Think they can stay out of trouble?"

"Hope so."

"Does it make you worry about having kids of our own?"

"Of course not. She patted him on the knee and teased. "Our children will be perfect."

Chapter 48

Addie and Derek rode their bikes into the Tilton's yard and left them at the edge of the woods. They walked through the forest along the familiar worn path and entered the meadow. Dry golden grass brushed against their legs as they crossed the field. A goldfinch landed on a tall stem and picked seeds from the tip.

Derek reached for Addie's hand and led her to his thinking rock. He cupped his hands to make a step and boosted her then vaulted up and sat cross-legged beside her. They sat in silence for a minute listening to nearby birds chirping unseen in the trees. He put his arm around her and kissed her on the lips. She leaned against him and closed her eyes welcoming his deep kiss. Her arms wrapped around his back, hands kneading firm muscles. After several minutes they stopped making out and lay on their backs snuggled against each other staring up at the sky. Wispy clouds floated across a field of blue carried on the southwest wind.

The pleasant calm was interrupted by the distant wail of a siren. Addie sat up and turned, facing the direction of the sound. "Wonder if that's my dad."

"Is he on duty?"

"Yeah. He's working a twelve hour shift today. Mom gets cranky when he's gone a lot. Guess she's freaked out something will happen to him."

"I'm sure he'll be okay. He's been through the classes. Knows what he's doing."

"I know. Still, it's sort of scary." She shifted around and lay back across his thighs. "I think she misses him a lot, especially at night. It does seem weird without him at dinner. He's always been there." The sound of the sirens grew louder then faded away into the distance.

His fingertips stroked her hair. He took her hand, brushed it across his cheek and kissed it. "I miss you when you're not with me. I think about you all the time." He reached behind her, raised her up and kissed her lips again.

"I love being with you." She melted into his embrace, lips searching hungrily.

Chapter 49

Sirens blared at the station. Nick put the cap on his shoe polish, shoved his foot in his half-polished boot and tied the laces. One man picked up the remote and turned off the TV. Nick got off the sofa, and hurried to the coat rack right behind them.

They were grabbing jackets and helmets when Battalion Chief Grant Cleary walked out of his office. "Forest fire, Carney Lake area, southwest Kitsap County. All local companies are responding."

Cleary left the garage, siren blaring as soon as the door opened. The engine roared to life. Nick pulled on his heavy yellow jacket and helmet as he took the passenger seat. They left the driveway as the flashing red lights of the command vehicle disappeared around the bend far ahead.

Cars pulled aside waiting for them to pass. Nick thought about the past six months. All the hours of training, Time for the real thing. A gray smoky haze drifted across Carney Lake Road bringing a pungent smell that filled his senses before they reached their destination.

FIRE, the sign with an arrow, was taped to an orange gate post beside the dirt driveway. The gate was open. They turned in and the truck lurched ahead down the rutted dirt road. Half a dozen engines and two tenders loaded with water were there already, a small army of firemen pulling hoses.

Nick climbed out. Stopped, eyes wide. Soaring flames shot skyward. He felt a blast of hot air on his face. A tree exploded with a thunderous crack sending a cascade of sparks like fireworks raining down, feeding the roaring inferno.

"Come on!"

Nick's heart raced. Adrenalin kicked in. He'd fight this fire like it was threatening his own home and property. His family. He grabbed the hose.

Information

Geoduck poachers pose a serious threat to native wildlife. The State of Washington Department of Fish and Game is under constant pressure to catch the criminals. Large amounts of foreign money spent on the black market encourage exploitation of this local mollusk.

For more information on geoduck and other wildlife poaching read, <u>Shell Games: Rogues, Smugglers, and the Hunt for Nature's Bounty</u> by Craig Welch, Harper Collins Publishers.

Lushootseed language is one of two main divisions of Salishan language spoken by Coast Salish Indians. It was a dying language before the efforts of the late Vi Hilbert, upper Skagit elder and native speaker, who worked to create verbal recordings. Thom Hess was a linguist with the University of Washington who specialized in Northwest native languages. They created a lushootseed dictionary. Now there is a revised, much expanded version by Dawn Bates. Classes are available online through local tribes.

Lushootseed words used in this story were altered to accommodate the English language alphabet. Many lushootseed sounds cannot be represented by letters or symbols from the English language.

Acknowledgements

My sincere thanks to many people. I apologize if I overlooked anyone. Members of Lakebay Writers for invaluable critiquing, encouragement, and moral support throughout this lengthy process: Loren Aikins, Max Aikins, Keith Bezona, Leslie Bratspis, Kristi Clark, Dick Dixon, Charene Goodhue, Dix Hare, Amy Landa, Gordon Moser, Arthur Rose, Carl Tucker, Carolyn Willis, Teri Wolf, and Marjie Wood.

Watermark Writers: Jerry Libstaff, Kamryn Minch, Irene Torres, Linda Whaley, and Carolyn Weily.

Jackie Crenshaw, who kept me posted on historical, cultural, and current events involving the Squaxin Island Indian Tribe. To Ted Moran who explained the art of native carving.

Members of the Key Peninsula Fire Department, District 16: Fire Chief Tom Lique, Battalion Chief Chuck West, Receptionist Vanessa Taylor, Firefighter Paramedics Zack Johnson and Brent Adams and Fire Administrator /Volunteer Firefighter Paramedic/ Anne Nesbit.

Special thanks to Raina Callahan, RN for explaining procedures and equipment at St. Anthony's Hospital, Gig Harbor.

Key Peninsula Community Services and Food Bank staff: Penny Gazebat, Kathy Gil, and Brett Higgins.
YMCA Friends and Servants Program Coordinator, Dennis Taylor.

Olympic Mountain Rescue, Mike Baum

Dottie Beaver, David Mikelson, and Ted Olinger

Girl Scout Camp Leader, Karen Fortner.

Mark Peabody, whose computer and software expertise kept my computers and printers running and came to my rescue numerous occasions, sometimes in the middle of the night.

Jan Walker, an editor of exceptional patience and talent who guided me through the process, again.

Karen Lovett graduated from the University of Washington with a Bachelor of Science degree in Zoology. She was a research technologist at Fred Hutchinson Cancer Research Center until moving to the island of Okinawa, Japan with her former husband, a U.S Naval physician. She studied fashion design when she wasn't scuba diving or traveling throughout Asia. She has also spent time in England, France, Holland and Scotland.

An all-breed rabbit judge with the American Rabbit Breeders Association, she has judged rabbit shows throughout the United States and Canada.

She plays guitar and enjoys writing poetry and songs, painting, walking in the woods, gathering wild mushrooms with other members of the Kitsap Peninsula Mycological Society, swimming, water aerobics, or spending time at the beach. She maintains her rabbitry, gardens and orchard on a small farm on the Key Peninsula in western Washington.

She is a staff writer for the *Key Peninsula News* and is a member of Lakebay Writers, Key Peninsula Writers Guild, and Watermark Writers. She is currently working on her third novel.

Her first book <u>Beneath the Surface</u> was published in 2012 by Plicata Press.

CPSIA information can be obtained
at www.ICGtesting.com
Printed in the USA
FFOW03n2314090314
4099FF

9 780984 840069